A POWERFUL FAMILY CAUGHT UP IN CONFLICT, DIVIDED BY SHOCKING SECRETS, HELD TOGETHER BY A SPECIAL LOVE . . .

The Dinner Party
Howard Fast

W9-AHK-871

Books by Howard Fast

THE DINNER PARTY
CITIZEN TOM PAINE
  (A Play)
THE IMMIGRANT'S
  DAUGHTER
THE OUTSIDER
MAX
TIME AND THE RIDDLE:
  THIRTY-ONE ZEN
  STORIES
THE LEGACY
THE ESTABLISHMENT
THE MAGIC DOOR
SECOND GENERATION
THE IMMIGRANTS
THE ART OF ZEN
  MEDITATION
A TOUCH OF INFINITY
THE HESSIAN
THE CROSSING
THE GENERAL ZAPPED
  AN ANGEL
THE JEWS: STORY OF A
  PEOPLE
THE HUNTER AND THE
  TRAP
TORQUEMADA
THE HILL

AGRIPPA'S DAUGHTER
POWER
THE EDGE OF
  TOMORROW
APRIL MORNING
THE GOLDEN RIVER
THE WINSTON AFFAIR
MOSES, PRINCE OF EGYPT
THE LAST SUPPER
SILAS TIMBERMAN
THE PASSION OF SACCO
  AND VANZETTI
SPARTACUS
THE PROUD AND THE
  FREE
DEPARTURE
MY GLORIOUS BROTHERS
CLARKTON
THE AMERICAN
FREEDOM ROAD
CITIZEN TOM PAINE
THE UNVANQUISHED
THE LAST FRONTIER
CONCEIVED IN LIBERTY
PLACE IN THE CITY
THE CHILDREN
STRANGE YESTERDAY
TWO VALLEYS

QUANTITY SALES

Most Dell Books are available at special quantity discounts when purchased in bulk by corporations, organizations, and special-interest groups. Custom imprinting or excerpting can also be done to fit special needs. For details write: Dell Publishing Co., Inc., 666 Fifth Avenue, New York, NY 10103. Attn.: Special Sales Dept.

INDIVIDUAL SALES

Are there any Dell Books you want but cannot find in your local stores? If so, you can order them directly from us. You can get any Dell book in print. Simply include the book's title, author, and ISBN number, if you have it, along with a check or money order (no cash can be accepted) for the full retail price plus $1.50 to cover shipping and handling. Mail to: Dell Readers Service, P.O. Box 5057, Des Plaines, IL 60017.

HOWARD FAST

The Dinner Party

A DELL BOOK

Published by
Dell Publishing Co., Inc.
1 Dag Hammarskjold Plaza
New York, New York 10017

Dell ® TM 681510, Dell Publishing Co., Inc.

ISBN: 0-440-12047-0

Reprinted by arrangement with Houghton Mifflin
Company

Printed in the United States of America

December 1987

10 9 8 7 6 5 4 3 2 1

KRI

To the memory of J. Krishnamurti

ONE

Senator Richard Cromwell awakened, and with a sigh of resignation accepted the fact that it was five o'clock in the morning. He had not yet glanced at his music-first-tinkle-and-then-firm-alarm Japanese bedside clock, nor was it necessary. It was five o'clock. Senator Cromwell was fifty-seven years old, and ever since he had turned fifty-six he had awakened in the morning at five with a bursting bladder. He had mentioned this once to Dr. Gillespie at the club bar, and Gillespie had said, "Well, you're fifty-six, take it or leave it," whatever that meant. Stumbling sleepily into his bathroom and urinating, the senator recalled the brief passage with Gillespie and murmured, "Horse's ass." It was a cold summer morning. The senator closed the window and rolled back into bed.

The five o'clock awakening was not all negative. It gave him the right to a delicious half hour, warm and secure under the covers, with his mind free in the easy confusion of awakening. At first the senator tried to slip back into a pleasant dream he had been having about a college play long ago, and in the dream playing the lead in some vaguely familiar plot. But the dream eluded him and faded, and the senator's thoughts returned to his present self. He began to weigh what he considered his good and bad aspects—aspects, not deeds, for where deeds were concerned he thought of himself as a pretty decent sort who did the best he could, which was not easy in these last years of the twentieth century. He would still be short of his seventy-fifth year when the century rolled to an end, and this turned his thoughts to the world that would follow, the world of the twenty-first century. Computers: he always fixed on computers when his mind wandered into the future—instruments he revered and hated. The computer world was a place where snotty kids knew everything and nothing.

In all truth, the plain fact was that he had two computers, one in his local office and another in his Washington office, neither of which ever felt the touch of his own hand. Having an army of help, any one of them only too eager to spring to the keyboard at his bidding, he simply refused to confront the machines. Not that the senator underrated the computer. The fact that within its electronic mind was stored the name and background of everyone who had ever contributed a dollar to one of his campaigns, chilled, rather than cheered, him. The computer was a part of a future cloudy, unpredictable and menacing.

Enough of such notions. The senator switched his thoughts to one Joan Herman, five feet eight inches, blue eyes, blonde hair, very nice even though her pubic hair was dark brown, one hundred and thirty pounds, and smart enough to be his personal secretary, and close-mouthed and pretty enough to be his mistress. Developing the mental image, he began to feel deliciously horny; and knowing that he faced an important and difficult day, he cut the dream short, rolled out of bed, and steeling himself with thoughts of some proud and manly Roman senator of old, plunged into the bathroom and into a cold shower.

Agony and joy in his courage, as he bit his lips to keep from screaming with the shock. That was it: how many men of his age could roll out of a warm bed and into an icy shower? True that he took only thirty seconds of it, but how long is a second when you're under an icy cascade? Fine, stimulating thoughts. Although he was fifty-seven, he didn't feel it; he felt like a twenty-seven-year-old as he rubbed himself down. Life had become easier, healthier, and certainly more productive since he and his wife, Dorothy, had accepted the reality of separate bedrooms.

It was not yet six o'clock, the sun just blinking at the trees on the other side of the horse meadow as the senator finished shaving. He had decided to run, and he pulled on a comfortable old sweat suit and a pair of sneakers. He never could adapt to the new running shoes that the kids used, nor did he feel any need for them. He didn't jog; he damnwell ran, while most of his peers shuffled across the golf course.

It occurred to the senator, as he walked through the quiet house, through living room and dining room and pantry into the kitchen, and then into the garage, that when people slept, the house slept. He marked that as an interesting thought, possibly something that could be worked into a speech one day.

"At least sometimes I try to be original."

His two-door Mercedes was in the farthest stall of the four-car garage, and that was good. He could slip off without waking anyone else now at ten minutes to six, and that eased the small guilt he felt—although why he should feel guilt when all he intended was to run one mile on the high school track, was an interesting question.

He refused to probe for what else was on his mind. "Only running, nothing else," he told himself as he touched the button that raised the garage door. "Only running."

Truth was that he had almost decided to give up running. "In fact," Dr. Gillespie had warned him, "you're pitting your strength against your condition. You're a strong man, football in college and all the other memories of what your body did at that time, but now you're thirty pounds overweight and you run ten times during the summer, and sit on your ass ten months of the year."

It was six miles to the high school running track, and after the first mile the senator had done away with Gillespie, and turned his thoughts to the dinner party this evening. Tracy Youman, the third most important hostess in Washington, had once remarked to him that a proper and successful dinner party was a work of art. "It has always been that," Mrs. Youman explained, "as long as civilization has been around, but most hostesses don't give a moment's thought to the dinner party as an art form."

Richard Cromwell had tried to pass that along to his wife one day, and she had responded by snorting that the last person to offer anyone advice on any art form was that "vulgar bitch, Tracy Youman." At least "snorting" was the word the senator used when he passed Dorothy's response on to Joan, who for all her ill will toward Dorothy could not pic-

ture her snorting. Dorothy was about five feet
and five inches, round faced with gray hair
and green eyes, doll-like even now in her
forty-fifth year, and gentle of voice.

Well, he could be sure of one thing, the food
and the service would be excellent. Dorothy
would see to that.

It was ten minutes after six when the senator pulled into the parking lot at the high
school. His was the only car present. There
were at least a dozen early morning runners,
but the earliest would not arrive before a
quarter to seven, something that pleased the
senator. It pleased him to be the first. It
pleased him to start his run alone, and it
pleased him to see the old red brick buildings
of the school as his backdrop. Beyond this, he
would have been enormously pleased if the
throng of boys and girls who inhabited the
school during the winter months could have
come pouring in, later to tell their parents
that they had seen Senator Cromwell, in an
old sweat shirt, just like anyone else, running
the track. That would have connected. He
frequently harped on the art of connection
with his staff; connect, make ropes that bind
you to the people. In his fantasy, he accepted
the fact that he would have to begin his run
about three hours later in the day. He could
easily adapt to that—but since it was summer,

no amount of adaptation could fill the empty high school.

He ran for fifteen minutes, at least a mile and a half as he calculated, and then breathing hoarsely and sweating, he dried himself as well as he could. A gently warming shower would have been the right thing now, but the school was closed and the town would not pay a custodian to keep the place open for those who used the track and football field. Actually, he was not much bothered by the film of perspiration that covered his body under the workout suit. The soft cotton lining reminded him of the sweat shirts that were once de rigueur for every kid in athletics; but that was a long time ago, and when he had tried to buy an old-fashioned sweat shirt recently, he could locate only a modern imitation, thin as paper.

He climbed into his two-seater and relaxed gratefully. Gillespie be damned; the senator felt good, and relaxing now in his car, he saw the first of the runners drive in, park, and climb out to begin the run. Johnny-come-lately. He was beginning to feel a subtle warmth of horniness again, and he picked up his car phone and called Joan. She answered fuzzily: "My God, Senator, do you know what time it is?" She always called him "Senator." That had been agreed upon, even when they were alone, so that there could be no slip into overheard intimacy.

"Six-forty," he said cheerfully.

"I watched a damn late show. I didn't fall asleep until one."

Her voice came alive as she spoke. She had a rich, low voice, one of the things he liked about her. Whoever called, her voice on the phone mollified and soothed. This is no cheap fling, the senator had told himself, not once but fifty times. This is a damn wonderful woman.

"Well, I'm up," she said. "Where are you—in bed?"

"No way, Miss Herman. I am not in bed. I have shaved, showered, and run my mile and a half, and right now I'm sitting in the two-seater at the high school parking lot. How about that?"

"It sounds dreadful, so it must be virtuous. Come on over."

"Oh, how I would love to. Can't. This is a difficult day, and I must show for breakfast."

"Ah, well, so it goes. Anyway, the place is a mess and I don't think there's an egg in the fridge. I hate this apartment." Her home place was in Washington. Her father had been a rather highly placed bureaucrat in the Treasury Department, and she had been born and raised in Georgetown. This small apartment in the senator's home town was a necessary convenience, both for business and pleasure. Miss Herman, who was thirty-three years old, had been married and divorced twice, and both the senator and Miss Herman knew that she would not marry again unless it was to become Mrs. Richard Cromwell.

The barrier to that end was not Dorothy Cromwell, but the senator. He dreamed dreams. "Do you know," he said to Joan once, "no one wanted a divorce more than Jack Kennedy. It might have given him the kind of contentment that never existed in his life, but the way I hear it, Pope John said to him, you will not divorce and you will be president."

But today, driving back to his home, the recollection was of small comfort to Richard Cromwell. He drove slowly, passion and zest melted, leaving him with a small stinging pain in his chest, which he brushed aside as morning gas. He worked on his recollection, justifying himself with memories of Kennedy. God, he had loved Jack Kennedy, and now the bastards were hanging the Vietnam War on him. *Instead of a cross, the albatross about his neck was hung,* instead of a cross, Vietnam about his neck was hung—but he couldn't think of the title. Scraps and bits of poetry floated through his mind. It was more than thirty years since he had opened a book of poetry. Dorothy reacted to poetry. *Leave thy father, leave thy mother, leave the black tents of thy tribe apart? Am I not thy father and thy mother, and what need hath thou of their black tents who hath the red pavilion of my heart?* How would Joan react to that? Dumb astonishment, probably. "Senator, are you feeling well?" She'd be justified. Why on earth had he resurrected that sophomoric chant? The red pavilion of my heart. Oh, Jesus, he was doing the mental handsprings of some thirty-year-old yuppie sex jockey, and it was not him. He didn't sleep around, and alongside some of his colleagues he was close to being a monk, so why was he engaging in this mental guilt whipping?

He was home now, around on the driveway to the rear of the house, where the four-car garage bordered on Dorothy's vegetable garden. A month or so ago, an interviewer had scratched around among the local real estate people and learned that the senator had refused an offer of two and a half million dollars for his house and the five acres of lawn and plantings and swimming pool and tennis court that went with it; and as a result of this, Cromwell had spent an extra hour talking the magazine writer out of printing it. He pleaded that when his mother-in-law built the house, or rebuilt it more properly, it had cost less than fifty thousand dollars, and that it was really his wife's house, not his, and that he was not to blame for the years of inflation that followed, and that he actually did not live in a two-million-dollar house. He won his point and the worth of his house remained unrevealed, and in any case, the man who had made the offer to buy had been a Texan, which put the price in a special category.

Nevertheless, he lived well. The car alongside of his in the garage was a chauffeur Cadillac; and on the other side of the Cadillac, a Buick Executive station wagon; and after that, Dorothy's four-door Volvo. Outside the garage, three more cars, a Datsun pickup, which Baron MacKenzie, chauffeur, gardener, and man about the place, drove; an ancient Volkswagen which his son, Leonard, would not part with; and the old Ford driven by his daughter, Elizabeth. Seven cars in all, and if another nosy newspaper man had scratched around the way the magazine writer did, he might have wondered how a United States senator could run the place on a salary of seventy-five thousand dollars a year. Strangely, for reasons the senator did not fully understand, nobody ever remarked on this; and even if they had, the senator bore no guilt. He had married a very wealthy woman. Others had done the same. It was respectable and even admirable in his circles, since more and more men in politics were not of the old Eastern establishment and thus faced the necessity of building their own class position in a society where rich was admirable and poor was unenviable. Still and all, most voters were far from rich, and a senator needed voters. Wealth would not make them mistrustful, only envious, and envy was not the best vote-getter.

The senator sighed, accepted the fleet of cars without further mental demur or internal conversation, and walked into his house.

TWO

Baron MacKenzie set his alarm for half past six each morning, but this time he was awake a few minutes before the alarm sounded, and he reached out and turned it off.

"You don't have to do that," his wife, Ellen, said. "I'm awake."

"The best few minutes are right now," MacKenzie said, pressing his face into his wife's warm bosom. He was a big man, and the only way he could keep all of him in the bed was to sleep on the bias.

"I'll be on the floor in two minutes," his wife complained. "I am not a linebacker."

"You want to be rid of me, presto, you are rid of me." He rolled out of bed and made his way into the bathroom. The servants' quarters were pleasant enough, including their own bath and shower and a small sitting room, which contained armchairs, couch and television, as well as a wall of shelves for their and their kids' books. They used to have a second bedroom, where their daughter, Abbey, slept. Their son, Mason, had slept in the sitting room, where the couch opened into a bed. But now both kids were gone, and Nellie Clough, the white housemaid, slept in what had been Abbey's room.

The MacKenzies' quarters were comfortable enough, certainly miles better than the bedbug-infested flat in East Harlem where they had spent the first five years of their marriage before they gave up the struggle to raise two kids in New York, bought a stack of out-of-town papers, and eventually answered Dorothy Cromwell's ad. That was twenty-three years ago. "Nevertheless," MacKenzie said, coming out of the bathroom, "it gets to me. We are servants. We have spent our lives as servants. Every time I stand in front of the mirror and shave this ugly face of mine, it gets to me. I am no goddamn cotton-picking sharecropper. I am a high school graduate and a trade school graduate. I am a first-rate mechanic and machinist—"

"Stop it!" Ellen snapped at him. "I been hearing that sad litany too damn long. I tell myself he's a nigger and he got the right to sing the blues. But enough is enough."

"Now don't you ever use that word 'nigger' at me. Never. Never. Never."

"I will use what I want to use. Tell you something, Mac, and this is the last time I got to squeeze it into your dumb black head. We busted the system, busted it wide open. We got us a job where we could put away better than half of what we earned, and that's the only job that could do it for us, and we got a daughter who is a pharmacist and who is married to a pharmacist, and they got their own store, and we got a son who is interning in one of the best hospitals in this state, and that, you poor dumbbell, is revenge enough to cover at least a dozen of them nigger-hating Dixie states—"

He fell into bed and put his arms around her. "Shut up. You are too smart. I should have never married a smartass fox like you."

"I can just imagine what you would have married if I hadn't got there first." She pushed him away. "Just stop that. I am not going to drag my ass around all day."

"I got a date for tonight?"

"Nighttime is a proper time. You're too old to be so horny."

"Oh? It's supposed to wear off?"

"Come on, Mac. We got us a large day. We got that big dinner party tonight. You got to pick up her folks at the airport, and then you got to do the silver, and I still have three meals to get out. So just pick yourself up out of this bed and get dressed."

MacKenzie sighed, rolled out of bed, pulled off his pajama top and then peered out of the window as the two-seater drove into the garage.

"Who is that at this hour?" Ellen wondered.

"The senator. Been out running, I suppose."

THREE

Dolly," they called her, everyone, and that was possibly because she had never liked the name Dorothy. Dolly suited her. She weighed only a hundred and twenty-two pounds, yet she gave the impression of being plump, perhaps because of her broad hips and round face. Since college, Sarah Lawrence in her case, she had worn her hair in a pageboy bob with bangs across the front. A very small nose made her face quite pretty, and her hair, which had once been black, was now at age forty-five iron gray, contrasting pleasantly with her pretty and unwrinkled face. She was one of those women who expressed authority without irritation, and who appeared usually to be poised and content.

On this morning, Dolly had set her alarm for six forty-five, and she had already showered when the senator drove in. Her bathroom faced the front of the house, and she saw his sleek little Mercedes swoop down the driveway and around to the back. She guessed that he had been out running, and as always his energy and determination amazed her. His determination was like his ambition, boundless—as, for example, in his approach to baldness. He had begun to lose his hair in his late forties, and he immediately started the process of having patches from various hairy parts of his body surgically transferred to his scalp. It had worked quite well, and now he had a proper head of white hair, befitting a United States Senator. Perhaps she was amazed because she had so little of what she thought of as ambition. She had never considered her fight to exist as a woman a manifestation of ambition.

She almost never wore make-up during the day, thankful that her skin remained good and healthy, and even more grateful for the fact that she could put herself together in a few minutes. On this day a shower, a toothbrush, and a comb through her hair did it. She then slipped into a blouse and skirt, and ran down the steps and outside to get a breath of the cool morning air before it turned warm, or hot and muggy if this were to be an uncomfortable summer day. But it had begun as a glorious morning. Dolly took such weather as a gift, and she whispered aloud, "Oh, I do feel enriched—so enriched." She walked the length of the long driveway and back, not as exercise but because she had no appetite for breakfast unless she had used her body first.

Ellen MacKenzie had put up the coffee pot, and the aromatic smell filled the big kitchen. She was cutting bread for toast; Dolly would have no presliced bread in her house.

"I'll set the table on the terrace," Ellen said. "It's warm enough, isn't it?"

"Oh yes, just right. And don't let the kids drive you crazy."

"No, ma'am. No way."

"Did the meat come?"

"Yesterday. I put it in the big fridge in the pantry."

Turning to the pantry, Dolly said, "I do hope he sent us four small legs, properly filleted and dressed." Ellen stared after her, puzzled, as Dolly opened a door of the big refrigerator, bent down, and confronted an enormous fresh ham.

"Mistake," she said. "Ellen, he sent us the wrong meat. Did you tell him exactly what I wanted, four small legs of lamb, filleted and dressed?"

Ellen sighed and shook her head. "I do hate to get into the middle of things and I should have asked you; but the senator said that you knew about the fresh pork."

Damn liar, she left unsaid. You did not call your husband a liar in front of your housekeeper. "He asked for it?"

"Yes—yes, he did. Do you want me to call the butcher?"

"No, he won't deliver today. I'll run over there myself. Just pour me a cup of coffee. That's all I want, and find a big bag or something that we can put the ham in."

The ham was heavy, at least fourteen pounds, and as she stepped out of the back door, MacKenzie appeared and took her package.

"It weighs like a sack of potatoes."

"It's a fresh ham."

"Don't see many of those these days. I do love fresh ham."

"It's going back."

"Oh? Do you want me to take it to town."

"No, I'll do that myself."

Dolly took the Buick station wagon. The senator made few public appearances in the Mercedes; his public image sat better in the Buick though he would not have complained had Dolly taken the two-seater. She had no feelings about a German car, but her father, who had been an infantry officer in the Seventh Army in World War II, detested the car enough for her to shy away from it. She never understood why she had to please her father when he was not there to be pleased, she simply accepted it as one of her minor quirks. Anyway, the fact that it was so definitely the senator's car and not the family's made her uneasy the few times she had driven it.

Driving to town, she tried to make some sense out of the puzzle of the switched meat order. Not only had Richard never tampered with a meat order before, or indeed with any process in the kitchen, but he loved lamb as Dolly served it. She would have the butcher bone the lamb leg, then remove the slightly tougher small end and trim away any excess fat. She would then marinate it for about four hours in wine with onions and spices, after which it would be broiled instead of roasted and served in slices like a roast of beef—often to guests who mistook it for tender beef, the slices being pink at the center.

The butcher, Mr. Schiller, shook his head about the fresh ham. "I'll take it back if you want me to, Mrs. Cromwell, but I don't know what I'll do with it. I had to send to the packer for it, special, and I don't know if they'll take it back. I don't get many orders for fresh ham. You know the way people are about it."

"Then I'll keep it," Dolly agreed. "The kids are home, so we'll eventually eat our way through it. But you will find me four small legs of lamb."

"Absolutely. I'll have them out at your place in an hour and a half—tops."

Dolly felt foolish, lugging the ham back into the kitchen. She should not have tried to return it. It was ridiculous, as if she could not afford both cuts of meat at the same time. She had done it out of sheer pique; and Ellen's gentle inquiry as to whether the ham would be served after all, elicited an irritated response.

"No! The lamb will be here in an hour. Put it to marinate as soon as it comes." And then, ashamed of the sharpness of her response, she hugged Ellen and said, "I'm sorry, I'm sorry. I guess this is my bitch morning."

"No, no, not at all. You always get a little up tight when your folks come."

"It is not my folks," Dolly said, breathing deeply, "it's the whole weird business of this dinner party tonight, and then on top of it this silly charade of changing the meat. Did I tell you who's coming?"

Ellen shook her head. Dolly treated her sometimes like a sister and sometimes like a servant; it made her subject to intimacies she did not seek and frequently did not welcome, yet there was the pleasure of being leaned on and depended on. Ellen was a giving woman; giving enriched her; and in her own way, she loved Dolly as much as a black woman could love a white woman who was her employer. But always there was that nugget of ice that forms in the craw of an intelligent poor person listening to the "sufferings" of the rich.

"Well, if it's not distinguished, it's important. We're having Webster Heller, Mr. Secretary of State, and that idiot wife of his, Frances, and we're having Bill Justin, Heller's assistant, and add to that Pop and Mom, whom the White House hit squad desires to see, and which is no reason for them to enter the enemy camp, unless Richard has decided that he's no longer their enemy. And Bill Justin is bringing wife Winifred, who is a malignant brilliant cat in human form—they say she runs the man—and of course Pop will insist that both kids be at the dinner table, and you know my father."

"I certainly do," Ellen replied. "But you mentioned yesterday that there would be ten at the table. That's no problem."

"Or eleven?"

"Oh? But that ain't a problem either. That's a big table. When Mac puts in the three boards, it sits sixteen comfortably."

"When they're people," Dolly agreed. "But I'm not sure at this point that politicians are people, and this number eleven is a friend of Leonard's from Harvard, a brilliant young man, they tell me, and his name is Clarence Jones and he just happens to be black."

"Oh."

"Yes, you can say that again."

"Does the senator know?"

"I don't think so. They came in at about ten, exhausted. You had gone to bed and Richard was not home yet. We put him in the middle guest room. Any sound from there?"

"Not yet."

"They're probably sleeping late. Hope so. Where's my husband?"

"Breakfast on the terrace."

"There I am bound. Just toast, cottage cheese, and a cup of coffee."

FOUR

Richard Cromwell, already at the breakfast table on the terrace, hunkered over a plate of six small sausages and three eggs, the eggs fried sunny-side up, crisp edges, just the way he liked them, and with this he had toast and imported ginger marmalade. Dolly was constantly amazed at the amount of food he consumed, three large meals, dessert, rich pies and puddings—all in open contempt of the recent nutritional discoveries, which in private he would refer to as "cult junk." He supported the beef industry, which, he felt, had been cruelly damaged by "unproven" propaganda against red meat, "the guts and strength of America," as he had once put it. With all of this, he was not fat but well built, tall enough to carry thirty extra pounds without showing it, and as yet undamaged by his diet. For a while, years before, Dolly had tried to change his eating habits, but that only served to annoy him and make their relation-

ship a little worse than it had been; whereupon she simply gave it up and provided him
with the foods he cherished. This was no great
imposition on the household, since even during summer days when Congress was not in
session, the senator ate few meals at home.
Occasionally, Dolly felt that she was watching
a slow but determined suicide.

Today, as she joined her husband, carrying
her plate of dry toast, she made no comment
about his breakfast, and by a hard hammered-
out agreement, he did not mention her toast.
The senator felt good, open armed, so to
speak, filled with the beauty of this part of the
world, the low, swelling hills, the green mead-
ows, the song of birds and the hum of insects
—and the curious sense of virtue and righteousness that comes to runners, the feeling
that God and the world has lifted the mantle
of guilt that hangs like a sweaty blanket on
most decent people. He put it into words:

"Morning, Dolly. Isn't this just one remark-
able son of a bitch of a morning?"

"You might say that." She gave him twenty
seconds or so to think of pouring her a cup of
coffee, and then did it herself. Understandable; Richard was filled with himself. His
manners were not his weak point. His father
had been an underpaid bank teller, and early
on Richard had been taught to rise when a
woman entered the room, and to cut his meat

with his right hand and then switch to his fork. His mother had been Irish, born there and come to America from Belfast as a small child, and where his constituents were Irish, Richard could put on a mellow brogue and beg that if his sainted mother had been forgiving enough to marry a man called Cromwell, surely his voters could see their way to voting for him. For his mother, manners were strong evidence that she had not succumbed to the bitterness of poverty, and if she had seen her son ignore his wife's need in this manner, she would have been furious.

Dolly was less than furious—indeed, she was not bothered at all. If her relationship with her husband puzzled her friends, it puzzled her equally; but today there would be no time for introspection, too much to do. Having poured her coffee and sipped it, Dolly said, "Richard, what possessed you to cancel my meat order and substitute fresh ham?" She was not hostile, but utterly intrigued. "I never suspected that you knew we had a kitchen, much less a butcher. How on earth did you find out who our butcher was?"

"I asked Ellen."

Mock humility. "I am silly. Of course you asked Ellen. And I suppose the mystery of the meat is just as simple?"

"Oh, absolutely. You're not angry, are you?"

"Suppose you explain."

"Simple," the senator assured her. "Just think of the fact that Webster Heller, the secretary of state, is dining with us tonight. First time. Well, that's not important—what is important is his desire to see your father, and that must be damn important or he wouldn't drag his assistant for Central America with him. On the other hand, it's my house that makes the connection, our dinner table, and whatever it has to do with your father, it's equally important to me."

"For heaven's sake, Richard, they're not our party. If one wanted to be overdramatic, one could call them the enemy. They are guests who want to harangue Daddy. They will be greeted with hospitality. They will be given as good a dinner as this house can provide. But there my responsibility ends. And I still don't know why you bought that damned ham."

"Will you listen? Will you listen one moment. I am coming up for reelection, and that will put me in the position to have at least one dim shot at the Oval Office. I've dreamed about that long enough, but there's one issue that's very important to me. If I bring it up in the House, it will mark me too left. I need the center for the election."

"Why on earth should you even think that the election is in question? You're finishing a

second term in this state. It's our state." *Ours.*
In what way, she wondered, even as she
spoke? What does *ours* mean anymore? Sitting in the sunken, brick-floored terrace, the
clipped hedges enclosing things so neatly and
precisely, the terrace, beyond the hedges the
herb garden, with its careful patches of basil
and dill and chives and mint and thyme and
parsley, the big Colonial house, one small corner of which was two hundred years old, she
realized that the world was not this—no
longer this, no longer even aware of this.

"Oh, no," Richard said. "Not so quick.
You've heard of targeting. These bastards
have all the money in the world, and they use
it. They pick a senator they want to destroy,
and they target him. They drown him in television commercials, they dig up his past and if
he doesn't have a past, they create one. Well, I
don't want it to be Richard Cromwell."

"And you're going to tame the beast tonight?" she asked, smiling.

"Maybe. Maybe neutralize him a little
bit . . ."

"How? Good heavens, how?"

"Appeal to compassion. Anyway, I didn't
invite them here—I mean it wasn't my ges-
ture. Bill Justin—"

That pissant, Dolly thought. She found it
difficult to voice crude language, as much as it
was the manner today, and even the name of

the assistant secretary rubbed her nerves as a coin scraped on glass.

"—well, Bill Justin called Joan and mentioned that Webster Heller was staying at his home for a week or so, and that—"

"I know how he happens to come here."

"But you see, Dolly, it makes a connection. I might even say a basis for quid pro quo now exists. They want something damned important from your daddy. I want a small but important favor from them. It's an opportunity for me, and I need it."

"Well, be that as it may, I have a dinner party to prepare for, and I want to know why on earth you ordered the ham?"

"It's Webster Heller. He's crazy about fresh roasted pork, and I remembered that a couple of months ago I overheard one of his assistants telling someone how much Heller liked fresh roast ham, and how it was these days that you never see a fresh roast ham, only the smoked and the boiled; you know, you're standing around on the Hill, and you overhear something. You're not listening, you just overhear it, and I thought to myself what a neat ploy to just happen to serve Heller with his favorite meat. You know, nothing earthshaking but one of those small touches that goes right to a man's heart."

"The small touch is fourteen pounds—"

"I know I should have spoken to you, but you weren't around, and—"

"And the brilliance of your notion overwhelmed you, and you acted."

"Hey, are you angry?"

"Not a bit. I just tore into town, practically got Schiller out of bed, and then like a true idiot had to lug the ham back with me. However I did order the meat I had planned to serve and thank heavens he had it."

"You mean that damn filleted lamb."

"Just about the most delicious meat money can buy."

"Dolly," the senator said, "before we get into a real squabble, tell me why you won't serve the ham? Does it louse up your menu?" His question was plaintive, and when he was plaintive, with just the edge of a whine in his voice, she pitied him. It was a side he revealed to no one else, a small boy in a large, confusing world, where he just happened to be a member of the most important club in the world; or at least this was Dolly's measure of her husband, and with it went a suspicion that more than one member of the United States Congress built the same façade of knowledge and power over inner fear and stumblings that were not unlike the reactions of a small boy.

"My father and mother are coming," she

said gently. "They are Jewish. You may have noticed, I have never served ham to a Jew at my dinner table."

"What!" His exclamation was so intense that Dolly burst out laughing. Now Richard was angry and indignant. "You're telling me that in the past twenty-three years, in which time we sat at the dinner table with maybe five, six hundred, maybe a thousand Jews, you never served ham?"

"No, I never did. And you never noticed."

"Why? I never knew a Jew who didn't eat ham."

"You might have," she said quietly. "You don't know, really."

"Are you talking about those dietary laws? Dolly, I don't think you even know what Jewish dietary laws are."

"Richard, it's not a matter of the dietary laws. It's a matter of a decent respect for what might or might not be your guests' preference—without prying into their belief."

"But it's your father and mother."

"Exactly."

"But, Dolly, I just happen to know what their beliefs are. I've had lunch and dinner too at your father's club and at mine, and I've seen him eat ham and bacon."

"That was not my house."

"Dolly, your mother is not Jewish; as far as I

know, you never set foot in a synagogue, and now you're throwing this Jewish thing at me." Grimly serious, he said, "Don't ever throw this kind of thing at me. I have faults. Anti-Semitism is not one of them."

"I wish you could understand."

"Oh, the hell with it . . ." And then his voice trailed away. Around the back of the house and toward the swimming pool, in their bathing suits, three people appeared, two young men and a young woman, and one of the young men was black.

"Who is that?" he asked blankly.

"The black kid?"

"I know who the others are."

"Well, that young man's name is Clarence Jones. He's a student at Harvard and a close friend of Leonard's. He's there on scholarship —not one of those special preference things, but the old-fashioned kind that you win by having more brains than the other kids."

"Lenny's guest?"

"Right."

"For the day?"

"Do you mean," Dolly asked, "is he leaving before dinner? No, he's staying. Lenny invited him for the weekend, and since today is Friday, I suppose that means until Monday. He's a delightful boy. Why do you ask?"

"Well, I suppose the three of them could

have their dinner first. They won't find much amusement in a party of old folks."

"Come on, Richard," Dolly said, "do you really think they'd miss a chance to break bread with those two old pirates you invited here tonight? Anyway, Daddy doesn't come here to see us; he comes to see Leonard and Elizabeth, and if they weren't at dinner, he'd raise hell. What are you worried about?"

"You know what I'm worried about."

"I'm not sure."

"It's bad enough to have a Harvard liberal loudmouth son who thinks I've sold out the human race, but a smartass black kid from the same reservation—well, Web Heller just isn't that quick. This kid could cut him to pieces, and there goes your dinner party, and my plans."

"Why should he?"

"Why? Did you ever meet a black man who didn't think that this administration is out to destroy the black population?"

The trouble was, Dolly realized, that outside of Washington cocktail parties and dinner parties and various receptions, she had known too few black people to have any clear notion of what they thought. Those she had encountered at various affairs had, like most political people, disguised or hidden their thoughts behind walls of clichés or platitudes, and now she could hardly accept the fact that a guest of her son would deliberately provoke another guest.

"Do you want me to speak to Leonard?" she asked Richard.

"No. If it comes up, I'll handle it."

FIVE

Elizabeth Cromwell was twenty years old, going into her junior year at Sarah Lawrence, five feet nine inches tall, and reasonably beautiful. Her brown hair was streaked by the sun, and as the summer wore on, her skin would turn berry brown. Her good looks and obvious good health attracted men; her manner put them off, too thinly veiled sardonic humor and too much evidence of intellectual superiority. Too many men who came on to her came off rather quickly, stung and petulant and sometimes angry. Her brother, Leonard, was more disarming. Two inches over six feet, slender, good-looking, he had a gentle, amiable manner that hid a sharp, inquisitive mind. A couple of years older than Elizabeth, he adored her. He was very thin, a long bony body and black unkempt hair over a round, button-nosed face.

His friend, Clarence Jones, was shorter, broader, and coffee brown in color. Both of them were first year at Harvard Law, and both were oddly alike in having the same round head and small, turned-up nose.

Elizabeth and the two men were in their bathing suits, carrying robes and towels, their bodies bare to the warm morning sun; and as they came around the back of the house on the path that led to the pool, they were about sixty yards from where the senator and his wife were having their breakfast.

"Shouldn't I be introduced?" Clarence Jones wondered. "I never met your dad."

"Rejoice for a while longer," Leonard said bleakly.

"Oh, come on," Elizabeth protested, "he's all right."

"Yes?"

"I mean you're giving Clare all the wrong notions. Pop is polite and pleasant and he doesn't rub people the wrong way."

"No chip on my shoulder," Clarence said mildly.

"Right now, let's swim," Leonard said. "We'll meet him."

"As you say."

The swimming pool was nested in a wall of flowering shrubs, which gave it privacy without casting shadows. It was fifty feet long and thirty feet wide, a large size for a private pool, a diving board at one end, and the pool itself was positioned and decorated with great charm. Since he arrived at the Cromwell home the night before, Clarence Jones had been quietly yet intensely observing and studying a manner of life he had read about and seen in films, but never actually encountered before.

"Liz does her laps first," Leonard told him. "She gets the pool to herself for half an hour because she's selfish and rigid."

"Go to hell," Elizabeth said pleasantly, and dived in and came up screaming, "It's fucken, fucken cold! Didn't anyone set the heater going?"

"I set it last night, but it doesn't start heating until six in the morning. Once Mac starts putting the cover on at night, we won't have a problem."

Elizabeth had begun her laps without waiting for him to finish his explanation. She swam with a smooth, easy freestyle that brought a grunt of praise from Clarence.

"Man, she's a beautiful swimmer."

"I've raced her a hundred times. She always beats me. Men can swim faster, but I never saw a man who could swim with the style and class of a good lady swimmer."

Clarence was looking around, absorbing every detail, the striped cabana tent at one end, the outdoor shower, the lovely wrought-iron table and chairs on the poolside terrace, the telephone, the wheeled cart with its weather-protected small television, so that even here one should be near the glass tit on which all America sucked. "This," he said, "is what they call the good life, and you had no business bringing a poor black boy out here to taste it. When I was waiting tables at Casey's and brought you a beer, I had no idea that you had crawled out of a cornucopia to go slumming."

"Bullshit. You'll be the editor of the *Law Review* and you'll walk out of school into a job at some truly hotshot New York or Washington firm at a starting wage of fifty grand a year, so don't pull any Topsy shit on me."

"Topsy was a girl. The rich are always ignorant."

Nellie Clough, the housemaid, appeared. She was small, blonde, and cute; at least, Dolly always described her as cute, and she had an interesting Irish brogue. She was not impressed by Clarence's statement about the rich; her own faith in the rich would never be shaken. She had been with the family six years, and only once during that time had the senator crawled into bed with her. She had known girls in the old country where it had been every month and every week, and in one case, with Sir Roger Kimberly, every day of the week, although Nellie never knew whether to believe the girl who told her the story. Measured against that yardstick, the senator was a gentleman. All her very restrained and careful advances toward Leonard had so far produced no results, yet she smiled on him fondly as she told him that Ellen was out of patience today. "That's what she says," Nellie told them. "Breakfast will not be served at the pool, and not even juice or coffee, mind you, and after ten you get no breakfast at all, not a smidgen, because it is a day with no extra hours, which is what she says."

"Ah, Nellie," Leonard said, "you know I love you—"

"I know nothing of the kind."

"—and what harm—" imitating her accent "—in a bit of coffee and a crock of juice. Come on. Come on. Be a love."

"Ellen would kill me. You know the way she is." Pointing to Elizabeth, doing her laps, "She's at it again?"

"I can't talk her out of it. Even coffee. Just coffee—how about it, you lovely golden-haired creature?"

"All right. I'll try. I don't promise, but I'll try."

She departed, and Leonard stared at Elizabeth. Clarence mentioned the fact that Nellie did not appear to know he was there.

"She can't deal with blacks. She's used to Ellen and Mac, and maybe she pretends they're not black. But others—I don't know. To be plucked out of a peasant cottage in Ireland and dropped here—well, it's a peculiar transition."

"By the way," Clarence asked, "does Elizabeth know?"

"Know? Oh, you mean about me. No, she doesn't."

"She knows you're gay?"

"She knows. We've never talked about it, but I'm sure she knows. She's smart. She's a damn sight smarter than anyone gives her credit for, because when you look like that, you're not supposed to be smart. And the two of us—you know, I don't think we ever had a fight, you know, the way brothers and sisters scrap all the time and cat each other. We made a closed thing, and she was like a romantic love to me as far back as I can remember, and we did all our sexual exploring of each other with such innocence, like two loving animals, like you might think about two puppies, and sometimes I'd have daydreams of just Liz and me on an island, like those two kids in that movie—what was it, do you know?"

"The Blue Lagoon," Clarence said gently.

"So she has to know I'm gay—it's just putting two and two together, and there are other things between us that she knows and I know and we never talk about them."

"And your mother and father—they never put two and two together?"

"Bite your tongue, Jones. My father would have to pause, resign from the Senate and the presidency for at least five minutes, have a good long look at me, convince himself that I am his son, memorize what I look like—and then he'd remember that he never looked at me before, so how in hell could he put two and two together when the other two never was there? Does that make sense?"

"No, and you're shouting and Liz will hear you. Anyway, I don't believe you. The senator's a good man."

"She wouldn't hear a bomb explode, the way she's going. And don't tell me about the senator." He glanced at his watch. "Twelve minutes. Eighteen minutes to go."

"That's determination."

"That's a stainless-steel ramrod instead of a spine." Looking at his watch, he felt his pulse, counting the beats against the second hand of the watch.

"Do you feel all right?"

"I think so. I can go an hour, sometimes two hours without remembering, and then it comes home and my heart stops—it actually does, I mean I miss a beat or two or three—and my chest is filled with ice. Fear. My God, Jonesy, the fear is so fucken terrible, but I'm all right now. I'm all right. Daytime isn't so bad. The nights are awful."

"You have to tell someone, Lenny. You have to. You can't do this alone."

"I told you."

"That's what I mean. What about your mother? You never talk about your mother."

"Ah, my mother, dear, sweet Dolly. I love Dolly. I don't know about right now, right this minute. Right this minute I don't know whether I'm capable of loving anyone, even you. But Dolly has been all that a mother should be. She dedicated herself to being a mother, just as she dedicated herself to National Cancer, or to the End Poverty thing or Save the Children or Amnesty International or public television. She has a conscience large enough for every good cause this country produces, but whether there's any real ordinary compassion under that conscience I simply don't know."

"You're being pretty hard on her. She struck me as a lovely woman."

"She is a lovely lady. She's beautiful, and when I do tell her, or when somebody else tells her, it will be like cutting her heart out, because she adores me. But what is she and where is she? She goes on living year after year with a man she despises. She does this Jewish pretend. Her full name is Dorothy Shippan Constanza Levi. Somewhere the Shippans came into the family, and Constanza was the name of her first woman ances-

tor here in America who married Gideon
Levi in New York. Somewhere in the sixteen
hundreds."

"Just about when my folks came," Clarence
said.

"Right on. Oh, hell, why am I doing this?
Dolly is Dolly. She's a dear, and so she wants
to be Jewish. But it's like when I told her I was
a vegetarian. She didn't ask me why. She immediately fell into a game of menus. What
now? Mother darling, I'm gay, I'm a real hon-
est-to-God faggot, and I'll be dead in six
months or so."

"Cool it. Here's Goldilocks."

Nellie came striding up, proudly bearing a
plastic container of coffee, some plastic cups,
and a box of croissants. "Ellen saw me," she
explained, "but then your mother called her,
so I grabbed these and ran. You like them?"

"We do indeed," Clarence said, smiling at
her. She stared at him as if she hadn't seen
him before, and then she whirled around and
ran. "Which is power over women," he said.

Leonard, suddenly famished, handed a
croissant to Clarence and then bit into one
himself. He poured the coffee.

"Have you tried cocaine?" Clarence asked,
a stupid question that made him writhe inside.

"I've tried it." Stupid didn't matter to
Leonard.

"It doesn't help?"

"Not much, no."

Wet and glowing, Elizabeth was climbing out of the pool, and looking at her, Clarence felt that she was the most beautiful woman he had ever seen, and it made him wonder, as he had often wondered before, how it would be to love a woman, wholly, totally, to lust for her day in and day out, to become alive at the touch of her hand. Yet in the next breath, he said to himself, She is not that beautiful, and this whole stinking white world is filled with beautiful women, and I'm losing every sense of proportion sitting here in this lousy twentieth-century white paradise. He also remembered a time when his father had been laid off by the company where he had worked for twenty years, and he, Clarence, aged ten, had asked his father what God was like and wouldn't God help them? To which his father had replied, "I know what God looks like. He is a cold-assed blue-eyed blond white son of a bitch, and you hold out a hand and he'll kick in your head, like any rotten white boss I ever known." His mother overheard this and burst into tears. He had never heard his father talk like that before. They were church-going folk who never tolerated bad language in the home, and he and the other kids watched, scared and afraid even to whisper.

"Twenty minutes," Leonard said.

"Towel!"

He threw a towel to her and watched her rub herself dry. She was breathing deeply, totally alive with herself. "Give me time," she said. "I've only been at it a week." She shook out her hair. "What is that—croissants? Give me one. And coffee. That dear angel Nellie. Well, Jonesy," she said to Clarence, "what do you think of this big shit pile of money and class?"

"Given a chance, I could learn to live in a place like this."

"I bet you could. Money makes the world go round. But it costs. You don't have the right grandpa, you can't afford it. And the senator has to have a place in Washington. Respectable. A house in Georgetown, proper for proper entertainment." She took a sip of coffee. "Of course, it's small potatoes compared to Grandpa's modest way of life. He has seven homes."

"Come on, you're kidding."

"Didn't Lenny tell you?"

Leonard shook his head despairingly.

"It's the truth. Lenny is embarrassed as hell with wealth. I don't mind it. I can face right up to it. Myself, I don't think seven houses are a reflection of sense or sanity, but then I don't think rich people are very sane—or poor people, come to think of it."

"Seven homes?"

"Poor black boy can't believe it. I don't blame you. I'll give you a rundown. Old family house in New York City on East Sixty-fourth Street. Five floors, seventeen rooms, built by his granddaddy in eighteen ninety-six. Lodge in the Adirondacks, apartment in Paris, house on Cape Cod, house in Montecito —his granddaddy used to be buddy-buddy with old William Randolph Hearst, and built the Montecito place to be reasonably near him. How many is that?"

"Too many," Leonard said. "Will you forget the goddamn houses."

"Lenny is like my mother. They both have what Thorstein Veblen used to call the conscience of the rich, which is as much of a lie as everything else, because the rich have no conscience. I like to bring up old Veblen because nobody in our generation knows who he is."

"You impress me," Clarence said.

"Come on, Jonesy, you're too smart to be impressed by me."

"Will you come down," Leonard said plaintively. "It's wonderful to see you like this, and I hate to lay the worst kind of shit on you, but I have to."

She stopped her chatter, looked at him thoughtfully and waited.

"You and me. This is not for Mom or for the senator—do you understand. Just you."

"All right," she whispered.

"Begin with the fact that I'm gay."

Elizabeth smiled wistfully. "That's all, Lenny? I've always known it—a long time, anyway."

"I know. I wasn't sure."

"So what? Jonesy here is gay, and the poor bastard's black. Suppose Jonesy were Jewish —Jewish, black and gay, that would be something—"

"Don't kid about it," Clarence said.

She smelled it and sensed it. It was as if the gentle morning breeze had stopped, as if everything had suddenly turned into winter. She saw it in their faces, in their eyes.

"Oh, my God, what is it?" she begged them.

"Poor darling Liz," Leonard said, his eyes brimming with tears. "I have AIDS."

Elizabeth stared at him for an endless moment, and then Leonard saw her face collapse. Something tore away all the flesh and muscle that supported her beauty, leaving a crinkled, distorted mask of sorrow and horror. Leonard went to her and embraced her, clutching her to him while she buried her weeping face on his breast. He held her like that, feeling her sobs contort her body, and whispering to her, "It's all right, Lizzie. I didn't want you to cry. Please don't cry. You know what happens to me when you cry." He was crying. That's what happened to him when his sister wept, but it had not happened since they were children; and now clutching his sister, he remembered how, eight years old, he had felt his first intimation of mortality, a little boy alone in bed with the cold image of death.

"Don't cry, please."

Clarence, watching, found himself being drawn into their grief. Close as he was to Leonard, he could never let down his walls of defense for a white man. He had his own hours of terror and despair after the tests told him his own final truth, and being black, he kept that as well as other things inside himself. He resisted the forces drawing him to the brother and sister as long as he could; then he dropped into a chair, covered his face with his arms and wept. He was weeping for himself. How lonely it is to weep for oneself.

Leonard pulled them out of it. "For Christ's sake, there comes Dad! No tears, please! I can't face him with it—please!"

They had dried their tears and pulled themselves together as the senator came onto the pool terrace. He wore a pair of pink and yellow swim shorts, and in spite of being thirty pounds overweight, he was a fine figure of a man, broad-shouldered and well built. He shook hands with Clarence with an energy that excluded any sensitivity to what might have been going on before he arrived. He boomed a cheerful good morning to Leonard and he kissed Elizabeth with exuberance. "So you're young Jones," he said to Clarence. "Heard a lot about you, and glad you could come. Make yourself at home. We have a fine library and a nice selection of those movie cassettes that seem to be engulfing the country. Myself, when I want to forget the world, I take an hour at the billiard table." With that, he walked to the pool and plunged in and came up shouting, "Cold—cold!"

Leonard managed to smile and say, "You see, he never saw me. Never knew I was here."

SIX

Richard Cromwell swam two full lengths of the long pool before he realized that he had done an utterly deplorable thing; except for "good morning," he had not said a word directly to his son, whom he had not seen for two months. He was taken sick at the thought. How could he have done anything like that? It was not in his nature, and never before had he done anything like this—or had he? He tried to examine himself, to roll back his memory and make a picture of how he had treated his son through the years; but it was too difficult while he was swimming, and after the fourth length, he pulled himself out of the water hoping to repair the situation.

They had gone. What now? He loved his son, he loved both his kids; he threw this declaration of his feelings at himself, muttering in his mind, Just don't tell me I don't love my kids. Well, it was not easy to love Leonard. Other sons related to their fathers, played ball with them, rolled in the grass with them, went walking with them. Yes, there were times he could get Leonard to walk with him; he could count the times on the fingers of his hands; but that didn't mean he didn't love his son, nor did it mean that his son didn't love him. Or did his son love him? It had never occurred to him to ask himself that question. The boy was at prep school, the boy was at college, the senator was in Washington. I do my best, his apology to himself. But what now? What could he do now?

SEVEN

At ten o'clock, Dolly joined Ellen in the kitchen to go over the menu for tonight's dinner. In all the years that Ellen and Mac had worked for her, Dolly had never found a way to an easy relationship. She had grown up with servants, but they were white servants, and her mother had a distant, imperious way with them, a way that came from an era when the poor were poor and lived and died with it, and the rich were rich by the grace of God. But when it came down to black servants and today, a difference appeared.

There was a difference, subtle, but always there, as Dolly spelled it out to her Washington, D.C. analyst. He was one of the most expensive analysts in Washington, charging one hundred and fifty dollars for his fifty-minute hour, and with enough positive reputation to back that up. He had at least two dozen patients who were wives to elected and appointed officials in high places, and

Dolly often felt that the world might be at least slightly improved if the husbands were to take their wives' places. She irritated Dr. Philip Westfield when she referred to this. She irritated Dr. Westfield in other ways too— which was not supposed to be the case with a bright and reputable psychiatrist, and when she got too deeply under his skin, he ceased to be a Freudian listener and spoke out. As once when he said, "You make too much of this black business, we all recognize it. We live with it."

"What do you mean—you live with it? Blacks live with it. They suffer, not you." That finished her analysis for what it was worth. She decided that if she stayed out of Washington for a maximum number of days, it would be cheaper and more effective than analysis.

Apropos of her fluttering memories, she asked Ellen whether she had ever known anyone who was analyzed, and to her surprise, Ellen replied that her daughter was taking courses in psychology, and that after she had produced two children, and the store was doing well enough to hire a pharmacist, she'd like to go in for therapy.

"Good! Encourage her. Now let's get down to work," Dolly said. "You know, we're dealing with eleven now. The secretary of state and an assistant secretary. Be duly impressed."

"I'm duly impressed."

They sat at the big kitchen table, each of them with a pencil and work pad. For Dolly, a proper dinner party had to be a theatrical production in its own right, planned as such down to every detail. And details change. "I couldn't get the salmon," Dolly said.

"That's a shame."

"They had a few steaks, but not enough and I didn't like the look of it. I took sole instead."

"Just as good."

"Well, almost. I'll run through the menu again, and you tell me where we have a problem—if we do. Start with a quenelle of sole."

"Then we'll want a white butter sauce, won't we?"

"I'm not sure of it. But jot it down anyway," Dolly said. "I think we have everything. There are two jars of the caviar and the shallots are still good. Wine, vinegar, butter—we have a recipe for it somewhere."

"I think so, yes."

"Main dish, lamb, flageolets—do we have two boxes of flageolets? If not, we'll do wild rice. Very classy, but I dislike it."

Ellen went to the pantry and reported that there were ample flageolets.

"And chopped spinach."

"We have about five pounds of the fresh spinach, and I think there are eight boxes of the frozen stuff."

"Fresh spinach. My mother knows."

"Indeed she does," Ellen agreed.

"Now on the salad, I want your opinion. I thought of endive and sliced, peeled tomatoes."

"Endive?"

"Oh? Come on, speak."

"I feel it's in the same class as wild rice."

"Right. Pretentious and not great. No argument? Boston lettuce?"

"Arugula?" Ellen asked tentatively.

"Absolutely. But that wants a tart dressing."

"No question about that," Ellen agreed. They were always closer and easier when they worked. "Still lemon mousse for dessert?"

"Oh, absolutely. My father adores it."

"He had it last time," Ellen reminded her.

"With a lemon sauce. This time, raspberry sauce. Makes all the difference in the world."

"It does, sure enough. I spent an hour yesterday squeezing them berries through the sieve. Miserable seeds."

"But it's done."

"All done."

MacKenzie had come into the kitchen while they were discussing the menu, and he stood at the stainless-steel utility sink, scrubbing his hands. "Miss Dolly," he said, "did you notice anything driving the station wagon?"

"The brakes pull to the right—just a bit."

"Well, I got it. They'll pull straight now. When do you want me to go to the airport and pick up your folks?"

"Oh? No, I'll need you here, Mac. I want the silver polished, and I want you to see whether you can get the stains out of the dining room rug. I also want to talk about the meat."

"Miss Dolly, I done that boned lamb maybe two dozen times. I know just how you want it."

"She don't want it grilled through like leather, and you done that too," Ellen said.

"I'll send the kids to pick up Mom and Pop. Mac?"

"Yes, ma'am." He was miffed. He stiffened, looking straight ahead of him.

"You're my wine steward. You're the only one I can turn to about wine. What do we have in the cellar that's really good and goes with my menu?"

That pleased him. The senator had no real interest in wine or liquor. Social drinking was obligatory in his position, as was an occasional cigar under certain circumstances; his pursuit of youth drove him onto the running track and into the pool, never toward a bottle, and while he pretended to some knowledge of wine, what he had mastered came from reading the labels MacKenzie selected. It was

MacKenzie who maintained their small but excellent wine cellar, both here and in Washington. Now he said to Dolly, "Well, Miss Dolly, you better run the menu through for me again."

Dolly knew that he knew exactly what would be served for dinner, and that this was a sort of apology on her part for ordering him away from a pleasant ride to the airport and into the pantry to polish the silver and do other odds and ends, like extending the table and finding flowers in the garden that might be cut. She didn't mind. "Quenelle of sole, broiled lamb leg, salad, and lemon mousse. In the library, we'll have assorted nuts, cheese sticks and olives with the drinks."

MacKenzie thought about it for a moment. "We have a nice white wine. It's very dry, but light and nice, maybe the best white wine there is. Pavillon Blanc nineteen seventy-eight. It's a Château—Margaux, I think?"

Dolly, now as always, was impressed. Mac had been reading books on wine for years, and anticipating that she would question him today, he had already worked out the selections. Dolly nodded.

"For the quenelle," he said. "I'd use the same wine in the library."

"But not for the lamb?"

"I thought maybe some variety. I was looking for a rosé, but we don't have more than three bottles of any rosé and it wouldn't hurt to have something a little heavier with the meat, because most people think it's beef anyway, the way we do it. We got almost a full case of the Lafite-Rothschild red Bordeaux, nineteen sixty-four, and it's something we been saving for something real special, if this is that special?"

Dolly grinned and the two blacks began to giggle. "I don't know," Dolly said. "They run the country, but I don't know whether that makes them special. What do you think, Ellen?"

"Now don't go asking me what I think because trouble comes out of that. What I think is that Mac could get himself one of them jobs in a fancy restaurant when you retire us as a— what do you call it?"

"No retirement," Dolly said.

"Sommelier," MacKenzie said. "You like that suggestion of the Rothschild?"

"Absolutely. Now, you know, Mac, I want you to do the carving and the wine. Have Nellie serve, but you rehearse her about which is her left hand and which is her right, and you pour the wine. Now do you think we should have something with the dessert?"

"Just the mousse?"

"We have cigarette cookies," Ellen said. "Nice and light. I made them yesterday."

"I forgot about that." Dolly nodded. "Absolutely. Then we should have champagne. Do we have anything special?"

"We got a case of Cordon Bleu, and we got four bottles, I think, of Dom Perignon, same year as the Margaux, seventy-eight, and really high class."

"Good. Put them in the fridge and then get the boards in the table. I'll set it with Ellen just as soon as we can. You know about lunch," she said to Ellen, "put out cold cuts and a salad niçoise and bread and relish and that sort of thing. We can't bother with more than that."

"I'll hardboil some eggs."

"Wonderful, wonderful." Dolly sighed and leaned back in her chair and reflected on the curious ritual they were going through. Making a dinner party. Elizabeth had once said to her, "Dinner parties are ridiculous. You go through this endless fuss and bother, and this and that must be just right, with this wine and that sauce, and Mother dear, it's absolutely silly, and it's such a real, heavy class thing." But Elizabeth was wrong. It was a ritual, Dolly agreed, but not silly—indeed one of the very oldest rituals that had come down unchanged from the misty beginnings of civilization; and right now, sitting in her marvelous twentieth-century kitchen with its eight-burner restaurant stove, its small microwave subsidiary, its enormous refrigerator, its island work counter bearing eight-slice toaster, Cuisinart, Kitchenaid dough hook and two blenders, she remembered, for some reason, a story she had read as a child. In this story, a king had invited one of his powerful noble-men to dinner. It was a very elegant dinner, and course after course was served; but as the dinner progressed, the nobleman realized that no bread was being served, and he also realized that when the dinner was over, he would be killed. Thus the absence of bread on the table, since if one breaks bread with a guest, one cannot do him harm. The story had chilled her blood when she first read it, and now the memory of it sent a chill through her and caused Ellen to ask, "Are you all right?"

Dolly managed to smile. "Of course. I was thinking about bread."

"No trouble," Mac said. "I picked up half a dozen french breads day before yesterday. Four of them still in the freezer." But the thought of death, not bread, had chilled her.

EIGHT

I think we ought to go to someplace quiet, where we can meditate," Jones said.

"And what will that do for us?" Elizabeth demanded.

"It helps."

"It helps," Leonard repeated. "Nothing else helps."

"I don't know how to meditate," Elizabeth said, her eyes full of tears.

"It's easy, Liz."

They went to the old barn. The senator's place was five acres, and the old barn was hidden from the house by a roll of the land. The house that had once been its companion had burned down long ago, leaving only its fieldstone chimney, covered over with honeysuckle and poison ivy. The glade where the barn stood was reached by a narrow dirt road that wound through high, sweet-smelling grass, netted over with insects and birds, all of it succulent in the morning warmth. Once, when Elizabeth was eleven, her mother yielded to her pleading and allowed her grandfather, Augustus Levi, to buy her a horse. At that point, the old barn was hardly more than a pile of barely joined boards, but the senator had it rebuilt for the beautiful little filly that took up residence there—at least for the summer months. In the winter, it was boarded elsewhere. Leonard had never been interested in horses, and by age fourteen, Elizabeth had passed through her horse phase. The horse was sold and the barn abandoned.

They had changed into jeans and cotton shirts, all three of them dressed alike without thought or choice. "We'll sit cross-legged," Clarence said. There was an old decaying English saddle in one corner of the barn. "You can use that, Liz, if you have to."

"I can sit cross-legged," she said. "I've been doing it since age two."

Leonard had fallen into position, legs crossed, hands loosely clasped in his lap. They formed a triangle, the three of them, each at a corner.

"I pick a spot in the center for my sight," Clarence said. "I keep my eyes open."

There was a pungent, lonesome barn smell to the place, full of memories and the nostalgia of time and the pain of time. Why had Leonard picked this place? She thought of getting up and telling them that it was no good and that they must go elsewhere, but instead she asked Leonard, "Are you going to tell Mother and Dad?"

"I have to, sometime."

"Better if we don't speak. I'll speak a little —just to help Elizabeth," Clarence said.

"Sorry."

"Wipe your tears, Liz. It's this moment— only this moment. Nothing is happening now. Don't think about anything at all. I'll count my breaths. Ten."

She counted her breaths, one to ten.

"And now I stop counting," Clarence said, "but I watch my breathing. I watch it rise and fall, and at the same time, I make myself aware of my body. I sense toes, feet, legs—I go over my whole body and bring it into my consciousness."

It was a strange experience for Elizabeth, fighting with all her mental strength to empty her mind, not to think of Leonard and his fate, not to remember their childhood together, the games they played; the time when the two of them were lost in the endless halls and rooms of the Capitol building in Washington; the hours in this same old barn when the two of them groomed her horse; their secret talks and investigations; hard to put that away from her mind; yet it happened, long moments of nothing that washed over her like a very strange benediction.

"I let go of all the tension in my body, in my arms, my neck and around my head. . . ." His voice trailed away and Elizabeth raised her eyes to look at her brother. His eyes were shadowed. He sat very straight. She wondered how long he had been doing this. It didn't protect him. Nothing could protect him. He sat cross-legged, slender, erect, handsome, and pledged to death.

And silently he pleaded, fearful and wistful, Let it go away. But to whom? What gods listen to prayers? When he came weeping to his mother as a child, a bruise, a cut, a bump on his head, she could kiss it and make the pain go away, and then the cut or bruise or bang would go away; but now, remembering that terrible, icy line of Swinburne's, *Only the sleep eternal in the eternal night,* nothing could make the pain go away.

So easy for Jones to say, "Empty your mind." Jones had persuaded him into meditation. "It's bad enough that the world doesn't know what we are. We don't know what we are or who we are, and that's the thing to find out isn't it? The only thing."

Over the winter break, instead of going home, he had gone with Jones to a place in the Maine woods, which they called an ashram, and there for six days they had sat and meditated with thirty-seven others in the cold, short winter days, cold always and mimicking the Buddha, who had meditated for many, many years until one day he was able to say, "I know the answers to all the questions." But Leonard knew no answers. Not why and not how, and the only real prayer now was in thanks, since Jones, miraculously, was free of it. Or was he?

If Jones was clean, Leonard was grateful, yet suppose Jones had it too. Would it be easier, the two of them together; and for that thought, he punished himself. No, Jones must live and he must die. He had the mark of the beast, he told himself defiantly. He could be like that, defiant, death be damned, I am not afraid, resting peacefully for a moment in the memory of what an old Buddhist rashi had said, "Death? You ask where you will be? Where were you before you were born?" But only for a moment this kind of defiant indifference; then the quiet emptiness that comes sometimes out of meditation and then he remembered again.

He remembered the thing on his foot, the purple spot like a blueberry, and the old doctor who looked at it and then murmured softly, "Kaposi's sarcoma," but with such sadness in the two whispered words that Leonard's heart stopped; and then tests and more tests, but never even a suggestion of hope.

The only positive thing he could exact from them was an agreement not to inform his family; and in return he nodded to the old doctor's warning, "Your semen and your blood are deadly now. Remember. They have the power to kill."

NINE

Dressed now, Senator Cromwell set out to avoid being chosen to drive to the airport and pick up his in-laws. If Dolly pointed a finger at him, he would use the fact that his secretary, Joan Herman, was coming by in a half hour or so to take some letters and a few notes. When Dolly informed him that the kids would drive to the airfield, he felt relieved. At the same time, Dolly told him that she didn't know where the kids were, except that they were somewhere on the property because all the cars were in the garage. She was about to send Mac out to find them.

"I'll find them," the senator said. It was not that he disliked Dolly's father and mother; it was a gut feeling that they had contempt for him—and no more than a gut feeling because nothing in their attitude toward him expressed it. "But don't you see," Dolly explained to him, "they have contempt for everybody. For one thing, they are one of the oldest families in America. They look down upon such Johnnys-come-lately as the Rockefellers, the Vanderbilts, or the Boston crowd, the Lodges and the Adamses and the others. They are impossible, and my four brothers are impossible. I'm the only civilized person in the family. They look down on the German Jews and the Eastern European Jews, even though they accept them in marriage. They hide; they feel that true aristocracy does not look for publicity, and Daddy employs a very clever person to keep his name out of the media. So don't brood over it. We don't see them enough for it to be a real problem."

The senator had tried to live with that advice, but it was not easy. Dolly was a very rich woman in her own right, and Augustus and Jenny Levi, who were generous in gift giving, never offered money or discussed it, the single exception being the senator's campaign funds. Whatever their feelings were toward the senator, for his part, he was not fond of them. If he hated them, it was not a hatred he could admit to himself. The senator had learned long ago that in American politics, you do not hate people, and he had learned it so well that it was doubtful that he could summon up a strong, old-fashioned hate. In his business, politicians to the right of Genghis Khan were his *good friends,* people with the minds of Neanderthals were his *valued asso-*

ciates and people still residing mentally in a slave society were his *respected opponents.* Hatred, like love and honor and a decent respect for the opinions of mankind, was watered down and replaced with a process of being careful. And that same process led him to move heaven and earth to avoid being with his in-laws.

But his children were not to be found in the house, and he stormed into the dining room where Dolly had begun to set the table, demanding to know where they were.

"I don't know," Dolly said. "Did you look in the old barn?"

"Why?"

"Because they might be there," Dolly said patiently, as if it were the most obvious thing in the world.

The senator shrugged, left the house and started off toward the old barn. The day was hot already. The swarms of insects made him miserable, and he was sure that somehow he would get poison ivy. This he hated; he felt more vicious toward poison ivy than toward the Ayatollah, and he had even played with the notion of introducing a bill to rid the whole country of poison ivy. In his childhood, he had several painful sessions with poison ivy, and nothing could convince him that one had to touch it to get it.

Coming around a bend in the old dirt road,

the barn still a couple of hundred yards away, the senator suddenly felt tired. He had awakened early in the morning, hours that felt like days, he had run, he had swum, he had showered twice, and very soon he would have Joan Herman working with him in his study, doing a first draft of a bill he had been contemplating and arranging and rearranging in his mind; and in his house Joan Herman was a problem. Being in his house, under the nose of his wife, she appeared to explode with lust, luring him into love, or into what went by the name, behind locked doors, standing, sitting, on the floor, on the top of his desk—wherever. He should have gone to her apartment this morning. Why on earth had he asked her to come here?

"Lenny!" he shouted, deciding he had gone far enough. If they were in the barn, they'd hear him. If they were not, he'd look elsewhere. And then, when they appeared at the entrance of the barn, the senator remembered his welcome—or lack of it—to his son, and he quickly rehearsed some sort of apology.

It went badly, words to the effect of a bill he had been trying to formulate for days until it had become a residing obsession. His mind was on the bill. That was the poor substance of his apology.

"I understand, Dad," Leonard said. "It's all right. Is that what you wanted to talk about?"

"Well, sure. But I'll pass this on from Mother. She wants you to take the station wagon to the airport and pick up Gus and Jenny."

"What time is their plane?"

The senator looked at his watch and decided that they had at least an hour.

"I thought Mac was going to pick them up."

"You know the way your mother is before an important dinner party. She won't let Mac out of her sight for ten minutes."

"O.K."

They walked back to the garage with the senator, and no one mentioned the interrupted meditation. At the garage, Clarence excused himself, saying that it was just family and he'd prefer to remain here. "I'd like to spend a little time in the library, sir," he said to the senator. "It looks like a wonderful library."

"Feel free," the senator said. "There's plenty of time. We won't be having lunch until they come back and the old folks have rested a bit."

"Yes, I'd appreciate that," Clarence said.

"Enough of libraries at school," Elizabeth said to her brother. "I'll tag along with you. Can I drive?"

"Do you feel up to it?"

"I think so."

"What's this?" the senator demanded of Elizabeth. "Are you sick?"

"If you call it that. Same old thing."

Leonard nodded; blame it on the period, it answers all things at all times.

The brother and sister climbed into the station wagon and backed it out of the garage.

The senator hooked his arm into Clarence's and led him into the house, thinking, Damn it, things change, maybe not much but they change, and just try to think of this twenty-five years ago.

The senator deposited Clarence in the library, a warm, pleasant room, three walls floor-to-ceiling with books, old leather armchairs, a fine old mahogany library table, and three tall windows looking out over the lawn. The floor was covered with a very old, worn Aubusson rug, a fierce eagle, with lightning in its talons, woven into the center. "The rug," the senator explained, "was a gift to my wife's great, great-grandmother from the association of cotton-mill owners in Rhode Island—although why I do not for the life of me know."

And with this strange declaration, which left Jones puzzled, Cromwell begged his pardon and took off down the corridor from the library to the wing of the house that contained his personal bedroom and study. He heard his name called, and turned to see Dolly coming out of the door to the storage pantry.

"Hold up," Dolly said. "I saw her car outside, so she's here and she can wait. I thought you could give us the day."

"I shall. I only want her for an hour. I've been walking around with this Sanctuary thing in my mind, and I have to have something formalized on paper."

"So long as she doesn't stay for lunch."

"Good heavens, Dolly," he protested, "I can't get rid of her before one. How can I send her away without lunch?"

"She won't starve. Ellen will bring her a sandwich if you're that worried."

"No, no, no," he said worriedly. "My goodness, she'd see the terrace going to her car. You are setting lunch on the terrace?"

"Yes."

"Oh, it would be a slap in her face. Come, Dolly, let's be reasonable."

"I don't feel reasonable, and I don't give a damn whether you think it's a slap in her face. She could use one. Mother and Father and the kids will be here. I want the family. I don't want her. I don't want Pop to have to break bread with someone he knows you're humping."

"What?"

"Richard, this isn't the time or the place. I know. He knows. Other people know."

"For God's sake, Dolly, we can't talk about something like this here in the hallway."

"You're right. But I want her out of the house before lunch."

"God Almighty," he whispered, "how you must hate me!"

"No, I don't hate you."

"I'll send her home," he said hopelessly.

But that was easier said than done. Joan Herman was no fool. In fact, in spite of her position as the senator's personal secretary, she was in all truth his chief of staff, and when Richard had finished explaining how he could not possibly marshal his thoughts today, what with preparing for the visit from the secretary of state and Bill Justin, assistant secretary, she said coldly, "That's horseshit, Richard— pure, unadulterated horseshit," using his given name. She almost never used his given name.

Cromwell sighed and shook his head hopelessly.

"A little more explanation, sir. That bitch laid down the law to you."

Joan was unlike Dolly in all the ways one person could be unlike another. Dolly could not be put down; she was as secure in her social position as the Queen of England. Anything, any slanted remark, slur, imagined or otherwise, any bit of misdirected humor could destroy Joan. She was taller than Dolly; she was blonde; her figure was large-boned and rangy; she was strongly handsome rather than beautiful, and she constantly fought to be self-possessed, a quality Dolly enjoyed without ever considering it.

"Joan, this is not the place," thinking that neither was the corridor.

Joan commanded her voice, taking a deep breath and dropping it to just above a whisper. "There is no place, Richard. I haven't seen you for a couple of days, and I came here panting like a damn female hound dog, with some stupid fantasy that you'd fuck me right here on the floor. Oh, the hell with it!" And grabbing her purse and briefcase, she stalked out of the room.

The senator fought an impulse to go after her. He would not chase her through his own home, and the last thing he desired was a shouting contest, with Dolly and the servants as witnesses. This had happened before and he supposed that it would happen again. He needed her; she understood things that he did not understand, and she sensed the special gait of politics in a manner that was beyond him. Essentially, Richard Cromwell was a good-natured and easy-going man; he lacked proper claws, and he lacked the ability to think politically. He still was uncertain why the secretary of state had sought him out and intended to bring with him one of his heaviest guns, namely Bill Justin. That they wanted to talk to his father-in-law might mean anything. Joan had already suggested, a few days ago, that the subject was a road Augustus had contracted for in Central America. On his part, he was not sure; and he clung to the possibility that they might be equally eager to talk to him. He felt he had something that might best be said off the record, outside of Washington, over a good brandy and a good cigar. He had not spoken to Joan Herman about this. She might well have said, "Senator, love, you're not thinking politically."

He remained in his room, staring out of the window, until he saw Joan's car come around the house and go down the driveway toward the main road.

"My driving used to scare you to death," Elizabeth said.

"Oh? That's funny, scare me to death. I wish you would."

"Forgive me. It's because I don't believe it. I can't believe it. You're not even sick. You're beautiful—just the way you've always been."

"Funny, if I weren't gay, you wouldn't say that, would you?"

"Say what?"

"Beautiful."

"You mean that only a gay man would be beautiful to me?" Elizabeth asked.

"No, that's not exactly what I meant."

"You've always been beautiful," Elizabeth said. "You always delight me. You're decent. I used to tell the kids at school that I had the ultimate big brother—" She broke off and stood on her brakes, pulling over onto the side of the road with a loud screech of rubber, and then sat behind the wheel, weeping. "I can't drive when I'm crying," she whimpered. "Take the goddamn wheel, Lenny."

Leonard got out of the car and walked around, while Elizabeth slid out of the way. "Long legs. Nice. I don't have to adjust the seat."

"Don't talk silly!" she snapped.

"Why not?" He pulled back onto the road. "Silly is the prime definition, isn't it? I'm dying in a country where a community of cretins who call themselves the moral majority have defined my death as a judgment of God on my wickedness. These same dunces crusade against you having an abortion, calling it an act of murder, while they back an atomic policy that will probably wipe out the human race during the next few years. You can't expect me to be profound in such a framework. Come on, old dear—you know, they used to say that those whom the gods would destroy, they first make mad. Mad is too elegant a term for our present condition. Silly, foolish, stupid—"

"Lenny," she interrupted, "don't talk like that."

"How? Liz dear, they never invented any distinctive mode of speech for the departing guest. I'm not trying to be flip. I just find that words are meaningless."

"I love you so much."

"Then maybe," he said, "we're discovering what love means. You know, I can't tell you how many times I've asked myself what that word means—if indeed it means anything in America today. It was a garbage word, a fraud to cover every cheap TV product, every worthless encounter, every emotional swindle. Now—did you see the way Dad reacted, first at the pool, where he couldn't even relate to me as a person, and then the way he tried to make up for it? And it matters, because I want so desperately for him to put his arms around me and tell me that he loves me, because I can sort of understand him now and I can love him. Do I make any sense?"

"I think so—but I'm not thinking very clearly. I sit here and try to adjust to what you told me—"

"Liz?"

She nodded, rubbing her eyes.

"Liz, you have to pull yourself together.

You have to stop crying and behave like everything is normal."

"I will."

"Your eyes are red. No more tears, please. The old folks will be looking at you like you're going out of style."

"I'll try."

"And one other thing, Liz, when I break this to Mom and Dad, you have to hold them up."

"Oh, Jesus, don't lay that on me, Lenny."

"Who else? I've been living with death five weeks now, and it could be months more. I've faced it. I've been awake through nights of terror. They've never faced anything like this. I had to come home. I'm here. I look no different—not yet. I'm condemned to death."

"Lenny," she said woefully.

"No, no. You must deal with it. Will you try, Liz, please."

"Yes. I'm good at control. Not when something like this first hits me. I'm all right now. No more tears."

"O.K. Now let's talk about the old folks and this big dinner tonight. Do you have any ideas?"

"Only that it's about Central America. Mother says it's the road. And that stinking bastard, Justin, is only about twelve miles from here. I suppose Mr. Secretary of State is staying with him."

"Why here? Why didn't they ask Gramps to go to Washington?"

Elizabeth managed a smile. "That would make it official, wouldn't it? Gramps would tell them to fuck off. This way, they just happened to meet at the dinner table." She loved politics. Ever since she was in boarding school, she had seized opportunities—school breaks, long weekends—to go to Washington and hang out in and around her father's office. She tried never to be obtrusive, not to ask too many questions, and be a willing gofer for anything that was needed, newspapers, coffee, sandwiches, anything at all. At times, the senator found her to be a nuisance, but for the most part he *prided* himself on being the father of a lovely young woman who liked his company.

On her part, Elizabeth very early on decided that this was the game, the most fascinating and important game ever invented. From early childhood, she had listened to the talk in her parents' home, and as she grew up, illusions other children clung to washed away. At age sixteen, she said to Leonard, "This is what I want." When he asked why, she replied, "Because it's a wild game and fun." And at age twenty, she said, "Because you're not fighting the smart ones. The smart ones are like Gramps. The politicos are different, crafty, cunning, greedy for power they never earned. If you know the game, they are easy."

Keep her on politics, Leonard said to himself.

"They want him to give up the road, you know," she said.

"How can you be so sure?" Here he was, death crawling inside of him, and coolly manipulating the conversation to keep his brilliant sister from thinking about that death.

"I just know. All the winds blow in one direction at a moment. This is one of those lousy moments. Look! Look! Look!" They were driving on a section of the road where white lilacs grew. They were in late flower, half a mile of lovely blooms that breathed their scent into the warm air. "They're so beautiful," Elizabeth exclaimed. "I would want to be a lilac bush—just for a day or so. Lenny, do you remember reading a story called *Mr. Sycamore*, or some such thing, about a postman so tired of walking that he just planted his feet in the earth and grew into a fine sycamore tree. Let's do that, Lenny, I'll be a lilac and you'll be a sycamore—oh, God, why am I talking so crazy, like a kid?—"

On the edge of tears again. Leonard, nipping it, said, "Come down to earth, Sis. What are you telling me? That they're going to talk him out of that road he's building?"

"That's right."

"You're crazy."

"Am I? Kiss my ass in Macy's window?"

"No way. I always lose. I lost enough of these nutty bets to spend a whole morning kissing your ass in Macy's window. You never said which Macy's. Where would it be, New York? Then we got to make a trip there one day. Go straight to the manager. I'm Senator Cromwell's son, this is my sister. Set ourselves up properly. She's smarter than I am, and every time we make a bet, the loser kisses the other's ass in Macy's window. Right now, I have to kiss her ass in your—what window?" he asked Elizabeth. "If I remember right, it could be Seventh Avenue, or Thirty-fourth Street, or maybe Broadway too."

"Whichever gets the biggest crowd."

"In your Seventh Avenue window. I'm at least three hundred kisses behind. Let's say two hours in your window."

"Tell him it's good for business."

"What does he say?"

"He wants to know whether we'll have media coverage. Come on, you really believe Gramps will cave in? He has the highest fuck-you level of anyone I've ever known. He'd toss the president out of his house if he thought anything the old thespian said was inappropriate."

"Who knows. Maybe you're right," Elizabeth said. "I'm O.K. now. Anyway, it's not caving in. Do you want me to drive?"

"No. I'm better off if I'm doing something, and what do you mean it's not caving in? Of course it's caving in."

"You think of Gramps as being principled. He isn't principled, Lenny. He loves noth-ing—"

"Hold on. He loves us. Jesus, Liz, you can see that. His sun rises and sets with us."

"We're his, the way he sees it. You can call it love if you want to. We're like his homes, his yacht, his horses, but his center is power and money. It's like this Jewish charade he puts on. Do you know how many non-Jews came into our family in the past two hundred years? We're as Jewish as the Pope. But Gramps car-ries on like a first-generation immigrant Jew."

"That's true," Leonard admitted. "It does give him status. There's nobody else just like him."

"So he won't cave in. He'll do whatever the moment requires for him to protect his silly empire."

"I know. But I like him. He wants me to switch to MIT, and then go into the company. Can you imagine me an engineer?" Death had receded for a moment. Neither of them could hold firmly to the reality of death.

"Never," Elizabeth said. "Suppose I said to him, Gramps, Lenny is a poet and there's not a damn thing you can do about it?" Death broke through. Elizabeth burst into tears.

"Oh, no," Leonard said. "Lizzie, love, we'll be at the airport in fifteen minutes."

"I know."

"Will you please kill the tears, once and for all."

"I'll try, Lenny. Promise, promise." She dried her eyes. "How do I look?"

"Wonderful. You always look wonderful."

"You haven't even looked."

"I'm driving. Go on with that Gramps business. I never knew you went around shrinking people?"

"It's not shrinking. It's just looking and listening. I make a kind of game of it, ever since I was a kid and used to hang around Daddy's office in Washington. When I was seventeen I heard Senator Bassington say to Daddy, 'Cromwell, there are only two kinds of people around here, and they're both sons of bitches. The difference is that half of them are our sons of bitches and the other half are their sons of bitches'—pretty stiff, huh?"

"What did Dad say?"

"He said, 'You're wrong.' I was in the next room, so I couldn't hang around and listen to the rest, but that's what he said."

"Score one for the senator."

"Tell you something, Lenny. Up at school, a

bunch of us got interested in the Sanctuary thing. Do you know about it?"

"I'm not sure. I haven't been interested in much lately, not much of anything."

"All right. I'll try to sum it up. You know what's been happening in El Salvador with their death squads. In the last few years, they've murdered almost forty thousand people who opposed the government in one way or another, so thousands of men and women and children have fled from El Salvador and gotten up here to the States. Immigration has been picking them up and sending them back, which is like a death sentence. Then a few of them were given refuge in a church. That's where the Sanctuary thing started. Other churches and synagogues joined in, until there were hundreds of these Sanctuary churches through the west—something like an underground railroad. The government got very upset about this, and they took a man from El Salvador whom they had the goods on and who they could send back if they wished to, and they paid him and wired him with a tape recorder and sent him into a little church in Arizona as a spy and witness."

"You're kidding," Leonard said.

"Oh, no. This is fact, the *New York Times* and all that. Now, the church people are on trial, in a Federal court in Tucson, and they can be sent to prison for five years. Well, you know the way it is at school, and the kids get to talking about it, and this really bowled us over—you know, this kind of thing can't happen here. And then here's Liz, with her daddy a United States senator."

"Oh, no. You didn't promise anything, did you?"

"I'll tell you what I did. We would get batches of material, because we were all chipping in with money to send to Tucson, and I would pick off the best of it and send it on to Daddy."

"And?"

"Well, I just don't know," Elizabeth said. "I haven't mentioned it to him, but then why is he willing to have those deplorable two from the administration at our house? They want to see Gramps. Well, why didn't Daddy say, you want to see him, invite him to your place? But instead, Daddy went out of his way to set up this dinner party."

"Liz, the ins and the outs don't hate each other. They play footsie under the table. It would calm the senator's nerves to be buddy-buddy with the other side."

"No way. No good reason. He's no saint, but he'd never play the double agent. Never!"

"Mother loves a dinner party. She's wonderful at it."

"Not enough. No. Daddy has enough failings, but down there in that squirrel cage, he knows his way around. He really does. I've watched him. Now Congress isn't in session. But even if it were, it would take weeks to push a bill through that would help those church people. The whole thing is a cheap frame by the administration, and my guess is that Daddy feels that if he can get the terrible two to the dinner table in our home, and feed them nice and talk to them nice, he might just get them to call off the prosecution."

"Could they?"

"In a minute." She reached over and took Leonard's right hand from the wheel and pressed it up against her lips for a long moment, and then she said, gently, "He's a good person, the way things are measured in this stinking world, and you have to tell him, and he will die in his own way a thousand times, so please, Lenny darling, try to love him a little."

"Jesus, I love him so much already," Leonard cried. "Why can't he just once be a father to me?"

TEN

Do you know, there is something wrong in this house today," Ellen MacKenzie said to her husband, who was polishing dry and shining a set of champagne glasses. "There is something dark and sad."

"I am dark," Mac said, "and you are making me sad and sorrowful."

Ellen bristled. "How?"

"You are a pessimist. You always been a pessimist. I am an optimist."

"That'll be the day."

"O.K.—O.K., woman. Spell it out. What is dark and sad?"

"Vibrations."

"I wish," Mac said deliberately, "that I was one of them niggers could put his wife on the bed, ass up, and give her a dozen of the best."

"You ever use that filthy word in here again, I'll give *you* a dozen of the best."

"Vibrations. Vibrations. God help us. Furthermore, you used that same word right here this morning."

"That was different. God won't help you, because you don't have a sensitive bone in your body. You are Boobus Americanus."

"What? What on earth is Boobus Americanus?"

"Mencken."

"What's Mencken?"

"That other gentleman coming tonight, Justin, the man from the state department, I asked the senator was there anything special about his needs we should know, the senator called him Boobus Americanus, which is something this Mencken said. Put the glasses on the table there."

"So I'm that," Mac said thoughtfully. "How come, if I'm so stupid, I got two kids who are smart."

"My genes."

"Well, you are one smartass fox, I got to admit. What time do I go to the airport for the VIPs?"

"No time. The Justin summer place is about twelve miles away, and they'll be driven here. What I want you to do is get down the Federal plates, the ones with the blue and gold stripe and the eagle in the middle. We got nineteen of them, but tonight we want only eleven. They'll be place plates."

"We ain't used them maybe two years."

"They are too precious. One hundred seventy-nine years old, according to Miss Dolly. She decided to make them a gift to the White House, because the way the Levi's got them was a gift from—oh, what is his name?"

"Jefferson. Thomas Jefferson."

"How do you know that?"

Mac shrugged and spread his hands. "Anyone knows that."

"Well, if you break one—"

"You ever see me break a dish?"

He was grinning at her, fondly, and she said, "Oh, for heaven's sake, you are trying. Trying. And don't you dare put them in the dishwasher. Just wipe each one off gently with a warm-water cloth."

"Yavo, mein Führer."

"Oh, get out of here."

There was a tapping on the door of the senator's study. "Come in," he said. Dolly opened the door and came into the room, and for a moment stood waiting, her whole manner hesitant and even apologetic. The senator's study was a comfortable room, a tufted leather couch, a pair of deep leather chairs, paneled walls, two excellent paintings, one a Thomas Eakins of boys swimming naked in a creek, and the other an unusually large George Inness Hudson highland scene, a gift from his father-in-law. There were also two

Audubon bird prints, a gift from Dolly out of her inheritance. Her great-grandfather had a full folio of the bird prints, and on his death in 1890, the prints were divided among his children. Eventually, eight of the prints came to Dolly. Six hung in various rooms of the house and two were in the senator's study. The rich rose and ivory Chinese rug gave a glow to the study. Dolly loved the room. She had put it together herself, picking up the rug when she and Richard were in Hong Kong, and finding the Eakins at an auction in London, and bidding for it and getting it at a wonderful price because he was American and not too desired then—before Eakins jumped to six and then seven figures.

The senator, who had been gazing out of the window, turned as she entered. He was such a big, good-looking man, Dolly thought, well, not exactly good-looking, his nose too heavy, his face too wide, but casually handsome in light gray trousers and a black golf sweater.

"You're very angry at me, aren't you," Dolly said.

"No—"

"I say awful things. I have a terrible temper."

The senator shrugged. She hated to have contention in the house when the children were home and even more so when her parents came. He had never been fully aware of Dolly or able to understand her movements and motives. At best, he was aware of her devotion to order, propriety, indeed to conservatism; on the other hand, in Washington, she despised the conservatives she met socially, their manners—or lack of manners— their taste, their gauche and naked drive for power, the furniture in their homes, the way they did their hair, their use of overpriced jewelry, their impassive, nonregistering faces whether she spoke of the clean, pure influence of the Shaker movement on American art or the fact that Sam Houston could quote the entire *Iliad* by heart. They were without history, ruling a country whose past was not simply a mystery but a handful of myths pasted on haze and confusion; and the senator could never be entirely sure that her devotion to his party was not simply a part of her contempt for the other party.

"I'd like you to help me," she said. It was as close to an apology as she could get, not an apology for what she had said but only for the manner in which she had said it. "The seating?"

He nodded.

"Oh, you're not speaking. Is it one of those days?"

"I'm speaking. Of course I'll help you. But the seating's a small matter."

"After lunch—I'll still have so much to do. If you could spend some time with Mother and Father?"

"Sure."

"And maybe get to talk with Leonard. That would be so good, Richard. He seems so sad— I think there is something dreadfully wrong."

"Oh, no, no. You worry too much about the kids. They both look wonderful."

"How can you say they look wonderful. Do you ever really look at them?"

"Dolly," he said tiredly, "if it were another day, I could take off to my office or whatever. Today I have to be here. Can we sidetrack this quarrel before it becomes irreversible."

"I don't want to quarrel with you."

"All right. I'm not an insensitive idiot, Dolly. I know there's a wall between Leonard and myself. I know I built it. I don't know how, but I made it, and I don't know how to climb over it."

"Why don't you forget about walls and just go to him."

"Yes," he said, recalling the times he had tried. You don't just forget about walls. They remain. "I'll try."

When she defeated him, when she touched the nerve that deflated him entirely, leaving a tragic and lost man, a frightened man that the world never saw—then she would be filled with remorse and compassion, finding in this

stressed, overweight middle-aged man someone that she had fallen in love with so long
ago, someone more than just a memory.

"You mentioned the seating," he said.

"Oh, yes. Well, I do need help. I had no idea
he was bringing this Jones boy home with
him. And now that he's here—"

"Of course."

"Time was we could feed the kids in the
breakfast room," she said, almost wistfully.

"What do you know about Jones?"

"He's Leonard's classmate at Harvard.
Jones loves what he's doing as much as Leonard hates it. Leonard's in law school only to
please you. You know that, don't you?"

"Don't turn everything back on me, Dolly.
I asked you about the black boy, Jones."

"Oh, Richard, I'm sorry. Why do I do it? I
don't know. About Jones—try to remember
his first name, Clarence. Leonard thinks he's
brilliant. Graduated cum laude. Very poor
background. Did it with scholarships and
such."

They had left the senator's study now and
were walking toward the dining room.

"Good voice and good speech," Dolly went
on. "I think Leonard mentioned that he's
from North Carolina. I'm not worried. Be a
good thing for our guests to break bread with
a plain black kid who isn't some overstuffed
Uncle Tom on show for the voters."

"It won't hurt."

"I told Leonard that it was black tie, and he didn't mind. He has an extra white jacket for Clarence, and they're about the same size. But the seating . . ." They were in the dining room now.

The dining room, as with the rest of the house, had been decorated by Dolly. She had decorated and furnished the entire house as, according to her lights, a house should be furnished and decorated. In Dolly's case, that meant a time frame between 1750 and 1820, and for the most part pieces produced in Philadelphia, New York, or Boston—with just an occasional intrusion from Great Britain. Other people might decorate differently; that was all right for others. The rich gray-mauve toile above the chair rail, the gleaming white woodwork, the mahogany table, the brass candle chandelier, and the twelve chairs, made in Philadelphia in 1793 in the style of Queen Anne, all of it sitting on a properly threadbare Persian rug, the walls exhibiting a group of American primitives that were a gift from her grandmother—this was proper and right for Dolly. "In Mother's world," Elizabeth had once explained to a friend, "nothing ages, nothing changes, nothing is new. It's wonderful but also ridiculous."

Richard Cromwell simply accepted it with appropriate reverence. To marry a rich woman is not as simple or as easy as some believe, and Richard Cromwell found himself in a foreign land where only the language was familiar. Only grifters, conmen, and out-and-out bums marry rich women and fall into it like a letter into a mail slot, using and spending with the pathological ease of middle-European noblemen; the senator was none of the above, and he had never made an easy adjustment to his wife's money or style of living. A teller in a midwestern bank, his father brought home a slowly increasing paycheck that started in the 'thirties at twenty-seven dollars a week. His whole boyhood had been skimped: shoes or new trousers, chopped meat or Spam, a movie for the family or medicine. Real poverty is formless, shapeless, chaotic, and the one good fortune of the senator was that he had a mother who was a rock of discipline and organization, and she had relentlessly fought and rejected the chaos of poverty. In many ways Dolly was like his mother, but at the opposite end of the social spectrum; that was why he had married her, not for her money.

MacKenzie had just finished inserting the boards that widened the table to its full extent. "If you would just hold the other end, Senator, we could get rid of the cracks."

The table came together properly. Mac-

Kenzie excused himself, and Dolly spread the place cards on the table.

"You and I at the two ends," she said. "We have to hang it on that. Ordinarily I'd say give me the two lords of Pennsylvania Avenue, and you'd have their wives."

"Why not?" the senator wondered. "As a start."

"Because Augustus Adams Fillmore Rosenberg Levi is being picked up at the airport by our two kids this very moment." It gave her a reason to smile and signal that she would like to be friends, at least for today.

"Good heavens! Is that his real name?"

"Every last bit of it."

"You never told me that. Nobody has four given names."

"Pop has. My grandfather was a peculiar man."

"That's the trouble with an old family," the senator said. "They get peculiar."

"Oh?" She regarded him thoughtfully.

"I say that in awe. And respect. My word, Dolly, four names. I'm envious. My family never had enough money to even begin to be peculiar. A middle name, mine is Joseph. But no more."

"Your daddy was a lovely man, and a gentleman. Sometimes, you're like him, Richard. You can be very funny and very sweet. Sometimes," she temporized.

"When you decided I was having an affair, why didn't you say something?"

"To what end? I don't want to divorce you."

"Why?"

"God knows—we're doing the seating, aren't we?"

"Yes. Sure. You feel that Gus will be offended if he's not sitting at your right hand?"

"Something like that."

"Suppose you put Winnie Justin on my left. She's bright and a bit nasty but she's good-looking. Gus is impressed with a smart, good-looking lady, so he could sit next to her, and then you put Liz on the other side of him, and he ought to be happy as a clam."

"We're eleven. That means five on one side of the table and four on the other. Who sits between Liz and me? Or is it the five side?" She slid the place cards around to match the senator's suggestion.

"No, I think the four side."

"That will put Gus in a pet. When he comes here and the kids are home, he'll want a spot between Liz and me."

"Dolly, I know that your father has met practically everyone in this country and almost everyone in most other countries, and he knows Web Heller, but this will be the first time he's had dinner with Bill Justin, a nasty and powerful man. He's sitting down with two of the most powerful men in the country

—in fact with two of the men who run this country behind that charade they call the presidency, so it seems to me that what Gus would appreciate most is to sit facing these two major linemen. That way he can say his piece without twisting his head and talking across someone else."

"Possible," Dolly agreed, moving the cards. "If I put Heller next to me—and then who sits next to him?"

"Jenny. Your mother."

"O.K. Mom can hold her own with that cadaverous old bastard. Then on the other side of mother—Franny Heller?"

"Why not. I can take her. A little flattery and she melts all over her dinner plate. And then to my left, Clarence Jones."

"Good—good thinking. You'll have him under your wing." She slid the cards around. "We're left with Father, Liz and Leonard. But we make progress." She stared at the cards. "You want Liz next to Jones—or Winnie Justin?"

"If we put Liz next to Jones, then Leonard gets Winnie Justin."

"Oh, no. That won't do. Absolutely not."

"Then she's mine—right here, between Jones and Gus."

"Can Jones handle her? Leonard says he's enormously bright, but she is South and she has a sharp tongue and a reputation for bitchiness."

"Still, she's at a dinner table under her husband's eye. She'll behave. And Jones may surprise us."

"Well, here it is," Dolly agreed, moving the cards to form a miniature pattern on the polished surface of the table. On my right, Leonard, Liz, Daddy, Winnie and Jones. On my left, Heller, Mother, Bill Justin and Frannie Heller."

"It should work."

"You know how many perfectly rotten dinner parties we've been to? It's because few hostesses pause to consider that they're not simply serving food, but creating a work of art —I mean a theatrical piece." She looked at her husband questioningly.

"Yes. I suppose I'd agree with that. Certainly about the lousy dinner parties," thinking how strange it was that he, a United States senator, with all the weight of a suicidal world on his mind and conscience, should be occupied with the seating arrangement at a dinner table. But thus the whole world was occupied, he realized, eating, drinking, screwing, weeping, laughing, robbing, killing, and why should he be any different?

Dolly shrugged. "I apologize," she said bitterly. "I'm pleading my case that there's some reason for me to exist on this earth, that I'm some use to somebody."

ELEVEN

A bit earlier, MacKenzie had mentioned to his wife that he hadn't seen Jones at breakfast. Ellen was in the process of rehearsing Nellie Clough. Nellie knew, but each time she had to be rehearsed, and if she was not rehearsed, some disaster inevitably followed. "Mr. Mac-Kenzie," Ellen said—to Nellie he was always Mr. MacKenzie—"will carve in the kitchen and serve the meat. I will prepare the platter for the beans and chopped spinach. We'll go over that later. You will follow Mr. MacKenzie with the vegetable platter. Do you understand me, girl?"

"I know what to do."

"You do and you don't. The quenelle will be ready in the kitchen, and you'll serve that first as Mr. MacKenzie pours the wine." She turned to her husband. "None of the young people had breakfast. Liz and Leonard went off to the airport. Where is Mr. Jones?"

"He's just a kid, Ellen."

"Shoo off," she said to Nellie. "Did you do the bedrooms?"

"Indeed I did."

"Run the vacuum in the library—he's a guest in this house," she said to her husband, "and he will be Mr. Jones as long as he's a guest in this house."

"I think he's in the library."

"Nellie," Ellen called, "hold up with the vacuum. Do Senator Cromwell's office, just neaten and dust."

Nellie departed.

"Some people," Ellen said, "it seems to make no difference they eat breakfast or they don't."

"I'll ask him if he wants something, you know, like maybe a sandwich and coffee." He shook his head. "I come in there and say to this kid, Mr. Jones—"

"Oh, stop it!" Ellen snapped.

"I got problems," Mac protested.

"You make problems. Why can't you get it into your head that it don't make no difference, black or white?"

"Because," he said slowly, "I am black and Jones is black, and it makes one big motherfucken difference."

"I'll tell you something," Ellen said angrily. "You never use that kind of filthy language in front of nobody but me! How dare you? Am I a prostitute? What gives you the right to talk to me like that? All my life, I been trying to civilize you, and I am sick of it!"

"I'm sorry—" Mac began.

"Never you mind sorry! You get yourself into the library and ask Mr. Jones whether he's hungry! Mr. Jones—you understand me?"

MacKenzie nodded without speaking and left the kitchen hurriedly, asking himself why on earth he ever gave Ellen these opportunities to manhandle him. By his lights, he was being manhandled. He had raised a simple and obvious point, and had his head handed to him.

As a result, MacKenzie entered the library with a certain amount of truculence, and then was put off by Clarence's engaging smile. "Hello. Am I making too much of a mess here?" He had half a dozen books and magazines on the table.

"No, that don't matter. Truth is, Mr. Jones, we figured you missed breakfast and might like a sandwich or something."

"Oh, thank you. That's very kind of you, but Nellie brought us things at the pool and we stuffed ourselves." He remembered and said, "I do hope this doesn't get her into trouble."

"Not if I don't tell my wife."

"My name's Clarence. I'm not used to being called Mr. Jones."

"Clarence." MacKenzie nodded. "They call

me Mac." He was looking at the books on the table. He felt a desperate need to prove to Jones that he, Mac, was not a lump, a mindless servant, and at the same time he was hesitant and embarrassed at the thought of projecting himself toward this good-looking, slender young black man simply on the basis of their both being black. All the books and magazines were focused on one subject. He had to gird himself to say, "You must be a lot interested in quantum mechanics." His voice almost broke, but he got it out.

Clarence responded with a wide grin. "You, too—man, it's like religion. You know, my mama and daddy, all they ever wanted and dreamed of was me being a lawyer, and then in politics, like Julian Bond. He's their hero— of course, they're southern folk. They laid that on me and also I'm supposed to look like Julian, but I don't see it."

"Oh, you do, you do," Mac agreed.

"So here I am at Harvard Law and Mama and Daddy are happy, but if I had it my way, it would be physics and quantum mechanics. There's all the secrets of the universe waiting to be solved. And here—here's maybe a hundred books on the subject."

"That's right. And a new one comes in every week or so."

"But who is it? Is this Leonard's secret? He never talked about it, and heaven knows, I gave him plenty of opportunity, bored him to death. Is it Liz?"

"You mean, who studies them books on quantum mechanics? It's the senator. He don't go anywhere without putting one of them in his briefcase."

"Really?"

"Yes indeed, Mr.—Clarence. Truth is, I tried one once, but I didn't make it," he confessed. "I couldn't make head or tail out of any of it. I'm just too ignorant for that kind of thing."

"No, no. Unlearned. You have to have a basis, years of working at it."

"Just too old and stubborn," Mac said, grinning. "But the senator—I once asked him is it part of being a senator, he says no, no way, just a hobby of mine. It's my own way to . . ." Mac paused. "Now what is the word? Yeah, eternity."

"How little we know about people," Jones said, causing Mac to wonder why he spoke so sadly. "No, sir, Mr. MacKenzie. I'm not hungry, but thank you so much for tracking me down and asking me. I'll put the books back exactly where they were."

"Oh, no. About the books, it don't matter about the books. I'll put them back. Just feel free with them. We'll be serving lunch on the terrace somewhere between one and two, depending on whether the old folks come in on time. It's cool and pleasant here, so if you want to stay here, I'll be happy to call you when lunch is ready."

Jones thanked him, and then, back in the kitchen, Ellen said to Mac, "Well, did you find him?"

"In the library."

"Does he want a bite of something?"

"No. Says he ain't hungry."

Ellen was mincing garlic, an odor that Mac found distasteful and could never adapt to. He sniffed, made a sour face, and moved back.

"What's he like? You get a chance to say something to him?"

"Fine boy. Reminds me of Mason. Some of these young colored kids, I just look at them and feel pleased. Now he's a friend of Leonard. Funny thing, Mason and Leonard, they grew up here like brothers—but they never became real friends. Know what I mean?"

"I know you just standing there and flapping your lips. Miss Dolly is in the dining room setting up, and you certainly could be a help to her."

"Yavo, mein Führer."

"And don't you start that either."

"Well, heavens to Betsy, Ellen, I am just making a kind of observation on that fact that the senator's son comes home with a black kid, and it don't even stir a ripple in this house."

"Why should it?"

"I give up," he said, and stalked out of the kitchen.

TWELVE

I think we have it," Dolly said to the senator.

"I think you're having a bit of glee putting Jones next to Winnie Justin."

Dolly smiled at him. It was a treat when she smiled. Her whole face lit up and she became young and alive, as he remembered her from the time they married. "You did it," she said.

"Yes, I suppose I did. We're both wicked."

"We try." She laughed. "I've always felt that a dinner party improves with a bit of humor."

MacKenzie entered at this point, and Dolly said to him, "Mac, I hate to lay any more polishing on you, but the candlesticks—"

"Of course. I should have remembered."

"And then we'll set for lunch, outside. This is what keeping a restaurant entails," she said to the senator. "Whatever hard times we come on, let's never open a restaurant."

"Not likely, not at all likely," Mac said.

"You know," the senator said to her, "I'm

suddenly quite tired. Do you think I have
time for a nap before lunch?"

Her little joke about the restaurant had
cleared the air. They were back together, until the next time one of them exploded in anger at the other. She touched his arm. "Of
course. Of course, Richard."

Nellie was in the senator's wing of the
house, the part where he had his bedroom
and the small office that opened from it, his
cul-de-sac, his retreat from the world, to
which there was no other entrance than
through his bedroom. He had wanted it that
way; his cave; he kept the door locked for the
most part. Nellie had made up his bed and
was running an electric broom over the car-
peting. She cut the broom as he entered.

"I'm almost finished, Senator Cromwell,"
she said to him very formally, yet with an
intimacy that a woman adopts once she has
been to bed with a man not her husband, yet
someone gentle and considerate. She assumes
a relationship that is not catalogued; not a
mistress, not precisely a friend of the other
sex, not a sibling; a relationship both warm
and protective that speaks of the body she
gave him and his acceptance of the gift. Nellie
treasured it. The senator was unfailingly kind.
On and off, he lusted after her, her sweet,
round body and her shimmering gold-red
hair, her whiteness and softness. She never sat

in the sun. She had the Irish wisdom of a race that does not sit in the sun.

Nellie finished and gathered her cleaning things. "Would you like me to put your office to rights?"

"No, not today, Nellie."

"If I may say so, you look tired."

"I am tired."

"I could bring you a nice cup of tea."

"Thank you, dear. No." He sat down on the edge of the bed and kicked his shoes off, old loafers that were like old friends.

"Shall I draw the drapes?"

"Please."

She closed the draperies, and the senator sprawled out on the bed. Nellie thought of how nice it would be to bend over and kiss him; it remained just a thought. Nellie could think of an advance toward the senator, but she was incapable of making one. She took her cleaning things out of the room, closing the door gently behind her.

The senator closed his eyes and was asleep almost instantly, and then he was rocked out of sleep by the telephone. He could not have been asleep more than five or ten minutes, clutching a waking-sleeping dream of summer long, long ago; summer when he was just a kid, wading barefoot in the creek behind their home. It was the third ring before the answering machine clicked on, and then he heard Joan's voice, "Senator, I'm closing the office. Nothing today except Callahan, you remember the fat, beer-bellied gonif who wants to get in on the reservoir. The more I think of that reservoir scheme, the worse it gets. The survey came back today, almost four hundred families to be displaced or moved, and it's too many enemies for us to have in this state. Sorry about today, sorry about myself, and for heaven's sake, be careful with the Sanctuary thing. It's a very hot potato."

How did he always find women who loved him and would not hurt him? He didn't consider himself either handsome or lovable.

He reset the machine, dropped into the chair behind his desk, and thought of Joan Herman. A hard-nosed woman, totally cynical, believing in absolutely nothing, yet capable of loyalty and love beyond his comprehension. He needed her cynicism because he was incapable of it himself. He had once scribbled out the basis for a bill that would replace "The Star-spangled Banner," an impossible song he disliked, with "America the Beautiful," a song he had always believed should be the national anthem. Joan said, "Senator, who gives a fuck about what's in the song? This one is like apple pie and motherhood. You don't fool around with 'The Star-spangled Banner.'"

"It's an impossible drinking song. Francis Scott Key was a drunk."

"That doesn't win votes."

And Sanctuary. Why was it a hot potato? These people coming to dinner tonight were not of his party. He begrudged them the space at his dinner table, but he gave it to them out of respect for his father-in-law. Respect?

"That old bastard," Joan Herman had said, referring to his father-in-law, and never one to mince words, "has piss in his blood and ice in his heart."

THIRTEEN

Waiting at the local airport for the plane carrying their grandparents to land, Leonard asked Elizabeth whether she ever felt Jewish. It was the kind of question that under other circumstances might have provoked a clever, funny quip. Now it prompted her to stare at her brother for a long moment before she answered quietly, "It's crossed my mind. Why?"

"We're supposed to be Jewish."

"So they tell us."

"Has it ever bothered you?"

"No. Not really."

"I've never been in a synagogue," he said. "I mean—when this happens to you, you think about what you've never done."

"We were in a synagogue once," Elizabeth reminded him. "No, twice. Once when Daddy spoke at the Temple Emanuel in New York, and once in Newport."

"That doesn't make anything, Liz. You

know that. I don't even know what it is to feel
Jewish."

"I don't know what there is to feel. I'm sure
there must be something. I heard Gramps say
that according to Hitler's definition, if you
were one eighth Jewish, you were Jewish and
a candidate for the gas ovens. Gramps is I
think one sixteenth Jewish, if that means anything. Granny's father was a Congregational-
ist or something of the sort. I was never too
clear about it. Then Mother would be—"

"That's it," Leonard interrupted. "They're
coming in."

On this small county airfield, there was only
one rather unimposing airport structure. The
planes landed and the movable staircase was
rolled up to them. Augustus Levi's plane was a
727, blue and white with the word MACAMAW
painted in large black letters on both sides of
the cabin. Macamaw was the name of the engineering and construction company that Augustus Levi's great-grandfather had put together during the Civil War, building roads
and railroads on contract for the Union Army.

Noticing that his sister's eyes were beginning to tear again, Leonard said sternly,
"None of that, Liz. We have a long, hard day
ahead of us."

"You're not going to tell them?"

"No, no, no. We have to get through this

damn dinner party. It's important to Mother."

"How can you be so cool?"

"I've been living with it, Sis. You learn to live with anything."

"All right. I'm over this one."

The plane had rolled to a stop and was now swinging around to approach the installation. As Elizabeth and Leonard entered the airport building from the parking area, Augustus Levi and Jenny entered from the field side. Spotting Elizabeth and Leonard, Augustus strode forward and embraced his grand-daughter in a bear hug. His wife moved more sedately to embrace and kiss, first Leonard and then Elizabeth. Leonard had always feared his grandfather's handshake. It was bone crunching, and he still feared it, endur-ing it and trying not to wince with pain.

"Let's look at both of you. Stand back," Au-gustus declared. Leonard always felt that his grandfather had been named properly. Levi was six feet and three inches tall, a broad, barrel-chested man with a ruddy face that re-sembled the traditional cartoon of John Bull. His frame was large enough to support the roll of fat around his stomach, so he was never taken for a fat man, a large man but not a fat man, for all of his two hundred and forty pounds.

His wife, Jenny—Jean by birth certificate—

had been one of those tall, rangy women, golf
and skis and tennis and horses—wide shoulders that carry clothes with queenly grace.
Now, at age sixty-nine, she was still a fine-
looking woman, thirty pounds heavier than
the girl he had married, with the unassuming
arrogance that comes of having been born
rich and having been rich all of her life. Augustus was seventy-three, but he fought age as
he fought everything else, and if he displayed
a vigor he did not wholly feel, it was nevertheless a vigor he could command when called
upon. Leonard had often wondered how
these two self-satisfied and very large people
could have produced his mother, Dolly, who
was, in contrast, small, delicate, and prey to
endless uncertainties.

"You don't look good, either of you," was
Augustus's immediate reaction. "You need
sun and exercise! Kids today don't eat right!
God damn it, you're not on coke, are you?"
He spoke to them as he would have spoken to
a job-boss, but whereas the job-boss would
have cringed in fear, both Leonard and Elizabeth broke into their first real laughter of the
day. He adored them, and possibly they were
the only things in the world that he gave a
damn about, these two slender, beautiful
creatures who were out of his genes and his
blood. On their part, he was their large, gruff,
and totally malleable pet bear. Jenny was

something else, a grandmother, loving, though not too demonstrative; always in the shadow of the man she had married, yet tall and queenly enough to be her own person.

The luggage came off the plane, five suitcases for their single night at the Cromwells, and Augustus went off to have a last word with his pilot. When he returned, Leonard was hauling a suitcase into the station wagon. Effortlessly, Augustus tossed the other pieces into the car.

"Should we wait for the pilot?" Leonard asked.

"No. We carry a navigator who doubles as a co-pilot now. They'll find their way into town. I do wish I could spend some time with you kids and play some tennis. By golly, it's three, four years since we played tennis. Think you could beat me, Liz?"

"I'd give it a good try."

"Well, maybe this afternoon."

"You haven't touched a tennis racket in years," Jenny said, "and you're not going to this afternoon."

"Listen to her!" He was in marvelous good humor.

"Why can't you stay?" Leonard wondered.

"We're on our way to Switzerland. It's business, not pleasure."

"Oh, I envy you."

"Come along."

"Have you opened the house at Klosters?"

"No," Jenny said with annoyance. "No. Nor shall we. It's cold and drafty and falling to pieces, and I don't know why we don't sell it."

"It's so beautiful," Elizabeth said. "You remember, Lenny—that great big fireplace."

"I remember how cold I was," Leonard said.

"We'll stay in a proper hotel in Geneva," Jenny said. "I will not go near Klosters. He believes he's thirty. I will be seventy years old come October, and I am aware of it."

But Leonard's thoughts were riveted now on that day in Klosters—he was eight years old, chilled to the bone, and taken into that strange old half-timbered lodge through the wild, whipping snow. A fire roared in the great fireplace, but he could not warm himself and he kept shivering with the cold of death. Death—the cold, cold breath of death.

Jenny babbled on. "Believe me, nothing I'd like better than to take both you darlings with me and show you off to some people we know in Switzerland and France. Nothing ups the status like two gorgeous grandchildren, and I'm at a point where I don't hide my age—in fact I am not a little proud of it, and no face-lift. Ugh. Disgusting thought, taking your flesh and stretching it out until you look in the mirror and you truly don't know who you are. You remember Maggie Blakely—the one from Virginia whom your mother used to invite when we visited in Georgetown—well, her face job turned her into an utter stranger, I mean her own mother wouldn't recognize her, and while the new face was rather decent looking, the confusion of explaining who she was became a nightmare to her—"

Elizabeth began to cry.

"Will you shut up," Augustus told her. "Will you please shut up."

"It's nothing," Elizabeth said. "I'm just silly emotional, and it's all of us being here together today—"

"I understand," Jenny said. She was sitting in the back seat with Elizabeth, while her husband sat next to Leonard, who was driving. "I do understand, my dear," putting an arm around Elizabeth and drawing her over against her breast. Jenny could remember how fretful and maudlin she herself would be during her menstrual periods; long gone, but she could still remember. Certainly the same thing. When Augustus turned to stare at her questioningly and worriedly, Jenny nodded wisely to reassure him.

"She'll be all right," Leonard said thinly. "Don't worry, Gramps. She'll be all right."

FOURTEEN

MacKenzie came into the dining room with a basket of flowers from the garden. He had selected white lilacs and peonies of white and pale rose, a great mass of sweet-smelling and beautiful blooms, and at the sight of them, Dolly clapped her hands in delight. "How wonderful! But, Mac, what am I to do with them? It would break my heart to cut them back, yet they're much too big for the table. They'll make a fine bouquet for the sideboard. But then, what shall I do for a centerpiece? I remember when I was a little girl, reading a story about some great Italian chef who worked for a grand duke or some such person, and simply ran out of ideas for centerpieces. Then his nephew talked him into giving him a tub of butter which he carved into a splendid lion. Do you know, the boy became a famous sculptor, and I can't for the life of me remember his name and we don't have a tub of butter or a sculptor. What then? Come, Mac, be creative."

"Do you recollect that glass eagle made by the Corning people that the Red Cross gave to the senator for heading up their drive?"

"Wonderful! Order of Cromwell or something."

"Ma'am?"

"I've just decorated you. Come on, Mac, to work. Get the eagle and then the big Wedgewood vase for the flowers. Then wine and water—three glasses for each setting."

MacKenzie went into the kitchen to dress the flowers and fill the vase, a lovely piece of pale blue and white china.

"How is it going?" Ellen asked him.

"I haven't seen her like this in ages. She's high as a kite."

"Thank goodness, the way it's been."

"Any reason for it?"

"None that I intend to gossip with you concerning it. Here, be useful."

"Useful. I live my life like a goddamn screwdriver, which is useful and screws now and then."

Nellie Clough came into the kitchen on the last note, and she broke into giggles.

"And what is so funny?" Ellen demanded coldly.

"Nothing, Miss Ellen, absolutely nothing."

"I got to take this vase in to Miss Dolly, and then I'll return and be useful."

He returned with Dolly, who said, "Would you believe that I forgot about lunch?"

Ellen pointed to a tray piled high with settings. "Let's get this out, Miss Dolly, and then we'll brood over it."

Dolly was counting the settings. "Seven, Ellen. You have only six."

"Oh? That's right." She added a setting, wondering what devil's urging made it so difficult to remember that Clarence Jones was a guest, and telling herself that this was not the first black man to dine here, not by any means. "For heaven's sake," she said to MacKenzie, "don't stand there. Take the tray out to the terrace," and then disliked herself for using Mac to cover her own insensitivity. "You go with him," she told Nellie, "and set up on the large round table." When they had gone, she faced Dolly and apologized.

"I don't know what gets into me."

"You're a little hard on Mac, aren't you?"

"It's his fault, he's so kind and patient. He is, you know."

"I do know, of course, Ellen."

"Like the senator. Same type. And that just leads me to dump on him."

They were old friends, these two, going back years, with no proper servant-mistress relationship but something else shared in that curious sanctum called a kitchen. Dolly stared at Ellen for a long moment, and then said, "You cut up the cold chicken?"

"Oh, yes."

"We won't serve. Make a buffet on the baker's stand and let them pick. My father likes the chicken just cut in chunks with celery bits and the mayonnaise on the side. We have potato salad, and you put together a salad niçoise and a platter of sliced tomato. You mentioned hard-boiled eggs and they'll do fine with the tomato, and do a plain tuna salad just in case the kids want to be kids. We have a big piece of cheddar and a cut of stilton. Daddy likes stilton. Thin-sliced black bread and some rolls. And get Nellie to help you."

"You're nettled with me," Ellen said. "You certainly are nettled with me."

"I am not," Dolly said firmly. "So the senator's kind and patient?"

"I think so."

"I'm sure you do." Then Dolly went back to the dining room and began to arrange the flowers. The senator found her there. He had changed into a white shirt, pale gray flannels, and sneakers. He came into the room and stood quietly, watching Dolly whose back was to him. She was wearing a pink peasant skirt, a white cotton blouse, and sandals. A shaft of sunlight, filled with a dizzying dance of dust motes, caught her and made the senator think of the French impressionist painters and their obsession with sunlight. The flowers danced in the sunlight, and glowed as if they were lit from within.

"I sometimes think this is your favorite room," the senator said.

"It is, I suppose," she answered without turning, continuing to move the flowers, as if there were some perfect arrangement that she must find. "And it's the most valid. Every piece in the room has been in the family since at least—well eighteen ten at least."

"And that's important to you?"

She turned slowly to face him, and said, "This morning, Richard, all that fuss about the ham—well, it was my invention, you know. I get so angry with you, and then I have to hang it on something; but still it was real. Damn it, Richard, I am Jewish. That may be a recent decision on my part, and it goes in the face of all the Jews I do not like. I was born a year before Pearl Harbor, and until World War Two was over I never had an inkling that I was Jewish. Well, maybe an inkling, no more. I didn't even think of Levi as a Jewish name. I was fourteen years old when I first read about the Holocaust. Slow process."

"I try to understand."

"I don't think there's any way to understand family relationships. I don't understand my father and mother. I gave it up. I don't even know whether I love them or hate them."

"I think you love them," the senator said uneasily, wondering where this was leading. He had always felt a certain awe regarding Augustus Levi, a man so absolutely certain of himself that he sometimes sent a cold shiver down the senator's spine. In the Congress of the United States, Cromwell had known a good many men who were possessed of absolute certainty, and this he feared so much that he felt the only real and enduring evil on the face of the earth was unbending certainty, unshakable orthodoxy.

Dolly was putting the lace doilies in place, and the senator mentioned that she never used a tablecloth. "Mom used tablecloths," he said. "I have good memories of them. It meant an occasion, I mean a special occasion."

"Yes, of course. But I couldn't bear to cover this beautiful old wood. It adds so much."

"Well, nothing's exactly the way it used to be. I mean in the lower depths."

"Lower depths? Richard, your people were utterly respectable middle-class people."

"They were what our president likes to call the moral majority. My father was so moral he'd die before he'd ask for a raise. Do you know, he never worked up to fifty dollars a week. Bank tellers are the foundation of utter respectability. Mom was given to prayer; she worked prayer like no one I ever knew, and when I won my first election, she said to me, don't ever say that prayer won't bring what is prayed for."

"You mean she was praying for you to become a politician?"

"Of course. She was Irish."

"Touché. Could you take the silver chests out of the closet and set them here on the buffet? Or should I call Mac?"

"Bug off with Mac. I was up at five o'clock this morning. I ran at least a mile. I swam. I showered, and I'm still ambulatory."

"Apologies, right down the line," Dolly said. Somehow, these few minutes of the two of them alone in the dining room had turned into the best bit of relationship that she could recall in many months, if not years. What small magic was working on them she did not know. An hour ago she had been ready to bite his head off, and now she was regarding him fondly as he swung the heavy silver chests up onto the buffet. She had to admit that he was a fine figure of a man, gone a trifle to fat, but still a large, strong well-muscled man. She liked men to be physical.

"I will never forget," he said, "the first time I had dinner in your mother's house. I was just out of college and in uniform—thank goodness. I didn't have a decent suit."

"I guessed as much," Dolly agreed.

"Your father glanced at me as if I were an insect."

"Typical of him. You were not an officer. He relaxed when he heard you were Judge-Advocate. Afterwards, he told me he felt that was a sign of intelligence."

"You're being creative." The senator grinned. "You never mentioned that before."

"Scout's honor." She had opened the three chests of silver that Richard had lifted to the sideboard and was studying them thoughtfully. "Take a look. Do they need polishing?"

"No," he decided. "You know, that damned, idiot senseless war in Korea—"

"You didn't even look."

"Sure I looked." He lifted a fork. "Pristine. By golly, that night at your home, twelve spoons, eighteen forks, seven knives, all huddled around my plate—"

She turned to smile at him. "You felt that way. I bet you did."

"I told Mom about it. 'What are they?' she wanted to know. I said, 'Rich' 'Oh,' she said. 'That I don't mean. Are they Catholics or are they Protestants?' Do you know, I didn't know. She asked me did I see a crucifix? Specifying that the rich ones kept them in the bedroom. Next time, I was to slip into a bedroom and see."

"They need polishing," Dolly said. "Poor

Mac, he polished the serving dishes and the coffee stuff this morning, and now again."

"Ah, they don't need it."

"Some do. It's no great deal." Then, unexpectedly, she went to the senator and up on her toes and kissed him lightly. And then she hurried out of the dining room.

I'll be damned, the senator said to himself. I will be everlastingly damned. He dropped into a chair, waiting and trying to decide whether to follow her into the kitchen. She didn't come back to the dining room, and after a few minutes Richard left the room and went through the house, outside, and then rather aimlessly to the terrace, where MacKenzie and Nellie were setting the table for lunch. For a few hours where nothing much happened, the senator said to himself, it's been quite a morning.

FIFTEEN

After his talk with MacKenzie, Jones replaced the books on the shelves where he had found them. The library opened onto a screened porch that extended to the rear from one wing of the house, and Jones, filled with curiosity about the house but tentative about exploring it, opened the door from the library to the screened-in porch and went through. The porch was furnished with colorful summer furniture, an overstuffed couch covered in yellow and pink print, big chairs, wicker rockers—the single porch larger than the entire home of his childhood. He had never been in a house like this before, and he had the curious feeling that people who lived in such circumstances were basically defenseless. In the place where his childhood had been spent, death was a frequent and usually cruel visitor, fought on unequal terms, feared, hated, yet accepted. When Jones was still a kid, only nine years old, his great-grandmother, old as time, had told him the story of how her granddaddy, a slave on a Carolina plantation, had faced his owner. His owner had a shotgun and pointed it at the slave and told him to get down on his knees and take back the words he had spoken. Never, you white bastard, the slave had said, and the owner killed him with a shotgun blast in his face.

"Pride," the old lady told Jones. "You face death, you got to have pride."

Not that it made much sense to Jones or served to ease his own deep fear, and anyway, pride was an ancient word, hardly current anymore. Jones knew, as Leonard knew, that he, Jones, could be editor of the *Law Review* before he graduated. There he was, tall, good looking, black, but not too black, and smart and well mannered enough to become a Supreme Court justice's clerk, or go with a super Washington or New York law firm, or go back home and join a firm in Carolina and do politics there. No more nonsense about pride that got a stupid slave a shotgun blast in his head. You pushed death away. No death. Man, you were making it. Until death nudged you back. And then, by God, pride didn't help you one damn bit.

Jones left the house through the porch, walked around to the terrace, an outside place with a striped awning over it to keep out the sun, where lunch would be served. The awning covered the half where the table had been set; on the other half were the outdoor lounges. The senator, armed with a newspaper and his reading glasses, had dropped onto one of the lounges. When he saw Jones, he motioned toward the lounge beside him. "Sit down, Clarence, unless you mind the sun?"

"Some black people do," Jones said. "It makes them darker. I don't mind being dark as the night."

The senator regarded him with interest. Was he being arrogant, impolite, challenging —or just plain straightforward? "And of course, we strive to be darker. Suntan is one of the many silly habits of our time."

Smiling, Jones dropped down beside the senator and said, "Yes, but for us it's kind of flattering. White folks want to be darker. I've never quite understood. But whites are not easy to understand."

"True enough."

"I've been prowling in your library," Jones said tentatively. It was not easy for him to sit beside the senator and carry on a conversation. He forced himself to at first. If he sat in silence, he could see the senator telling his wife about the surly black kid Leonard had brought home with him. "It's a great library."

"Well, not great but eclectic, my taste, my

wife's, and of course Leonard's and Elizabeth's. Almost no law books, which is a pity
because I hear you're making your way at law
school. But I keep most of my law library in
Washington—in my office, and in my home in
Georgetown, and a sort of digest library in my
local office here."

"I wasn't looking for law books," Jones
forced himself to say, suddenly terror stricken
and wondering what insanity had led him to
accept Leonard's invitation. Suppose Leonard decided to blurt it all out today, to tell this
man, his father, and his mother, and the others that he was dying. I can run away, he
thought. I can get them to drive me to the
station before Leonard comes back. And with
that, he asked the senator, "When will Leonard and Elizabeth be back?"

The senator glanced at his watch. "Any moment now. Are you all right?"

"Yes, sir." He sighed.

"You're sure."

"Yes, sir." There were then a few long moments of silence, during which the senator
looked at him as comfortingly as he could,
realizing how awkward he must feel.

"Would you like to look at the paper?" the
senator asked him.

"No, sir." And then Jones added, "I wasn't
looking for law books in the library. I was

looking at the books you have on quantum mechanics."

"Oh? I thought you're a law student."

"Yes, sir. Quantum mechanics is my hobby."

"Hey—mine too," the senator said with pleasure. "How is it you didn't go in for physics?"

"My father and mother's dream is for me to go back down south and go into politics."

"I can understand that," the senator told him. "Some of us do what our people want. I did. But I got interested in physics in the army, which was my time of boredom. Armies are the most useless and worthless adornments of our so-called civilization, and aside from death and maiming, their chief product is boredom."

Jones was staring at him.

"Doesn't conform with my voting record?"

Jones didn't say anything to that. He didn't know how to handle the turn the conversation had taken. He looked away, across the lawn to the pool. Contradictions still troubled him, and here in this place, there were simply too many for him to deal with. Why had the senator chosen him for this particular discussion, and how was it that a man who appeared to have this kind of sensitivity could be so mindlessly insensitive to his son? Or was he? Or was he, Jones, so ignorant of the ways of white folk that he was operating on the basis of a series of misjudgments?

"I use it as a counterfoil to despair," the senator said, very tentatively, posing a question with each word—leaving out what he might have said about the fate of a Catholic who was not a Catholic married to a Jew who was not a Jew. "Do you know what I mean?"

Why me? Jones wondered. He wasn't at all certain that he knew what the senator meant. His own despair was the despair that comes with death both senseless and imminent—but no such death faced the senator.

The senator smiled. "I'm not talking about virtue," he said, "I'm simply referring to things the way they are. Trouble is, no one who hasn't buried his head in quantum mechanics has any notion of what I am talking about. Do you, Mr. Jones?"

"I'm not sure."

"But you agree that it poses ontological problems?"

"Oh, yes indeed, sir," grateful that he could make some reasonable observation.

"For example, when we face a situation in which contradictory states of being appear to be linked together, and an object—for want of a better name—is both a wave and a particle, well then one can take some small comfort in the possibility that this nest of lunacy we call society is less reality than illusion. But of course it isn't. I think quantum is a game—a last-resort game." His smile was quizzical now, and Jones simply did not know what to say.

MacKenzie, coming out onto the terrace with a tray of food, said, "Senator, Mr. and Mrs. Levi are here."

SIXTEEN

Jones felt released when the senator went into the house to welcome his guests. Mac-Kenzie appeared again with a cart of drinks and ice, soft drinks and hard. Nellie followed him with a tray of coffee service. "We'll serve lunch at half past one," MacKenzie said. "I ring a bell, so you can feel free to wander." He grinned at Jones.

"Thank you, Mr. MacKenzie."

"Call me Mac. Everyone else does."

Jones was wearing blue jeans, sneakers, and a white-knit short-sleeved shirt. "Am I all right, I mean the way I'm dressed?"

"Just fine. We don't dress any special way for lunch, but Miss Dolly don't like bathing suits."

Leonard came out of the house and called to Clarence to join him. They walked around the house to the herb garden. Dolly wanted some parsley.

"How did it go?" Leonard asked him. "I felt

guilty, leaving you with all these high-class honkies."

"Honkies," Jones said. "I hate those lousy words. They come out of self-hate. I'm glad you left me alone for a couple of hours. It was fine. I read a little. I met Mr. MacKenzie and had a talk with him—a nice man, believe me, and I had a kind of weird talk with your father."

"Weird?"

"Not exactly. No. You know, he asked a few questions—just ordinary, I'll-be-polite-to-this-black-kid kind of stuff, because these days most people lean over backwards, and then he found out that I was interested in quantum mechanics and it turns out it's a hobby of his."

"But weird?"

"Maybe a little. You get into that kind of thing, and reality begins to get very hazy. Are we real or is it all illusion?"

"We talked about that many times."

"I know. But with him, it was different. He was very nice to me, I have to say that."

"He can be, I suppose," Leonard said. "About this quantum stuff, he heads a sub-committee on atomic energy or something related to it. I forget the exact title."

How could he forget the exact title? Jones wondered.

"I guess a week doesn't go by without some physicist having dinner with us—"

"You're away at school," Jones interrupted.

"Well, before then. When I was just a kid. Clare, are you pissed at me or something?"

Jones put an arm around him. "Oh, no. No."

"Because I'm sick?"

"Oh, Jesus, Lenny, I love you. You know that."

"Yeah—sure."

"You know, Lenny, maybe I shouldn't stay overnight. I barged into this big, important dinner your mother is giving tonight, and I'm really forcing my way into the dinner table. Who says they want a black guy there? It may embarrass them. Where do I come off sitting down with the secretary of state?"

"Oh, bullshit. Who is he? What did he ever do that's worth talking about?"

"He's secretary of state."

"Jonesy, if my father doesn't want you at the table, he'll tell you so."

"Look," Jones said defensively, "every notion I have about what your dad's like comes from you."

"Hold on. Let's not fight over it."

Jones shook his head. "Forgive me, Lenny —oh, God, please forgive me. I forget and—" He stopped himself short.

"You forget and you begin to treat me like a normal human being who isn't on his way to the abattoir. I treat you like a normal human being."

They stood for a few moments facing each other, silent, and then Jones nodded. His eyes had filled with tears.

"Jesus Christ, don't do that! If I have one month left, I want to live it like a person, not like some damned creature walking into the gates of hell. Like poor Marty Helsen, who was left alone, isolated, because no one wanted to go near him."

"I try."

Leonard took a long breath, sighed as he released it, and bent his head. "I know. My father's a complex man. You sit down and you're next to him. I can't do that."

"Have you tried?"

"I tried, I tried. Look, forget it." They were at the herb garden now, a complex of brick paths and beds, old brick shot through with white lime. Dolly had designed the garden out of eighteenth-century drawings and twentieth-century memories of her own.

"Parsley," Leonard said. "Which is it?"

Jones glanced at him, as if to ask how anyone living here all his life could not recognize parsley.

"I know. I'm not a gardener. Anyway, she wants the broad leaf stuff, and that's different."

"There." Jones pointed.

"That's mint. Even I know that." Pointing, Leonard said, "Try this one for size."

"This is mint."

Leonard tasted it. "Parsley."

"I never saw parsley just like that," Jones said.

"Another marvel of the rich."

Elizabeth stepped out of the kitchen door and called to them, "Mother says, Where's the parsley?"

"If I had a place like this," Jones said, "I'd have me a nigger to pick the parsley."

"That means you're treating me like a normal person. You're hostile, you're nasty, and you stand on your right to talk stupid."

"Right on."

"Oh, Jesus, don't go away, Jonesy. I need you."

SEVENTEEN

Augustus Levi managed to get Dolly aside on their way out of the house to lunch on the terrace, and said to her, "Who's the black kid."

"Student. Friend of Leonard. Law at Harvard. Very bright."

"Joining us for dinner?"

"Yes," staring at her father and waiting for his reaction.

"That little shithead Justin, who runs the state department south, hates blacks and so does his wife, who's some kind of southern belle."

"Oh? Do you mind?"

"Me? You're talking to Gus Levi, kid. Nothing I like better than to shove one up his lousy little ass, if you'll forgive the language?"

"You know I won't, Daddy, and for God's sake, don't talk like that in front of Clarence. He comes from a decent Christian home, and you know there's nothing more proper than proper church-going blacks."

"If you say so, Baby."

"I do say so. Emphatically. Especially at the dinner table."

"And at the lunch table?"

"Absolutely."

At the lunch table, Augustus Levi dominated the scene, not simply because of his enormous bulk, but also in the singularity of his dress. He always voted for singularity, feeling it had profound psychological effects. Now, with everyone else in casual clothes, he wore a stiff and creaseless seersucker suit over a white shirt and a school tie, which in this case was Harvard. He also had gone on to get his degree in engineering at the Massachusetts Institute of Technology. He wore spotless white shoes and a pale lavender handkerchief in his outside breastpocket, and under the handkerchief, on the face of the pocket, a small MIT symbol. Thus he announced two antecedents out of the trunkful of varied awards and honors that he and his family had accumulated.

He said to his daughter, "Dolly, you look damn wonderful. If you'd be sensible and dye your hair, you'd pass for thirty, and your kids don't eat enough. Anorexia is one of the stupid ailments of our time. Your place looks decent enough, but your trees want pruning."

"Yes, Daddy," Dolly said quietly, conducting a conversation with her mother and only half aware of what her father was saying. Elizabeth and Leonard were suddenly convulsed with laughter—to the amazement of Jones, who ate his food in uneasy silence. They adored the old man. Jenny had developed throughout her life with Augustus the ability to hear nothing that he said—unless it was prefaced with a booming salutation: "Jenny, pass me the salt!"

"You're not supposed to have salt. You know that." She passed him the salt. "I do hope you're keeping the salt down tonight," she said to Dolly.

"Mother, you know it wouldn't help. He'd only put the salt back onto the food. The chicken salad has no salt. He's adding it."

"How's your golf game?" he was saying to the senator, who did not adore him, but endured him.

"Not my game. You know that, Gus."

"Of course, and that's a mistake. That's where the business of America takes place, on the golf links."

"You know what his blood pressure is," Jenny said to Dolly. Jenny, five feet and nine inches tall, had been one of those golden American girls. At age sixty-nine, she was a full-bosomed maternal figure of a woman, one hundred and fifty pounds and stout enough not to require a face-lift. Dolly had heard rumors of her father's adventures with a sex therapist who gave him injections of testosterone, but she dismissed them as the kind of gossip public figures endure—although, in all truth, her father attempted a low profile in all gossip and publicity. She still saw her mother as a beautiful and desirable woman, and perhaps she pitied her more than she loved her. If someone had asked her what were her feelings toward her father, she would have stated without hesitation that she loved him dearly; but asking the question of herself—which she rarely did—Dolly would come up with an answer far less certain.

Now she put her hand on her mother's and said, "I know what Richard's blood pressure is."

"At least he doesn't embrace the salt shaker."

"Well. You know . . ." dropping her voice, "Daddy is immortal, Richard isn't."

"What a thing to say!"

"Mother, just a silly joke."

"Tennis," Augustus was telling the senator, "puts your adversary on the other side of the net. That's why it's a game for doctors and rich bums. Not for politicians."

"Grandpa," Elizabeth said, "I am not a doctor and I am not a rich bum—at least I don't think so—and I love tennis."

"Then we'll thank God you're not a politician, Baby. What I mean to convey to your father is that you don't work a deal on the tennis court."

Hearing out of the nonlistening ear, Dolly ventured that tennis was less a sport than a religion.

"Not my tennis," the senator said.

"That's true. Richard isn't compulsive."

"Nor do I make deals," the senator said.

"Hah!" That was from Dolly.

"Sometimes, sometimes," the senator admitted.

"We're all of us corrupting young Jones here," Augustus told them.

Dolly busied herself with feeding. "There's a buffet of delicious things, Mr. Jones. The salad niçoise is delicious, even if it is just plain old tuna fish and green stuff and the bread is still hot. We make our own mayonnaise and we're famous for it at least for a mile down the road. And the potato salad is not just potato salad. See for yourself."

How nice of her, the senator thought, to put it that way and put the black kid at his ease.

"No, sir," Jones said to Augustus. "I don't think I'm being corrupted. Enlightened, perhaps."

"You'll find nothing enlightening here," Elizabeth said.

"Really, Liz," from Jenny.

"Still, I hear you're going into politics."

"Maybe. Yes, sir—if I ever get out of law school, if I ever pass my bar. That's what my folks want, but there's plenty of work down home for just a plain country lawyer."

"Don't ever put down a plain old country lawyer," Augustus said. "Sam Ervin was that, but nothing plain about Sam. He was one of the smartest men in Congress and the best damn constitutional lawyer in the country."

"Do you like the idea, Mr. Jones?" the senator asked him.

"Oh, Daddy," Elizabeth said. "The poor man's name is Clarence."

"Sir?" Jones wondered.

"I mean, Clarence, do you like the idea of politics?"

"Well, sir . . ." He hesitated and thought about it.

Jenny, who rarely listened to her husband's discussions, was worried about the dishes that would be used for dinner. "They're museum pieces. I should have given them to the White House," she said to Dolly. "I thought about it, but the White House wasn't interested in a hundred pieces of dinnerware. I never thought you would use them."

Jones said, finally answering the senator's question, "I do and I don't." He smiled, sheepishly but winningly. "This would be the wrong place to question the integrity of politicians in general."

"Not at all," Elizabeth protested. "Daddy agrees with you."

"Oh, come on," the senator protested. "There are politicians and politicians."

"And if they're millionaires, they don't take bribes," Leonard said.

"Not so quick, sonny, not so quick," Augustus said to Leonard. "A politician needs the votes, and that tends to keep him human. These two fellers coming to dinner, they're appointed. You don't need votes for that."

"It's not a thing widely understood," the senator said. "Maybe it's the big flaw in our constitution."

"Gramps," Elizabeth said, "what do these two good old boys want with you?"

"There's an example of what all that nonsense about women's rights has done. In my time, a young girl at the table with her elders would not dare to come up with a question like that."

"It's not a table," Elizabeth said, "it's lunch on the terrace, and I'm not a young girl, I'm a grown woman."

"And they're not good old boys but a couple of barracudas."

"The trouble is," Jenny was saying to Dolly, "that until Jackie Kennedy got into the White House, no one gave a second thought to how it was furnished. Anyway, who was there? Eleanor was above such things and that Truman woman never got her feet out of Kansas—"

"I think it was Missouri, Mother."

"However. And poor Mamie—"

"Mother, I'll be delighted to give you the dishes, and you can give them to whatever institution you like."

"What nonsense!"

Watching Leonard with quick glances or out of the corner of her vision, Elizabeth marvelled at his control. He and Clarence Jones had plunged into an argument with Augustus about the theoretical possibility of a politician with total integrity. The young men argued against it, and Augustus dismissed the concept as being an unreal conceit.

"You want to equate the politician with the crook. That's an old American legend, still vital, and it serves to ease the burden of voters who are being plucked dry by the gang in Washington, but my daddy was a friend of Al Smith, and by my daddy's lights no finer or more decent man ever stood in politics. Sure, there were people who called Al Smith a crook. It doesn't matter."

Elizabeth had lost track of the argument. She was watching Leonard and fighting back her tears, and smiling at the same time at Leonard's verve.

"You're telling us," Leonard said, "that the

system is admirable because it's crooked? Or in spite of?"

"A little of each."

"Gramps, I just don't know what you mean." He turned to his father. "Do you, Pop? Do you know what he means?"

Elizabeth realized that an unusual thing had happened. She had never heard him call the senator *Pop* before. It had once been *Daddy* and then it became *Father* and then it slid off to nothing, and speaking of Richard, Leonard would refer to him as the senator. Nor was Cromwell himself unaware of the word. The question had been addressed to him. And somehow, out of the part of her mind that heard the conversation through the screen of her mother's chatter, Dolly became aware of it, and as she turned to listen to the others, Jenny fell silent. Only Jones and the grandparents remained ignorant of the small thing that had happened.

"I think I do," the senator said, in answer to his son's question. "There's something profoundly important in what he says, but possibly it's profoundly awful as well."

Leonard asked Jones, "Do you make it?"

"I'm not sure. Mr. Levi," he said to the old man, "did you ever hold public office?"

"The closest I ever came to it, aside from various panels put together for the nonsense that panels confront, was as an officer in

World War Two. I suppose that was public service of a sort, but nobody ever had to vote for me. No, young man, I'm an engineer, not a politician."

"Daddy, you're being isolated," Elizabeth said.

"It's happened before."

"And Gramps never did answer my question."

"Lizzie, you don't want a world where every question is answered."

"Only Buddha set foot in that kind of world," Leonard murmured.

Augustus grinned at his grandson. "Oh? Tell me about it."

"He knew all the answers to all the questions," Leonard said slowly.

"There's someone I'd like to have on my payroll."

"You can't hire him."

"The way I see it," Elizabeth said, "if those two worthy diplomats wanted to have dinner with you, you want to have dinner with them. Otherwise, you could have told them to bug off."

"And miss a chance of seeing my grandchildren?"

"That's right, Daddy," Dolly said. "You need an invitation to come here."

"The trouble is," Augustus said to the senator, "that when you come from what we in

America, in all our lousy pretentiousness, call old money, you find your kids being born with more money than you have." And seeing the expression on Jones's face, "Clarence there is puzzled. Unfortunately, it's not your problem. My father, blessed with more money than God, left a bundle of it to my daughter—cutting my parental influence to absolute zero."

"Augustus," Jenny said severely, "this is not the place to discuss money."

"Any place, my dear, is the proper place to discuss money. It's the air we breathe and the food we eat."

"Suppose we switch to the food on our plates," Dolly said with some annoyance, turning to her children and Jones. "You're not eating. You're playing with your food."

"Not hungry."

"Mummy, you're absolutely right," Elizabeth said. And to the two young men, "Come on, kids, eat something." And to MacKenzie, hovering in the background, "Tuna fish, Mac. I can always eat tuna. It's the mother's milk of our childhood."

"The things you say, really," Jenny said. She disapproved of the way her daughter did things. She felt that one couple and one servant hardly suited their position, as Jenny called it; neither sufficient servants nor a proper house, referring to the sprawling Colonial structure as a mess of cottages stuck together. She had come from an old New Hampshire family and had married what her father always referred to as "the rich Jew." Once, during the courtship, Jenny's father got around to asking Augustus where the family's money came from. "Junk jewelry," Augustus said. "We used to peddle it here and there." Jenny was furious with him. The fact was that the Levis, Sephardic Jews, had come to Philadelphia from Cuba in 1692. By the middle of the eighteenth century, a trickle of Polish Jews found their way to Philadelphia, and poor as they were, uncouth in their beards and sidelocks and Yiddish tongue, they became an embarrassment to their elegant Spanish-Jewish brethren who had settled in Philadelphia a few generations before. Avrum Levi, born in 1714, discovered a profitable answer to this predicament. He outfitted each Polish Jew with two donkeys and two bags of what Augustus called junk jewelry, consisting of mirrors, trinkets, glass beads, knives, and clay pipes of Dutch design in the shape of a human head—which they traded to the Indians for beaver skins. While some of the Polish Jews failed to survive in the wilderness, others did so and in the course of things, struck it rich and laid the basis for many a fortune. Very few of these families survived as Jews; they intermarried and in a few generations lost their identity. The Levis also inter-married, but Augustus converted back—as he put it.

After lunch, Augustus, ignoring his wife's plea that he lie down for a nap, informed Richard that he would like the senator to take a walk with him. As always, the senator was awed by his father-in-law's energy. "I'd much prefer the nap Jenny suggested," Richard said.

"I'm too old to nap and you're too young to nap."

"I'm up since five this morning."

"So am I," Augustus told him.

They settled for two lounge chairs along-side the swimming pool. The swimming pool, roughly rectangular, rimmed with cut granite pieces to match a granite overhang at one end, gave the impression of a natural forma-tion, at least to a degree. Instead of detracting from it, the pool added to the charm of the little glen.

"Always liked this pool," Augustus said. "You built it about fifteen years ago?"

"Somewhere then."

"What did it cost you?"

"About forty thousand—with the landscap-ing."

"Cost you a hundred today. Do you all swim?"

"In the morning mostly," he replied, wondering whether the old man's purpose was to discuss family health.

"I swim. Can't get Jenny into the pool or the ocean."

Augustus was silent for a minute or so, while the senator closed his eyes and began to drop into a doze.

"Richard!"

"Oh, yes?"

"About this dinner tonight—how did it happen?"

"Justin's mother has a big summer place near here—up in the hills, one of those old turn-of-the-century minicastles. The old lady spends a month or so there with an army of servants, and I suppose Justin pays filial homage there each summer. She's as rich as Croesus, and Justin is an eager little bastard. Well, Heller and his wife are with him for a few days, and this past Monday, Justin calls me here and announces that Heller would be simply delighted to see my father-in-law. But you have met him, haven't you?"

"A good many times—enough to know he pisses standing. That was years ago. I don't like to mix with those fellers."

"Well, not just to meet you. But to sit down and talk. So I asked Dolly to put together this dinner party. I told Justin that we'd be pleased to have them at the house, but it would depend on your schedule. Since I owe them nothing, I could be cavalier about it. When you agreed, I invited Justin and Heller. I suspected that you agreed because you wanted to talk to them."

"You were right. But if I know you at all, Richard, you set it up because you wanted to talk to them."

"That's possible," the senator agreed.

"About what?"

"What are we playing, Gus? You tell me your dream and I'll tell you mine?"

"You can guess what they want with me. I can't guess what you could want with those two wolves in wolves' clothing. Unless you're planning to defect?"

"That will be the day. No way, Gus. The day I decide to step over the line and become a Republican and join your set of thieves, I'll toss away my toga and earn an honest living."

"Hear! Hear!" Augustus said goodnaturedly. "After that excellent lunch my daughter provided, I cannot berate you. Not that your son of a bitch is any better than mine; but we're richer. Your boys are easier to bribe."

"Are they? Well, about this dinner tonight, I would say, Gus, that they want to talk about the road."

"I think I always underrate you, Richard. That bovine exterior and the way you fumble around for words throws people off the track."

"That makes me out to be devious. Do you really think I'm devious, Gus?"

"No, I can't say that I do. I think the way you are is there. You don't alter it."

"I don't know whether you're being nice or nasty."

"And I still don't know what you want out of our revered secretary of state."

"All in good time."

"Ah. Well, I won't press you."

"What about the road?" the senator asked.

"We'll see. I have two hundred million in it —almost one quarter of a billion dollars. That, Richard, is not play money."

"It certainly is nothing I ever played with."

"And you're going to be close mouthed?"

"For the moment."

"I might be of some help," Augustus said.

"I hope so."

"All right. Enough of that. What about Leonard? He looks like hell."

"He's always been too thin."

"What's with the two of you? Why the hell can't you be father and son?"

"Always subtle, aren't you, Gus? Why don't you ask me how many times a week I sleep with your daughter?"

"I'd like to."

"Yes, and I'd like to deck you, except that I

never punched anyone, and it's late to start. The reason we've never had a real fight is that you're Dolly's father, and I'm not going to start one now."

Augustus grinned at him. "You know, I like you, Richard. I always have, and it's no news to you that I'm a nasty old bastard." He put out his hand. "Shall we start again?"

"I'm willing."

"You know, Richard, we don't split on the money question. I've never objected to this political game you play."

"Thank you for your overwhelming kindness."

"I am totally and indecently rich, and pretty old, and when I go, I don't take two nickels with me. My sons inherit, and my daughter has a nice pile put aside for her, on top of the boodle her granddaddy left her. My father never cared for the boys, which is why he left so large a bundle for Dolly."

"I'd just as soon not review comparative financial standings in your family. Are you going to tell me that I married my wife for her money?"

"No."

"Thank God for small pleasures."

"I turned it around, you damn fool. I was specifying that you and Dolly want nothing from me. That makes you unique in my eyes. I like it. You don't have to brownnose me. You can tell me to fuck off any time you want to."

The senator nodded. It was a long time since he had been this furious about anything, and he did not trust himself to speak.

"Damn it, Richard, will you get off your high horse!"

The senator controlled himself. His anger subsided, and he said slowly, "Let's walk again, Gus."

"Too hot to walk."

"Then let's go downstairs in the house and shoot some pool."

"I want to talk to you. I'm not finished."

"We'll play pool and talk. It gives me a chance to think, and maybe pool is the one thing I can beat you at."

"Maybe."

The pool table was in a room that had once been part of a large basement. When modern heating systems made coal storage space unnecessary, and electricity and refrigeration made root and apple cellars a thing of the past, Dolly's father turned most of the cellar space into a billiard room, and when Dolly's mother gave them the house as a wedding gift, the billiard table came with it. It was a deep cellar, nine-foot ceilings, and great twelve-inch-square oak beams to support the house above. Dolly had added to its attractiveness with dead white ceiling between the beams, white walls, and a floor of oak-stained eight-inch wide boards. The pool table was an old one, made in Milwaukee in 1901, by Stien and Scherson according to the gold plate on its edge. It had huge, bulging legs, and it nestled under green billiard-room lamps.

"You did beat me once or twice," Augustus said. "You don't practice, your skill goes. I started playing on this table when I was twelve. At eighteen I could beat a hustler. But I don't play anymore, not at the club, not at home—home. The pool table's in Switzerland. I don't know where the hell is home these days."

"Straight pool?"

"Good enough."

The senator racked up the balls, and then nodded at Augustus, who was chalking a cue he had selected.

"You break," Richard said.

"You're a gentleman. It's something I've always admired about you, Richard. I'm no gentleman." He was feeling his cue, and then lining up the white ball for his breaking shot. "Definition of a gentleman. He treats the lowest, the poorest, the most unappetizing with the same attention and courtesy he might give to that actor in the White House. No, I'm no gentleman." He made his shot and the balls broke widely. "Do you know, Richard," he said as he studied the board and planned his shot, "I'm going to lay the whole thing out for you. I might as well. I don't want any loud noises at dinner tonight."

"I thought you would."

Augustus didn't speak again. He fixed his attention on the table and ran the whole set of balls. Cromwell watched him with amazement, the old man's steady hand, his detachment and his uncanny judgment of ball and cushion. "I don't do that too often," Augustus said. "Maybe half a dozen times in a lifetime. Maybe it's the table. I know this old table. Your turn."

"The hell with pool," the senator said. "You're too hard an act to follow. Let's sit and talk."

"Got any cigars?"

"I keep a box of Don Diegos here."

"Cuban?"

"I don't smoke Cuban cigars."

"Come on, Richard, they smoke them in Congress and in the White House too, for that matter."

"When the dunces who run our foreign policy make their peace with Cuba, I'll smoke Cuban." He took the cigars out of a closet and offered them to his father-in-law. "Anyway, these are just as good."

"If Jenny comes down here, she'll cut my heart out."

"Take your chances. It's an uneasy life we live."

They dropped into two brown leather chairs at the end of the room, lit their cigars, and leaned back comfortably.

"Never played pool when you were a kid?" Augustus asked.

"Nope."

"Missed something." He tasted the smoke. "A lovely cigar, Richard. I don't deny it," he said, referring to the matter at hand. "It's about the road."

"They never liked it."

"You know—right from the beginning, it caught my imagination. A highway across Central America, linking the oceans. Only old Goethals had a dream like that."

"It's a very high-class dream. It certainly is."

"You're not going to say, I told you so, are you, Richard."

"No."

"I admire your presence."

"You build roads. I'm a politician."

"Don't tell me you don't have dreams. I never had one like this before. It's like building that tunnel they're going to have, connecting England with the continent. And this is historically overdue. You know that. Everyone in Congress knows that. A broad, fine, weatherproof road, ocean to ocean, with a rail line running alongside. It would change the whole history of Central America."

"That's just it."

"Damn it," Augustus said, "those two old buzzards could have come to my office, they could have subpoenaed me down to Washington—why here?"

"Here it can be social. The velvet glove and all that crap. You know what they're going to say. The wrong time, Gus. Politically inadvisable. The Pentagon garbage. A lot of talk—but the way I see it, the essence will be—forget it or we'll close you down."

"Like hell they'll close me down!" His cigar had gone out. He lit it again and said, "I suppose they could."

"I'm not sure they could. You're working for local governments."

"With money borrowed from us, Richard."

"Yes, everything is our money. All the same, we could put up a terrific fight in Congress—and we might just win."

"We? Who the hell is 'we,' Richard? Are there thirty men on your side of the house who'd stand up against those war-mongering bastards? Name them. Your damn party has shit in its blood. I'm a Republican. I hate those gross bastards who have taken over the White House. I hate them because they're stupid and greedy beyond measure, and because they could burn us all in some senseless holocaust. But I am what I am. I'm rich, I intend to stay rich, and I belong to the party of the rich —and by God, through the years we haven't done too badly—until this crew of bloodsuckers took over. What have your boys done? You gave us Korea and you gave us Vietnam and you've left a trail of blood and suffering right through the twentieth century, with your crazy Johnson and your dimwitted little haberdasher Harry Truman. You make wars and we pick up the bodies and end them. Your people created the Pentagon and the C.I.A., and now you're trying to sell the American people the notion that we were responsible for all of it."

It took the senator a minute or two to react to a kind of anger and eloquence that he had not experienced before from his father-in-law, and in the interval he fought to control his own anger. He managed that, and he managed to say, coolly enough, "Do you really believe that?"

"Oh, Lord, Richard, I am not putting you on trial. You're a decent good man. But what I said is history, not opinion."

Cromwell took a deep breath, and then lit his cigar, and puffed deeply. You don't inhale a cigar, but when you do, there is nothing in the world like it. Calm, calm, calm. You can help this man. He can help you. What he said was not totally false, nor is he so different from the crowd in the White House. Like him, they disdained to hide their position. If they lied, it was boldly and blatantly, and only fools believed them. If they hated welfare, they did not disguise their hatred with euphemisms. They needed hungry workers to break the unions, and they needed small wars to keep the industrial military complex in good standing. And when his own party aped them, his own party lied.

His anger faded.

"You're sore as hell, aren't you?" the old man said.

"No—no, I don't cherish illusions any more than you do, but I dream that perhaps it can work a little better. I think I could get at least a hundred voices in Congress to speak out for you—but that wouldn't make much difference, would it?"

"What do you think, Richard?"

"No. I'd never get a majority. If they want you to give it up, well, they know how to twist arms. The C.I.A. can grow more damn accidents than an army of black cats. Your shipments would stop, your machines would blow up, and your ships would have all sorts of interesting accidents. And your workers would develop a habit of getting themselves dead. What are you in for right now? I mean out of your own money."

"It's not pocket money. We draw our own

plans based on our own surveys. No other way to sell the bonds. That's already almost five million dollars. We've designed some new earth movers, bigger than anything that's ever been used, and we've placed orders up to—say sixteen million. We have a small army down there working on the right of way, buying property and clearing brush."

"Any of it guaranteed?"

"Those banana republics don't have a pot to piss in. The bonds that will pay for this are guaranteed by the U.S.A."

"And what are you in for—I mean what does it add up to at this moment?"

"About two hundred million. Now, understand, Richard, this is a toll enterprise all the way. We have floated a company, sold bonds, and intend to run it the way the Canal is run."

"Do you stand to lose?"

"That's it. We don't if we begin to lay down the road. At that point, Washington comes in with enough money to pay off our expenses, and they pick up whatever is left of the bond issue."

"But right now, the two hundred is down the drain."

"I don't think so. I think those two peculiar bastards will propose a deal."

"To save your two hundred million or to save the road?"

"What do you think?" Augustus asked.

"They sure as hell don't want the road." He studied his father-in-law with interest. "You won't fight them?"

"Richard, they may have crawled from under a rock, but it's my rock. You want something from them?"

"Yes. You don't have to cave in immediately. You can make it rough for them, because in the end they'll get what they want and what they came for. You can make a small deal."

"With you as the beneficiary."

"Not alone. Others will benefit."

"Tell me about it."

Richard nodded. "All right. I thought of bringing it up after dinner, but since you're going to give away the road, we might as well talk about it now. You've heard about the Sanctuary Movement?"

"I saw something in the papers. I haven't followed it." He lit his cigar again. "A good cigar, Richard, mellows even an old beast like myself. It soothes the savage breast. At another moment I might have said, out and out, that I don't give a fiddler's fart about your Sanctuary Movement. Now I've had a fine lunch and I've seen my favorite daughter and my favorite granddaughter, and I'm prepared to listen."

"We thank God for small favors. I'm very serious about this—believe me, Gus. I'll shorten the background. Since nineteen eighty-one, our immigration people have deported more than fifty thousand refugees back to Guatemala and El Salvador—almost half of them to prison and execution. The stories that come back to us are hideous and almost unbelievable, and the horrors are perpetrated by governments we back. This is at best a brief summary, but it is in response to this situation that the Sanctuary Movement came into being. Last year in San Francisco. Church people opened their doors to these refugees. They hid them, fed them, sheltered them—and not only Protestants, Gus, but Catholics and Jews, and in one case even an order of Catholic friars. Can you see it—there hasn't been anything like this since the old underground railroad of the days before the Civil War. Did I say it began in San Francisco —oh, it spread, California to Arizona and Nevada and Colorado until over two hundred churches and synagogues were involved."

"Why the synagogues—to soften me?"

"God damn it, no!" the senator exclaimed angrily. "The synagogues are involved. Does that surprise you? Do you expect less from the Jews than from us?"

"Finish your story, Richard."

He'd finish it, but he did not know why or to what end. The man sitting beside him was a stranger, a man worth more than a billion dollars who cleared a pool table on the break, who professed love for his daughter and granddaughter but apparently loved nothing, who was the least Jewish Jew the senator had ever met.

"You could guess, Gus. What was the name of the three-star general who said last month that the worst enemy the Pentagon faces are the goddamn churches—excepting of course the moral majority?"

"You're drifting."

"Sorry. Back to the point. The White House decided that this Sanctuary Movement, this revival of the underground railroad, this use of the church and synagogue, was, as the general specified, the major enemy. Whereupon, they ordered the immigration service and the F.B.I. to arrest and indict. Sixteen Sanctuary workers, a Presbyterian pastor, a Catholic nun, and a number of lay religious workers were arrested. Two of them are on trial now as we speak, in Tucson, Arizona. They have thrown a conspiracy charge at them, which could mean five years in prison on each count if they are convicted."

"Out of my line, Richard. I'm seventy-three years old; my heart is bad and I'm doing nothing to make it better and bleeding hearts leave me cold as ice."

"I'm not asking for money. I'm asking you to use the road to help me make a deal with my two honorable guests. I want them to call off their running dogs, to throw out the case in Tucson."

Augustus smiled and shook his head sadly. "Dolly once told me that she dreams of you in the presidency. Richard, Richard. It would be nice to see my daughter down there among the spooks as First Lady, but, Richard, you will never make it. You are sentimental and you are decent. I'm an old Yankee type, with two hundred years of dues paid in return for ice water instead of blood, but there's enough Jewish left to admit to myself that I run with a mean crowd. No decent, sentimental, honest man can be president of this country. You know that. You're asking for sympathy; that's not my line, and neither is compassion. I don't bleed for anyone, not here, not in Africa, not in Asia. I'm in this to have fun and make money. I've had my pleasures and I've made a lot of money. It's the name of the game, Richard."

"I can't even be properly angry," the senator said. "You're up front with the whole thing and you don't apologize. That's something to admire. You know, Gus, in all the years I've known you, we never talked about Jewish. I always felt it was something extraordinary, noble, a kind of Judophile thing that they have in England—you know, Einstein, Salk, Bernstein, Modigliani, great doctors and scientists and artists. I labeled it a kind of humanitarian vision—"

"Because you're a sentimentalist, Richard."

"Am I? Is that all it is?"

"Richard, I had two ancestors who fought in the American Revolution, which makes me a member of that pisspot organization that calls itself the Sons of the American Revolution. One was a Lieutenant Levi and the other a Captain Peretz. Both of them resident in Philadelphia. After Benedict Arnold did his thing and fled to the British, he had the *chutzpa* to petition General Washington, the same man he had tried so hard to scuttle, to allow his wife, Arnold's wife, to join Arnold in New York City, then occupied by the British. Well, war in those days was contrived and led by gentlemen who played by a set of silly rules, and sure enough, General Washington gave permission for his wife to join him. His wife was Peggy Shippen Arnold, a young lady of good position, as they used to say, and substantial wealth. And since the countryside between Philadelphia, where Mrs. Arnold resided, and New York, where Arnold fled to, was filled with angry folk who might not look upon Mrs. Arnold with the same generosity that Washington did, Congress sent along a military detachment to protect her. The detachment was led by Lieutenant Levi and Captain Peretz. And according to some letters I've read, both these gents fucked Peggy all the way from Philadelphia to New York— no small journey by horse and coach—raising the possibility that quite a few generations of Jewish Arnolds have been prancing around in England. What's Jewish? The kids? Or the behavior of the two officers? I find their behavior totally international. The lady wasn't raped. She enjoyed them with ladylike approval, and considering that, I can't think of anyone of the male sex of any nationality who would have behaved differently."

Suddenly, the senator was bored and a little disgusted by the rambling of the old man. Lasciviousness is without merit or beauty after a certain age, and the senator felt that he had paid his dues and listened for long enough.

"Why don't you get a bill through the Senate?" Augustus asked, as if to mollify.

"You don't do it with a bill."

"You can still try to work a deal with your dinner guests. I won't interfere. I won't help you, but I won't interfere."

"You don't feel anything about it, one way or another?" the senator asked.

"No, Richard. Nothing at all. And if you feel that's heartless of me, you're absolutely right. I don't give a damn for El Salvador or Guatemala—except that they are in the general area where I'm building a road. That arouses interest, not compassion."

"And if these people on trial in Tucson were Jewish?"

"Believe me, Richard, it would not make a damn bit of difference. If you find conservatives stupid—which many of them are—I find your liberals ridiculous and beyond the practice of reason."

"Then why in God's name do you cling to this being Jewish—which is farcical?"

"Because I love it, Richard. It distinguishes me in a very special way. We lost the name of Levi four or five generations back; I restored it. By blood, if you buy the nonsense, I am one sixteenth Jewish; but I cherish it. It's a profound fuck-you to the entire Wasp section of the establishment. If I didn't have it, I'd create it and lie about it. But I'm afraid you don't understand that."

"I'm afraid I don't," the senator admitted.

EIGHTEEN

When the junior members of the group left the luncheon table, Elizabeth whispered to the others, "Let's go up to my room. I have four tailor-made sticks of pure Acapulco Gold. It's very good stuff. We'll smoke a little and cry a little."

"It's kid's stuff," Leonard said.

"Lenny, a little kid's stuff won't hurt us right now," Jones said.

"It'll stink up the room."

"Come on, we're air conditioned. Blows it right out," she said, wondering that her brother, so stricken, should worry about the scent of marijuana, and the reaction of his parents to the fact that they were smoking it. They were children. She was the youngest of the three, but she was a woman and they were children, and it came to her that death was so much more terrible for a child, for the child knows that he is cheated and that the best thing in all the universe is taken from him before he has truly experienced it, and it doesn't matter that the child is twenty-two years old, and brilliant and sensitive and even wise, because it is never a wisdom that can confront death.

"It helps," Jones says.

"Joke," Leonard said. "Nothing helps. I'm terminal. You know how many times we talked about the atom bombs that the lunatics in the Kremlin and the White House are piling up, and we had that big discussion at school about time, and everyone guessed that at most we had five or six years before an accident had to happen, or the president would think he was a character in a movie, which he mostly is, and he'd press the button, and that would be the end of everything and all of us—and we sort of believe it, but we also feel that a miracle could happen and that something might save us."

"It might," Elizabeth said.

"But that's the difference, Liz. There's no miracle for me, not even the hope of one."

Calling back to her mother, who still sat on the terrace with Jenny, Elizabeth cried, "Mother—we'll be in my room if you want us for anything."

"Leonard," Dolly called after them, "do find some dinner clothes!"

"That's not so," Elizabeth said softly. "It's

not a matter of a miracle. They will find something, a vaccine, a drug—they must!"

"Dear Lizzie, I'm afraid not."

Jones reacted strangely to Elizabeth's
room. It was a large, beautiful room, with a
fireplace piled with wood and framed in a
white mantel, white woodwork, wallpaper of
dusty rose toile, Portuguese gros-point rugs
on the floor, framed eighteenth-century fashion prints, and a portrait of her great-grandmother done by John Singer Sargent. On the
bed was an ancient coverlet of stitched silk
that some poor Italian woman of a century
ago had dulled her eyesight to create. The
windows were draped with starched organdy,
and the painted electrified oil lamps went
well with the old cherry-wood furniture. At
first sight, the room threw him off, and he was
possessed with a feeling akin to panic, and he
stood in the doorway, searching within himself for the origin of his fears. Far, far back. His
mother had been a cleaning woman then; his
brother had been hurt. He ran to the house
where his mother worked, a skinny nine-year-
old black kid, and the door of the large house
being open, he went in, through the downstairs rooms, and then up the wide staircase to
a bedroom such as this, not like this but such
as this in confused memory. He had only a
glimpse of the room for then there came out
of a connecting bathroom, a great blonde

lady, half naked and toweling herself dry. Her scream echoed through the years.

"Come on in," Elizabeth said to him.

Leonard crossed to a window and stood looking out. "Ever notice the way Grandma Jenny walks? She sails—slowly, yet the feet don't appear to move, only the body. Rare in this country, but you see a lot of it in England."

Elizabeth was hunting through a drawer. "Trouble with hiding things is you forget where you hid them. I must have put these silly sticks away five years ago. You know why they do it in England—water all around them. Sailing and cricket."

"Oh, God," Leonard said.

"Sort of clever," Jones agreed, "but this poor black boy ain't never been to England. Ain't been much in white folks' houses either."

Leonard looked at Jones and shook his head. "Every time you pull that blackface routine, you're mad as hell. What is it now?"

"Memories."

"Stuff them," Elizabeth said. "They do no good and you can't eat them. Some day, when you're up on the appellate bench or maybe as house black on the Supreme Court, and you have ten years of being a law hooker behind you, you'll get rid of all those memories. Here they are." She handed out the marijuana. "Let's light up."

"How did you get that cynical?"

"Daddy's a senator. I love him, but he's a senator."

Elizabeth struck a match for her brother, but Leonard pulled back and said, "Hold on. This won't touch us if we keep thinking about this stinking AIDS. Maybe tomorrow I'll cry all day, but right now I'm with two people I love and I can open up and talk to you, but God Almighty, you have to talk to me and you can't keep looking at me with death on your faces."

Elizabeth dropped the burned out match. She struck another and lit her brother's cigarette. Jones took the matches from her and lit her cigarette and then his own. They inhaled deeply. They sat and looked at each other. They inhaled again. Jones was in a chair. Leonard sat cross-legged on the floor. Elizabeth sprawled on the floor, her back against the bed. She was dressed in jeans and a blue Levi shirt and she looked beautiful.

I would forget that I'm gay, Jones said to himself, and if you want to dream the way niggers always dream, dream that you shuck the gay and you marry this wonderful person. Just dream it good and strong.

"If we're going to sit in silence," Elizabeth said, "we might as well stiff the pot."

"Oh, no. No," Jones said. "I'll tell you a story. Long ago, in the days of the Arabian Nights, there was a smuggler named Ahmad Umahr, and he was unquestionably the greatest smuggler of his era."

"Is this another one of your creepy Sufi stories?"

"Sufi stories are not creepy. The Sufis are very wise, the result of so many of them being as black as I am."

"Naturally," Elizabeth agreed.

"So as I was saying, year after year, Ahmad Umahr would come to the immigration stations at the border, his train of seven or eight or ten donkeys loaded with firewood; and the border people would take each load of firewood apart, stick by stick, yet they never could find what valuable merchandise he smuggled. Then after forty years of successful smuggling, Ahmad, a very rich man now, announced that he was retired and would smuggle no more. Whereupon, a delegation of immigration agents came to him and said, Ahmad Umahr, since you smuggle no more and are retired, tell us what you smuggled? To which Ahmad replied, The answer is obvious. I smuggled donkeys."

Jones finished with a slow smile.

"Yes?" Elizabeth asked.

"No more."

"You won't tell us what it means?"

"He doesn't know what it means," Leonard said. "It's like all the rest of these Sufi and Zen stories. What is the sound of one hand clapping?"

"A smile," Jones said.

"I suppose your story is true about something. At our age, we are still young enough to reach out and try to touch something, but we always look for the wrong thing, like the immigration people, and then we stop looking."

"Why did you say a smile?" Elizabeth asked Jones.

"I don't really know. It was something to say."

"I don't know why you told us that silly story," Leonard said. "When I think about dying, which is almost all the time, what hurts most is that I've missed something of great importance, and I don't know what it is, not just the life I'll never have a chance to live, but something else that was here but I missed it."

"I know," Elizabeth whispered.

"We all missed it."

"What? What? You smoke this stupid stuff and your brain turns to jelly. You're both brilliant. Why don't you tell me what?"

They looked at him without anger. Elizabeth's face began to crinkle. "Sissy, don't cry," Leonard said. He had not called her that since he was a kid.

"I can't not cry." She jumped up and took an old plate with a Tenniel drawing on it down from where it hung on the wall. "We need an ashtray," placing it between them, and then she collapsed with her tears, as if all the bones in her body had lost their hard ability to sustain shape and weight and had become a mound of blue shirt and blue jeans and brown hair without form, as she sank to the floor. Leonard went to her and embraced her, kissing the back of her neck. Then he pulled back and dropped into a white wicker chair.

"I'm crying too," Jones said, "and look what you have done, Elizabeth. Here's a skinny old nigger boy who's seen all kinds of things and thought he was tough as could be, just sitting here in the white lady's boudoir and crying like a baby."

She turned to face him, drying her eyes with her hands. "Pretty funny." But she had stopped crying. "Well, that's what I needed, a good cry."

"Now that everyone's had their cry, could you talk like normal human beings?" Leonard asked.

"Human beings are not normal. Dogs are normal. Cats are normal."

"I know what you mean," Jones said. "We used to meditate a lot, every day, and for a while in the morning and at night too, and we were gung ho to find enlightenment or *satori,* or call it what you will, and we knew we would and we also knew we wouldn't."

"You explain that," Elizabeth told him.

"It's the same thing I guess as your daddy's obsession."

"How do you know what's his obsession?" Leonard demanded.

"We had a talk about the basic contradiction of quantum mechanics—light as a wave and light as a particle. You can walk down that road for a long long time and you come to the proposition that all is illusion, including us."

"It's the same medicine man trick your ancestors used to work when they were witch doctors in the Congo."

"Maybe."

The pot they were smoking began to have its effect.

"If you reach that place, wherever it is, and you become enlightened," Elizabeth said, smiling sadly, "what have you got?"

"I think they were witch doctors," Jones said. "That's why I'm so smart. It took brains to be a proper witch doctor—more brains than the medics up at school bring with them."

"What have you got?" Elizabeth said again. "Nobody talks to anyone and nobody answers anyone."

"When the Buddha was enlightened, little

sister," Leonard answered, "he said—I mean the Buddha said—that now he knew the answer to all the questions."

"Really—one answer?"

"I never thought of it that way," Jones said, "but it had to be one answer."

NINETEEN

Coming into the house with Dolly, Jenny said, "I don't like the way Leonard looks. They're both too thin, but Leonard's pale and he doesn't look well. What does he eat? Have you any idea what he's eating up there at Harvard? Do you know, Gus and I ate in their common room once. Dreadful food. Gus feels he must eat at the Harvard Club when we're in New York. Equally dreadful. Leonard probably eats nothing but junk food."

"Yes, Mother. I'll talk to him."

Jenny led the way into the dining room, forthright and straightforward as a general taking command, and staring at the table, she said, "Dolly!" a word filled with measures of criticism.

"Mother, they are only place plates."

"Do you know who gave this set of dinnerware to your family? To Ephraim Levi?"

"Supposedly, Thomas Jefferson. I'm not at all sure about that. The dishes were made in

England in the Federal period, long after Jefferson was out of office, and the only distinction Ephraim Levi had was that he was rich and that his father had the reputation of having gone to bed with Peggy Shippen Arnold."

"What an awful thing to say!"

"Mother, what a thing to do, and then to boast about it. Yich! I do not love Ephraim or his father, and I'm sure that Ephraim ordered these dishes when he was in London and then started the rumor about Jefferson. Our history hews to Mr. Clemens's definition: lies, damn lies and statistics."

"And who is Mr. Clemens?"

"Mark Twain."

Jenny disdained to reply; she circled the dining table, as if she were taking measure of each plate. The old plates were very beautiful, the white glaze pure and unsullied by crazing, the gold stripe as good as the day it was put on, and the gold and blue eagle fierce and proud.

"You don't know because I never told you," Jenny said, "that Mrs. Whittercur telephoned me after you wrote your letter resigning from the Daughters of the American Revolution, and it took me the best part of an hour on the telephone to persuade her not to put your letter in their files. She promised to destroy it. Dolly, darling, how could you call the Daughters a disgusting organization?"

"Because they are. And I wanted my letter in the files."

"But you can't do such things. What of Elizabeth? And won't her children cherish their ancestry? And don't you think it's a very important thing for Jews to belong to the Daughters?"

"No, I don't. And Mother, you're not even the slightest bit Jewish, and where Daddy stands is beyond me, but I do coddle him and go along with it, and you want Elizabeth's daughter—if she ever has one—to belong to the Daughters? I just don't understand."

"You never did," Jenny said, studying the table bleakly, "and if you have such contempt for tradition, why are you using the dishes tonight?"

"I will tell you why. There are two ill-mannered characters straight out of Balzac coming to dinner tonight, and my husband wants something from them, and I intend to make a point of these dishes in terms of helping, if only a bit."

"Balzac? What on earth has Balzac to do with this?"

"Oh, Mother, I am a beast. Forgive me for being so provoking." She put her arms around Jenny and, as always, went up on the very tips of her toes to kiss her.

"I'm tired," Jenny said. "I think I'll go up to my room and lie down for a little while."

"That's a good idea."

"And if you see Leonard, tell him to come to my room. I want to talk to him."

"Of course, Mother."

Jenny went up the stairs slowly. Slower each summer, Dolly thought. Poor dear.

Then she turned back to the dining room to stare at the dinner plates again. She had never been able to cultivate a love of things. She wondered whether she told the truth— that it was for Richard? Only a few hours ago, she had been utterly furious at him; she had been in a mood to leave him, to hate him until the end of time, to revenge herself on him, to make him suffer and to watch him suffer—all of it from a fire lit by the sight of what Dolly thought of as "that wretched blonde bitch's car." If the "blonde bitch" had been frivolous, or pretty and stupid in the manner of Nellie, Dolly could have dealt with it on a different level; but the fact that Joan Herman had a whiplash mind, an astonishing memory, and a knowledge of Washington that was invaluable, put her in a very special position; and added to this was the quirk in Dolly's character that had turned her away from the charades of politics. If she snobbishly damned Joan for her political instinct, she could not forbear from damning her own husband as well. In no other way was she a snob, but thinking of Joan Herman, she engaged in all the snobbish attitudes that she disliked so in the circles of millionaires and old money and new money that surrounded the senator.

And now, only a few hours after her wrath, she could think of nothing but the strange moment of intimacy that had existed between them in the dining room before lunch. At this moment she wanted to see him again, to be in the same room with him. It pressed like physical hunger.

He had gone off with her father, unquestionably to smoke cigars, since the only point that both of them agreed on was the satisfaction of a good cigar after a meal; and both of them knew that the billiard room was the only place in the house where they could have a cigar without arousing the anger of the women. The smell of cigar smoke confirmed her guess, but the room itself was empty, the smoked butts dropped defiantly in the brass ashstand.

She drifted through the house, looking for Richard, yet assuring herself that she was not looking for him. She heard the sound of voices from Elizabeth's room and more muffled voices from the guest room where her mother and father were supposedly taking an afternoon nap. She came to the senator's office, hesitated, then opened the door and entered. His office and his bedroom were both unoccupied, and Dolly walked slowly around each room, looking at the framed election posters; the signed portrait of Franklin Delano Roosevelt, for which he had paid almost a thousand dollars at an auction; warm letters from Tip O'Neill and Ted Kennedy, lovingly framed; a framed cartoon by Conrad, from the *Los Angeles Times*, showing Richard Cromwell in armor as Don Quixote, tilting at a windmill shaped like the White House, and another cartoon by Herblock depicting Richard as St. George cutting with his sword at a dragon with the countenance of Nixon. What a great moment that was for both of them, to see Richard as St. George! They were still madly in love then and they celebrated Herblock's salute with a splendid dinner at Belnicks and then walked back, hand in hand, to their house in Georgetown, their heads in the clouds where vision was clear and all things were possible.

She paused at his desk, looking at a picture on the wall behind it. It was an oil painting of John Peter Altgeld, done by John Sloan in 1897, and a gift to Richard on their fifth anniversary. Dolly knew that Altgeld was a hero of the senator's, but about Altgeld himself, she had known little until she bought the painting. She read about him after that, proud that Richard had chosen his portrait for an icon.

And now, from the painting, her glance dropped to the desk, where a long, yellow lined legal pad was covered with the senator's even, round handwriting. In spite of herself, she could not conquer her curiosity, or possibly suspicion: she read it:

Does no memory exist that this land was founded by people whose tremendous need was to worship God in their own way —and worship is not limited to mouthing prayers. Worship is a way of life, a living force in the creation of this country, and we are all touched by this ancient worship of theirs, and central to it was the fact that my church is a sanctuary. That was the force that built the underground railroad to confront slavery—the force of and the belief in sanctuary.

And now what has this government of ours done, but to put spies with recording devices into the churches where we gave sanctuary to those who fled from the murder squads of El Salvador, and then bring to trial the pastor of the church and his wife, for the sin of obeying the most hallowed word of God—

She heard Richard's step as he entered the room, and turned to face him, guilty and shocked at the liberty she had taken, the sheet of paper in her hand.

"You're angry. You have every right to be."

Richard shook his head.

"It was there. I was looking at the painting and remembering when I gave it to you, and I saw the paper—"

"I'm not angry. Why should I be?"

"I was looking for you."

"Oh?"

"Not for any reason. I didn't want to be alone." She paused and the silence stretched out. She put down the yellow sheet and the senator picked it up.

"What is it?" Dolly asked.

"Notes for a speech. I never really worked it out."

"For the Senate?"

"Yes. It wouldn't do any good. There are no more consciences to be shocked, memories to be prodded. Oh, they are the coldest bastards that ever set foot in Washington. I don't know anymore. Here you have Senator Richard Cromwell, who doesn't believe in God or in much of anything else, using the God he doesn't believe in to try to right the most shameful and vicious injustice this administration has yet pulled. If it makes no sense, what does? Where are we? Have we all accepted the fact that these filthy bombs will end life on earth sometime during the next few years— and if that's the case, why not kill your neighbor first and make a buck in the bargain?"

"Richard, stop it," she said gently.

He dropped the paper and gripped her shoulders, staring at her. He had stopped looking at her years ago, and what he saw was sudden and unexpected, though he saw her every day, a pretty, round-faced woman with hazel eyes and gray hair cut short, pageboy and banged in front, no different except in color than it had been twenty-five years ago, and never in a hairdresser since then, cut in the kitchen by Ellen.

"I want to kiss you," he said, almost plaintively.

She said nothing, only stared at him.

He bent, half lifted her in his arms, kissed her with his lips closed, and then when he felt hers soften and part, permitted his to do the same. They remained locked in the embrace for a few moments, and then the senator put his arm around her and led her toward the door that connected the office to his bedroom. No word was said. The senator closed the door behind him and locked it, and then they undressed, avoiding each other's eyes. He pulled back the covers, and naked they got under the covers, shivering a little in the air-conditioned room, and then buried themselves in each other and under the summer blanket, hidden from the world and each other. Their love-making was passionate almost to the point of frenzy, as if afraid that each would never see the other again, as if each had the need to bury himself and herself in the other, so that there would be one and not two of them after this.

Richard was awakened by Dolly's voice: "Good heavens—what time is it?"

He felt for his watch and found it. "Almost four."

"Oh, Richard, I haven't even finished setting the table. I'm going to take a shower right here."

He was awake now, embracing her body, touching, stroking. "Don't go away now."

"Oh, darling. Genghis Khan and Attila will be here in three hours or so, and I have everything to finish downstairs and I have to get dressed—oh, no, don't," she pleaded.

"The hell with those bastards."

"Darling, no, no—"

"When?"

"Tonight. Tomorrow."

"I will hold you to that," he said.

TWENTY

MacKenzie stalked into the kitchen and said sternly to his wife, "What do you think?"

"I don't think," Ellen said. "I have fed seven people at lunch, and two useless drones, which means you and that lazy Nellie, and I'm trying to finish the salt sticks for tonight, and I had to find Miss Dolly, and I been through the house and no Miss Dolly until I got to the door of the senator's bedroom, and from the sounds coming out—well, what do you think?"

"Well, they was either having a fight or fucking."

Ellen came to him, shaking her finger an inch from his nose. "MacKenzie—once more you use that filthy word, once more—"

"Well, how on earth do I say 'fucking' if I can't say fucking?"

"You say 'making love.' You know, you are a bum. You can take the bum out of the ghetto, but you can't take the ghetto out of the bum."

"Well, it ain't always love," MacKenzie said, grinning. "And you did not marry a bum. You married a dignified son of a people who were oppressed a damn sight more than the folks in Africa are oppressed by demented Dutchmen."

"A dignified son. That'll be the day."

"And I think it's beautiful."

"Well, so do I, but not on a day we have eleven for dinner. And what do I think?"

"What do you mean, 'what do you think?' How do I know what you think?" MacKenzie demanded.

"That's what you said. What do I think, when you come marching in like judgment day?"

"Oh. Well, I come by the door to Elizabeth's room, and the smell of pot is as thick as winter fog in Washington."

"Nonsense. The kids haven't smoked for years."

"After raising two of your kids, if I don't know the smell of pot I should be put out to pasture."

"My kids!" Ellen exclaimed. "You insinuating they are not your kids?"

"All I said is I smelled pot, and I don't want to think that this here smartass lawyer from Harvard brought it with him."

"Because he is black? You know, Momma was right. She said I could do better than some ignorant, musclebound colored man who never even finished high school."

"You are going too far," MacKenzie said sternly. "I am self-educated and a damn sight more educated than some of these college kids. And as far as your momma was concerned, she loved me. She said I was a natural gentleman. So you apologize for that, or I'll take a stick to you. There's always a first time."

"Take a stick to me? Good heavens, no." She threw her arms around him and kissed him. "I apologize, but don't never try to take a stick to me—no sir. Now get out of here. You still ain't finished with the silver. And send in that Nellie, and if them kids want to smoke pot, they ain't kids no more but adults. They got a right to do what they want to do."

Dolly entered the kitchen as Ellen was speaking, and the black woman turned to her, disconcerted and embarrassed. MacKenzie slipped out of the room, and Dolly said, "I know. I walked past the door."

"Mr. Augustus smells it, he will take a fit."

"I know. It's Daddy's single moral persuasion."

Ellen shook her head. "No way to talk about your daddy," she murmured. "He's a good and generous man."

"What's the strongest spray can you have?"

"Lysol, I guess."

"Give it to me."

Dolly took the can of Lysol upstairs and sprayed the hallway. Then she tapped on Elizabeth's door.

"Yes?"

Dolly said, "Open up, Liz. The hall stinks. I just sprayed it with Lysol, and I'm going to give you the can and with it an order to flush that junk down the toilet, open the windows, and spray the room with Lysol."

"Mommy, it's harmless."

"We'll discuss that after Grandpa leaves."

The door opened and Elizabeth's face appeared. Dolly handed her the can. "We haven't touched the stuff for years," Elizabeth said.

"I hope so."

"You're angry?"

"Yes. You're too smart to be silly."

"Just between us—please, Mommy?"

"If you wish. We'll talk later."

"Thanks. You're a dear." Elizabeth's eyes filled with tears.

"It's nothing to cry about," Dolly said.

Elizabeth nodded and closed the door. Crying still, she picked up the dish with the three butts and took it into the bathroom and flushed them down the toilet. The boys watched her silently as she opened the windows and sprayed the room. She then went back to the bathroom and washed her face.

"I feel so empty," she said. "I'm a pig to think about myself, but I feel so empty."

Leonard and Jones sat in silence, and the silence dragged on until Elizabeth said in vexation, "Will one of you say something—anything."

"While you were in the bathroom," Leonard said, "Clarence here tells me that he must go."

"Go? Go where?"

"I simply can't stay here," Jones replied. "No way, Liz. I can't. At first, I thought that possibly I could. Maybe there's some way. It would be interesting. It wouldn't be interesting, it would be cute. I dress up in Lenny's clothes and pretend. I can't pretend. There's just no way I can sit at that dinner table tonight."

"Are you scared?" Elizabeth wondered.

"Right on. Right to the point. Just ask the black boy—is he scared? I am the educated civilized product, not some junkie living and mugging on the streets of Harlem. I'm scared. I'm scared of what it could do to me. I'm scared that I'll stand up and talk nigger and say, you two mother-fuckers who run this country are as dirty and unredeemed as anything in South Africa, and my friend here next to me, my friend, Lenny, who is beautiful and sweet and never caused pain to anyone, is dying, and you malignant bastards who bring death to thousands in Africa and in Central America—you are sitting face to face with an innocent, with death, the same kind of death you bring to the ghettos where you squeeze my people—"

"Jonesy, Jonesy," Leonard interrupted, "that's all mixed up, and I know how you feel and you wouldn't say it anyway."

"I got to go away from here."

"Please, please be reasonable," Elizabeth begged him. "I'm putting a selfish thing on it, but how could we explain it if you went away? It's heavy. It would be like putting a knife into Daddy."

"He'll survive that," Jones said angrily.

"Why are you so mad?"

"You have to ask me that?"

"I do," Elizabeth said.

"I'll tell you, Sis," Leonard said. "It's me. Otherwise, it would be a great caper, and he could go back to school next year and tell everyone about how he had dinner with two white jackasses who are running the most powerful country on earth and who may just snuff all of us if the mood takes them. But he loves me. We are more than brothers; we are tied into one knot and it's full of death. You know what I am beginning to understand—I'm beginning to understand that I'm the only one who can face this. It's a fact of life—yes, death is a fact of life, and I am going to die and

I can face that. You can't. He can't. You are
beginning to learn about death, God help you.
Until now, it was literature surrounded with
all the shit words—nobility, heroism, selfless-
ness, sacrifice, idealism—a whole Christian
world staring at that figure of a poor, tortured
Jewish kid, nailed on a cross and dying, and
nobody knew what the fuck it was all about."

"Right on," Jones whispered, his eyes full of
tears.

"Now I know. It's the first truth I ever
knew."

"God help us," Elizabeth said.

"Not a chance. I need you next to me, Lizzie. Jones is going away. He's right. He has to.
But this is going to be the damnedest night we
ever had, and I want you next to me, standing
on your two feet and not crying. You always
were stronger. Don't cry, please, because you
rip my guts out when you do. I love you so.
What in hell do any of them know about love
when they say a faggot can't love a woman?
Love is love. It's all there is that makes any
sense in this lousy world. I love both of you."

"I have to wash my face again," Elizabeth
said, going into the bathroom.

"There are no planes tonight after eight,"
Leonard said. "There's one at six."

"It's a long drive, isn't it?" Jones asked.

"No matter."

"How about a bus station in town? Is there one?"

Leonard nodded.

"Good enough."

"I hate to see you ride a bus."

"Hell, Lenny, I don't mind."

"You're going home?"

"That's right. Momma and Daddy, they been asking and asking."

Leonard grinned. Elizabeth came out of the bathroom and wanted to know what was funny.

"Jonesy here, the moment he began to talk about going home, his damn southern accent returned."

"I don't have a southern accent. You have a northern accent."

Leonard went to him and hugged him. Then he said to Liz. "I'm driving him to the bus station. You hold the fort."

"All right."

"No more than an hour."

"What should I tell them?"

"Tell them I couldn't face it," Jones said.

Elizabeth embraced him and kissed him.

"We are all beautiful," Jones said. "We three, we are beautiful people."

"Sure."

"And you, Leonard Cromwell, you are not going to die."

"Thank you."

"They will find a cure. I tell you they will find a cure."

Leonard smiled. "Why not? We lie to ourselves about everything else."

"Drive carefully," Elizabeth said. Suddenly she realized that Jones shared death with her brother, and there flashed into her mind a vague, fleeting picture of both her brother and Jones racing their car into a wall or a fence or a cliff or off a cliff; but there were no cliffs between here and town, and she knew that her brother had never been suicidal. He loved life too much. They both loved life.

And of course Jones had AIDS. How could it be otherwise? Now, slowly, Elizabeth put it together, her tears for both of them, Clarence Jones the rock supporting Leonard, white man you can't do it alone, but I can, and I'll give you my own strength because death, the stranger to you, is my old friend, my people's friend; and then it came together and exploded and she cried out, almost a scream, "No, no, no. That's horseshit! No one can carry that off. Animals die alone, not people." She took a deep breath, wiped her tears, and thought, Please God, I'm wrong. He'll go home. That's why he left. He had to go home. Clarence had to go home.

The image of Jones at the table this night, classy ornament, testimony of fraudulent equality, well trained, well mannered, well spoken, framed itself in her mind, and she whispered, "Goodbye, Jonesy. You are wise. I'll think of you with love."

TWENTY-ONE

MacKenzie was in back of the house, at the herb garden, cutting a handful of sorrel, when Leonard drove by with Jones sitting beside him. After he had dropped the grass off at the kitchen, MacKenzie went up to the guest room Jones had occupied and confirmed his suspicion. Jones's small suitcase was missing, and drawers and the closet were empty. Since the large guest-suite was occupied by Augustus and his wife, Dolly had put Jones into what they called "the lady room," as opposed to a larger guest room with twin beds and its own bathroom. She felt she had to consider the possibility that one or another of her dinner guests might have to stay the night. If both decided to, she would have to put Jones in Leonard's room on a camp bed. She had explained this carefully to Leonard, hoping that Jones would not be offended or put off by the contents of the small "lady's room," the white rug, white Swiss bedspread, pink-and-white curtains and striped pink-and-white wallpaper. "It's very feminine, but we only have three guest rooms, and I must reserve the other."

"He'll love it, Mom. Jungle colors."

"What an awful thing to say! Anyway, pastels are not jungle colors."

But now the pretty pink-and-white guest room was empty, as carefully clean and neat as if it had never been used; and MacKenzie went to the kitchen and informed his wife of this latest development.

"Why?" Ellen wondered. "Why would he slip away without even a goodbye and a thank you?"

"Can't you guess?" MacKenzie asked.

"I certainly cannot."

"Take our own son, Mason. He grew up here with the Cromwell kids and he is a doctor now, which in my eyes puts him second to nobody. But can you see him pushing his way into a dinner table with the secretary of state?"

"Why not?"

"Because it don't matter that you are eating three meals a day and you got a job with white folks treat you decent—no, ma'am, because you are still defined by your people, who live in squalor and hunger and misery."

"You talk like a Communist," Ellen said.

"There you are. I just talk two words different from them White House coffee-colored Uncle Toms and I am a Communist." Getting no rejoinder to this, he said, "Should I tell Miss Dolly?"

"Since she got the table set for eleven, I just think you might."

"You know, I been reading this book out of the senator's library by Thorstein Veblen—"

"I got work to do and I'm in no mood for your self-education. Miss Dolly is in the dining room."

MacKenzie found Dolly in the dining room, going over service with Nellie. "Oh, Mac," Dolly said, "I'm glad you're here. I'm changing the service, and we won't do it the English way. I want you to carve the meat in the kitchen, quarter-inch slices and only from the high part of the leg. You do the first platter you slice, and Nellie will serve the vegetables, leaving Ellen free to make a second platter. Much quicker. I want you to do the wine. Nellie will serve the quenelle and you follow with the wine."

"Yes, ma'am, but I must tell you about Mr. Jones."

"What about Mr. Jones?"

"He is gone. Leonard is driving him."

"Where? What do you mean, Leonard is driving him?"

"Maybe to the airport, maybe to town. I just seen them drive out. Then I went up to Mr.

Jones's room. He had packed and cleared out."

"Mac," Dolly said, "rearrange the service for ten. I want to get to the root of this. I'll be back here. You might go over things with Nellie."

Nellie was disappointed. She had always nurtured a fantasy that one of the guests in the senator's home would come creeping into her bed one night. It had never happened, but most of Nellie's sexual fantasies had never happened, and ever since she first laid eyes on Clarence Jones, she had decided that this time her fantasy just had to be fulfilled. Now he was gone; no fantasy, no fulfillment, and after Dolly left the room, Nellie blurted out, "Oh, it is a shame—just a rotten bloody shame, he was such a nice lad."

Dolly, meanwhile, marched upstairs to Elizabeth's room, entered without knocking, and said to her daughter, who was sprawled on the bed, "Tell me about it. What drove that nice boy out of here?"

"Himself. He wasn't driven. He went."

"That's no answer, Liz, and you know it."

After a moment, Elizabeth replied, "I think he was frightened."

"Leonard says he was an honor student, and if he could face things out at Harvard Law, there is nothing at the Cromwells' to frighten him."

"It's different."

"You know, Liz, it's your own cockeyed code that holds us beyond the pale. You decide that our worlds are so far apart that there's no way to cross them. That doesn't express a very high opinion of us."

"No, that's not the way it is."

"Well, what way is it?" Dolly demanded, exasperated.

Elizabeth sat up. "You're my mother. I'm your daughter."

"And what does that signify?"

"Oh, Mother, you know what I'm talking about. There are levels. I can't just bridge them because I love you and you're intelligent and sensitive. Can you do it with your mother, with Grandma Jenny?"

"No, I suppose not."

Elizabeth got off the bed and went to her mother and held her and kissed her.

"That's nice," Dolly said, "but it doesn't get you off the hook."

"He couldn't face tonight, so he's running away. Do you understand? He's just a kid. He's over six feet but don't let that fool you. He's a brilliant little kid, and he made it right from the bottom with scholarships. But he's black and he's a kid from a North Carolina ghetto slum, and the way he felt today he could not bring himself to sit down with the secretary of state and Mr. William Justin. So he ran away. Lenny is driving him over to the bus depot in town."

Dolly was silent for a moment or two; then she nodded and said that she could buy it. "I'll talk to Leonard about it. I'm sorry. It would have been an interesting experience for him."

"Or a loathsome one."

"Elizabeth," she said, "whatever you may feel, these two men run our foreign policy."

"Yes. I always had the notion that the president had something to do with it."

"I don't wish to talk about that poor man. The important thing is whether Leonard will be back in time for dinner?"

"Leonard promised in one hour."

"Very well. And at the table, darling, try to swallow the sarcasm. I know you're a very clever and well-educated young woman, and you will find both these men rather dull and limited; so if you must engage someone with your wit, use Mrs. Justin."

"I love you when you're prim and proper," Elizabeth said. "I'll try."

Leaving the room, pausing at the door, Dolly said, "You wouldn't consider telling me what Leonard has gotten himself into? I am his mother, you know."

Elizabeth shook her head, not trusting herself to speak.

TWENTY-TWO

Showering, soaping his body energetically, the senator reviewed the day from the moment of his awakening at five o'clock in the morning. In the ordinary course of things, when one awakens at five in the morning, some days can be endless. In this case, it had also been extraordinary. The passage of sex with his wife still bewildered him, the explosion of passion puzzling, upsetting, and at the same time delicious; and as he dried his body, he found that the very memory of it was giving him an erection and filling him with renewed desire. If he responded, it would send him off, like a horny hound dog to find Dolly and lure her back into bed.

That was beyond the pale. He tried to review the facts calmly. He had long ago given up any pretense that he was capable of monogamy, and while he had taken a handful of women to bed, it was always the result of affection. He loved women. He loved to be with

women and talk to women and make love to
women, and now, suddenly and unexplicably,
he was once again in love with his wife, and
on top of all this he had a mistress, Joan Herman, whose fascination for him had by no
means turned cold enough to make him certain that it would not flare up again. There's a
mess, he thought, a beautiful mess, and ad-
dressing himself, told himself that he was by
any measure, the most worthless one hundred and ninety pounds of manhood that had
ever existed. This very morning he had become horny as a porcupine over the thought
of Joan Herman in bed, and here, less than ten
hours later, he was trying to convince himself
and face the fact that the affair was over. Of
course it was over; it had become shabby and
worthless, but when he examined that conclu-
sion, he was devastated. For years he had
been a member of NOW, and he was one of
the most prominent and aggressive support-
ers of the E.R.A.—and how did it all come
together with the events of today? He had
taken a detestable course with both his wife
and his mistress, and if today actually meant
some sort of a return—not to righteousness,
which he detested—but to sanity, he still
lacked enough faith in himself to believe that
he could carry through.

He decided to shave again, an unusual decision. Shaving to him, as to most men, was a ritual performed in the morning, and the senator's beard was not heavy enough to require a second evening shave. On the other hand, at least for Richard Cromwell, shaving required total concentration—which would at least for the moment take his mind off his confused sex life.

He shaved. Always when he shaved, he found his countenance intolerable, suffered it because a number of writers had described him as good looking, and wondered how anyone who looked like himself could be elected dog catcher. However, the act of shaving worked with his thoughts, and drying his face he turned his critical reflection upon his session with his father-in-law. And since this was a moment for self-examination with an added shred of honesty, he admitted to himself that he hated his father-in-law. The points he had given him in the belief that even a mean Jew had a streak of compassion hidden somewhere, were points without substance or meaning. He was as compassionate as John D. Rockefeller, Sr., the senator decided, and as much of a Jew.

But on his part he had played it wrong, and that appeared to be a habit of his where Augustus was concerned. Having agreed to playing a few sets of pocket pool, he washed out as

soon as the old man cleared the table on the
break, thereby frustrating the old bastard.
Surrender did not mean Augustus had won; it
simply stigmatized Richard as someone with
too little guts to play against a real hustler.
Also, he should never have broached the subject of Sanctuary there in the billiard room
immediately after he had washed out of the
game. If he had been thinking properly, he
would have saved the subject for the discussion that evening, throwing it in at a moment
when Augustus, facing the two men with the
senator beside him as family—well, that
would have put the matter in an entirely different framework.

His Machiavellian talents left much to be
desired, and this once again returned his
thoughts to his secretary, Joan Herman. She
was his Machiavellian right arm, and without
her he would be limited to naiveté and honesty, both death sentences in that strange
place they called the Hill.

All of which drops me into that uncomfortable space between a rock and a hard place,
the senator admitted to himself, and with his
bow tie hanging unmade around his neck, set
off to find Dolly and beg her to tie it for him.
That, he felt, was at least a trifle Machiavellian, for put to it, he could do his own bow tie.
But this way it provided what he felt he

needed at this moment, Dolly's arms around him as she bent over a chair, encircling him from the rear, while he meekly allowed her to tie his bow.

TWENTY-THREE

Jenny found Dolly in the dining room, putting the finishing touches on the table, new candles in the sticks, two low clusters of flowers, and a rearrangement of the place cards that eliminated Jones and put Elizabeth between Web Heller and Bill Justin. Jenny was moved to sit between Leonard and Augustus. "Which puts you," Dolly said to her mother, "next to Leonard and directly across from our two distinguished guests."

"And next to Gus. I could have been spared that."

"Mother," Dolly explained, "we want something very important to Richard from those two, and I think that a pretty young woman will serve to put them in a better mood—"

"Than a fat old lady."

"Mother, for heaven's sake, you are not fat and you're a very beautiful woman—"

"Matronly is the word."

"—and they will be looking at you and probably trying to rub knees with Elizabeth under the table."

"What a dreadful thing to say! I don't know what's come over you, Dolly, but you do say the most common things. Whether you like them or not, these are very important people and very highly placed in our government."

"Yes, Mother."

Prowling around the table, Jenny snorted at the card for Frances Heller, placed between Bill Justin and Richard, who sat at the head of the table. "You put her too far from you and me. She wants protection. She's so sweet and innocent."

"And stupid, Mother. Richard will protect her, and if at age fifty-two she hasn't learned to protect herself, heaven help her."

"You put her next to Bill Justin."

"Winnie Justin will be watching him like a hawk. And you were just defending him, Mother."

"Why are you so provoking? You know that I defend the office, not the man. Gus says he's a perfect swine."

"You're wonderful. Mother, you don't have a double standard—you have a triple standard."

"What nonsense. Why did the colored boy leave?"

"I suppose he was shy."

"That was no reason to leave. He was Leonard's guest. You could have fixed him a tray of sandwiches for his room."

Dolly sighed and shook her head. "You've been my mother for forty-five years and you still astonish me."

"Well, what is it this year?" Jenny asked, irritated. "Is it Negro or black or what."

"Mother!"

"I think I'd better go to my room and get dressed. We get into these awful quarrels and I know you're so displeased with me, and I never know why. It never happens with my other children. Why are you so difficult, Dolly?"

"Because I love you."

"That's no answer." She shook her head, petulant for a long moment, and then smiling. "Could Ellen help me dress?"

"She's up to her neck in things. Anyway, it would upset her. She's not a lady's maid, Mother."

"Upset her. Good heavens, your servants are servants, Dolly."

"I could send Nellie."

"That silly girl! Absolutely not."

"Then I'll help you myself. I have time now."

"I don't understand why you don't have a personal maid. You run such a large house—

there's plenty of room for servants. You should have a chauffeur and a personal maid."

"I'm sure," Dolly agreed.

"I don't need you to help me dress," Jenny said, aggrieved. "Gus will provide whatever help I need. You always make me feel beastly —you know you do. Have I ever refused a contribution you asked for? The world is just the way it is; I can't change it."

"Neither can I, Mother," Dolly agreed. "I don't want to make you miserable. I do love you. Can't I help you dress?"

"Absolutely not," Jenny said firmly, having established her position, and with that she stalked out of the room.

Dolly sighed and shook her head. She was the pivot of a seesaw, with her mother at one end and her daughter at the other—and every disagreement at one end or the other was of little consequence, and the realization pressed her on to the notion that her whole life was of little consequence. A few more passages through the seasons, and it was done. Her mother was an old woman, and she was middle-aged, and it all appeared to have happened in a moment when her back was turned. And then—whenever she thought of death a cold chill shivered its way through her body—and then what?

She walked around the table, slowly, examining it. It's really the only purpose I have, she

said to herself, to put together a dinner table.
If I were a waitress in a restaurant, I would be
doing the same thing, but I'd be connected
with reality. Here there's just no connection
with reality. On the other hand, she realized
that there was a true mythic connection in
what was happening this evening. Two of the
most powerful people in all of mankind's history on earth were coming to her pleasant old
country house. They represented a power
that dwarfed the Alexanders and Caesars and
Napoleons and Hitlers. They could press a
button and extinguish, not only mankind, but
all that lives on earth. They were the thunder
gods, and like her own father, they were neither Jew nor Gentile, not human in any as-
pect of prayer or hope or reverence. She
knew. She had been born into this and lived
with it and watched it. Now, dutifully she
walked slowly around her dining room table,
touching a fork here, a spoon there, a plate
just slightly off center on its doily of hand-
crafted Irish linen. She couldn't help but admire the fine old china, the glittering silver on
the burnished mahogany table, the splendid
correctness. All of it pleasing, as a work of art
is pleasing.

TWENTY-FOUR

I don't know how long I have," Leonard said to Jones, as they drove into town. "They couldn't tell me that. They weren't sure."

"I know."

"It seems unimportant, and I make this huge fuss about it. It helps not to know exactly when."

"You're a brave man," Jones said.

"The coward dies a thousand times. I have already died ten thousand times. Why do you lie to me, Jonesy?"

"I try to help you, Lenny."

"You have."

"When I get down home, I have to get a job. There's a lawyer in town, name of Ruddiman, a white guy and pretty decent, and he says I can have a job clerking with him for the summer for forty dollars a week."

"That's below the legal minimum."

"They don't fuss much with legal minimums down there. But Daddy spoke to the foreman of the loading section at the Coca-Cola plant, and they always take on hands for the summer months. The foreman, Jake Tinsel, said he'd take me on and they pay two-seventy-five an hour. Makes a difference."

"It sure does. What does your daddy say?"

"He needs the money and I need the money, but he says I can make whatever choice I think best. I'd learn a bellyful of North Carolina law, and that will count in the long run."

"On forty dollars a week, you won't do much traveling."

"Sure. I know. But you could come down. We got a good family, and they'd treat you like one of us."

"Even if they knew I have AIDS?" Leonard asked bleakly.

"We don't have to tell them."

"Are you out of your mind? You'd have to tell them."

"We spent the night at your home, and nobody told anyone anything."

"Because of the dinner. Only because of the dinner party tonight."

Then Jones was silent, and there was no more talking until they drove into town and pulled up at the bus station. Jones went inside and bought his ticket.

"About thirty minutes," he informed Leonard.

"Let's have a drink."

"You? You're driving, Lenny, and you're not that much of a drinker. What the devil are you thinking?"

"I'm not going to kill myself," Leonard said. "If that's what you're thinking, just blow it out of your mind. I'm scared, I'm not depressed, and there's still a chance in a million that they'll find some kind of vaccine." He left the car and walked around it to where Jones stood uneasily, and he put his arm across Jones's shoulder. "You talk to your mom and dad, and tell them I'm sick, and tell them that there's no danger to anyone else. I know what AIDS does to people. It scares the hell out of them."

Jones nodded, unable to speak, his eyes brimming with tears. He tried to say something, and his voice came out as a hoarse croak. He tried again, speaking slowly, controlling his deep, soft voice. "You never hurt anyone."

"It's not crime and punishment," Leonard said. "We don't hurt people. There's no judgment on us. Go home and tell them the whole damn thing."

"You know?" Jones asked mournfully.

"Of course I know."

"I wanted to help you."

"I know."

"I didn't want you to have the guilts. I'm stronger than you."

"I know. But there's no guilt, Jonesy. Go home."

Jones went off, and Leonard stood and watched as Jones walked through the ugly concrete building to the open side, where the bus stood waiting. He resisted an impulse to run after the black man and beg, Jonesy, Jonesy, don't leave me here alone. Let me go with you.

Then he got into his car and began the drive back, pleading in himself, Why? Why did it have to be us?

TWENTY-FIVE

Without any reason that she could put her finger on, Dolly felt a cold chill gathering around her heart. It was unwelcome and hateful. She had experienced moments of true exultation today. She had gone to bed with her husband, and he had made love to her. Perhaps five, six, ten years ago, he had made love to her that way, and it was possible that he had never made love to her before in just that way, so long ago, so hard to remember passion; but even if he had, this remained new, and for the past hour her body had glowed with delight. Now fear began to take the edge off her delight, and she turned it to Leonard. She had sensed that something was wrong with Leonard, a difference in his manner, a hesitation in response, an uncertainty that Elizabeth appeared to share. She had put it down to the presence of Clarence Jones. Her children, growing up as they had between her house in Georgetown and this country place for those times when the Senate was not in session, were not easily bemused. If anything, they were sophisticated to a point that sometimes irritated her and sometimes troubled her; but this intrusion of the young black man into a situation as delicate as this dinner party was either intentional or at least in good part irresponsible. She couldn't deny that his departure had eased things; but after all, she had never in word or deed allowed him to sense her discomfort—or had she? Or had Richard? No. She dismissed the thought quickly. Whatever one might say about Senator Richard Cromwell, the notion that he could be rude or thoughtless in relation to a black man was ridiculous.

Perhaps her father or her mother? Not her father, she decided; for all of his icy aloofness and disdain for morality, his manners were impeccable—at least in terms of strangers. How often she had heard him spell out his definition of a gentleman: a gentleman is someone who treats a common laborer like a prince and a prince like a common laborer. It was not a definition that Dolly agreed with, since she had come to believe that the quality of a gentleman is something more than a display of manners; but she was satisfied that no remark or manner of her father's could have precipitated Jones's departure. On the other hand, her mother had carefully avoided any conversation with Jones, but it was hardly likely that he would have expected conversation from a lady Richard had once referred to as the "queen Wasp of Wasps."

Dolly walked through the house to the senator's room, full of an overwhelming need to see him, to touch him. The door to his office was open, and as she entered, he called to her from the bedroom. He was standing in front of a full length door mirror, black shoes, black trousers, dress shirt pleated and rather elegant, white suspenders, and bow tie drooping from his neck.

"I tried," he said.

Dolly took over the bow tie. "Oh, come on. Crouch a bit. You're seven feet tall. Or do you want to sit down?"

"I can still crouch. Damn it, I can still do a one-knee bend."

"Puffery! You haven't done a one-knee bend in twenty years."

He watched her hands as she leaned over his shoulders from behind him and tied the knot. She was as manually effective as he was incompetent. In less than a minute, the tie was perfect.

"You're not even dressed," he remarked.

"Plenty of time. I'm a quick change; you know that. By the way, Clarence Jones bugged out. Leonard drove him to the bus station in town."

The senator thought about it for a moment or two, and then he asked why.

"I don't know, to tell the truth."

"Did Liz go with them?"

"No—just the two boys."

"Did you ask Liz why?"

"Yes. She said he was shy, scared, uneasy, embarrassed—what you will."

"She didn't indicate that it was anything you or I said, or Gus and Jenny?"

"No. Really, no. I think her explanation covers it. I must say, Richard, that I'm a bit relieved."

"Yes, it occurred to me that our two gents from the high places could take it poorly. Especially Justin's wife."

"But I don't want to feel better about it," Dolly complained. "Richard, what is wrong with me—with both of us? That beautiful young man, do you know that every step of the way he fought through on scholarships. His father is a plain working man, and in the South. Think of the brains, the natural elegance of that young man, and we were apologizing to ourselves for sitting him at the table with that old man who presides over the end of things."

"Dolly, Dolly, you can't think that way. This feeling that an atomic holocaust is inevitable is paralyzing. We're not that crazy and we're not that bad—and this guilt over the blacks isn't productive of anything. We were as bad as South Africa, worse in many ways, and we changed it."

"We?" Dolly demanded indignantly.

"Dr. King led it—yes, of course, but with a lot of help from a lot of black people and a lot of white people."

Her face crinkled and tears began.

"Dolly, why are you crying?"

"I don't know," she whimpered.

He folded his arms around her. "It's been a good day—the best day for us in a long time."

TWENTY-SIX

Driving back to the house, Leonard said to himself, I am not going to die, and that's it. That's the long and short of it. I've mourned enough and I've been frightened enough, and that has to come to a stop. He began to laugh, not hysterically, but quite naturally, elated by the fact that he was convincing himself of what was obviously untrue. That did not matter; at this moment he had convinced himself, and whether this conviction lasted an hour or a day, it was a marvelous relief. He recalled the time—he must have been twelve, Elizabeth ten—when he first read Barrie's *Peter Pan*. He and Elizabeth were reading it at the same time; sometimes he read aloud, sometimes she read aloud, and since in the book Peter declared that if one wished hard enough, one could fly, they both decided to agree with Peter. For months after that, they dedicated themselves to flying, wishing harder and harder and harder, and when that led to no results, Leonard decided that one had to wish from a higher height than a chair. They climbed to the top of the old barn, and then, wishing like all get-out, Leonard leaped off. The result was a broken leg, for which Leonard did not blame the book but rather himself for not wishing hard enough. The childhood dream had not truly left him, but it lived with his knowledge that it was a dream and no more—which also did not change the fact that one could punch a hole in time here and there and believe for a little while.

He still felt good as he pulled into his parking space, leaped out of the car, and went into the house. At Elizabeth's room, he knocked, tried the door, and entered.

"Lizzie?"

"I'm in the shower," she called back.

Leonard paced the room. He was full of energy. As Elizabeth emerged from the bathroom, wrapping a terry-cloth robe around her, Leonard declared, "Enough of this! I've decided not to die!"

She stared at him, speechless. Then, slowly, "Of course."

"I'm not crazy. If this lousy thing kills me, it kills me, but not with my help. I'm going to fight it every inch of the way. Maybe they'll win, maybe I'll win."

Elizabeth threw her arms around him, her damp hair falling across his face. "You'll win."

"Oh, Lizzie darling, I won't, but you know what I mean."

"I know what you mean." She stepped back, looking at him, examining him. "Remember all the fights we used to have?"

"Sure."

"Why did we fight, Lenny?"

"We were kids. Kids fight."

"You're such a great guy. I didn't ever want to fight with you. I have such guilts about it. It was always my fault."

"No. Oh no."

"Sure. You remember that time I kept punching you, and you would never hit me back, and I just kept on punching until I was so tired I couldn't punch anymore."

"Lizzie, you were ten years old. You couldn't punch hard enough to hurt a fly."

"You're sure?" she asked woefully, beginning to snivel. "You're not saying that just to make me feel good?"

"Lizzie, you were ten years old."

She began to laugh through her tears. "How did Jonesy take it?"

"You know, I'm all right. No more tears, please, please. Let's get through this dinner tonight. Now promise me, Sis."

"Yes, yes, Lenny. I promise."

"You promised before."

"Double this time, double. Now tell me

about Jones, and then I have to dress. It's almost six o'clock."

"I think he was right—I mean, if he felt that he could face a barrage of sly insults and innuendos, why should he stay? My God, Liz, this black and white thing stinks. Do you know— he has AIDS. He was protecting me, from guilt and sorrow, even more sorrow."

"And you believe that?" Elizabeth asked. "That would make him a very great person."

"We find the quality in death," Leonard said.

TWENTY-SEVEN

In ankle-length beige chiffon, white satin shoes with a two-and-a-half inch heel, and her great-grandmother's pearl and emerald necklace—chosen specifically for the purpose of intimidating Winifred Justin—Dolly was reasonably pleased with the way she looked. Her hair, in a style that was avant-garde half a century earlier, curiously added to her youthful appearance—the look of a bright-eyed Greenwich Village radical, recently graduated from Sarah Lawrence or Bennington. As she came into the kitchen, Ellen and Nellie clapped with delight, while MacKenzie nodded approval. The two women wore white service clothes; MacKenzie, a white jacket and black trousers.

Dolly returned the compliment. "We do look classy, don't we—like something out of that T.V. show—which is it?"

" 'Dynasty,' " Nellie squeaked.

"I'm sure. Now, Mac, you be in front when they pull up."

"Outside or inside?"

"Outside for this one. They'll be driving in a black stretch, and aside from the four people in back, there'll be two Secret Service men in front, one driving, the other sitting beside him. They will hop out and open the car doors. You stand just outside our front door and open it to usher them in. I know this is all very obvious and silly, but the senator wants it to be done very formally. Nellie, you will be just inside the door, and you will say, 'Follow me, please.' Just that. But if the ladies have wraps, and they probably will, Mac will take their wraps from them first."

"Yes, ma'am," Nellie said.

"And meanwhile, Mac, have the Secret Service men take the car around back. They may insist on sitting in the car or they may prefer the house. The back porch is screened in, so they would be comfortable there. Ask them whether they would like today's newspapers or some magazines, and whether they are hungry. Explain that since we will sit down to eat at eight o'clock, it would be more convenient for the kitchen to feed them immediately. What have you prepared, Ellen?"

"S.S. men are always hungry. There was enough left from lunch to feed ten, and I got two nice plates in the fridge and—"

"For heaven's sake, don't call them S.S. men. It makes them upset and angry."

"But where do I take the guests?" Nellie wanted to know. "Will it be the library or the living room?"

"The living room before dinner. After dinner, I'll take the ladies and Leonard and Elizabeth. . . ." The sentence died. She and Ellen stared at each other. "Oh, heavens—I just never thought of it that way."

"We ain't done it that way for ages," Ellen said, her tone very tentative. "I don't think we ever done it—did we?"

"In Washington, do you remember, when we had the two Supreme Court judges."

"Yes. Yes, that is so."

Dolly glanced at the big kitchen clock. "Let me talk to the senator." She kicked off the high heels saying, "Remind me," and then fled through the house to the senator's room. The door was closed, and without ceremony, she flung it open and burst into the room. The senator was standing in front of his desk, quite handsome in his white jacket, declaiming to the wall, "—no, sir, mercy is not a stranger to us, and God help us if we toss compassion to the winds. What is left then, sir, what honor, what pride—" He was staring at Dolly and speaking at the same time. "Practicing. You look beautiful. Where are your shoes?"

"In the kitchen. I can't run in high heels."

She was used to his exercises in elocution and demanded no explanation. "We have a problem."

"Urgent?"

"You bet. I was working out last minute stuff in the kitchen, and I explained that, as you suggested, I take the ladies into the library and leave you and your two buzzards at the table. Cigars and brandy and all the rest. But we didn't know that Lenny was coming home. What on earth do I do? I can't ask the boy to leave with the ladies. That would be a dreadful put-down and I simply will not do it. What is this all about? Do you know? And can Leonard stay with the men?"

"You know what it's about, Dolly. Your father is beginning to build a road across Central America. My guess is that they want it stopped without any public fuss."

"But you'll be there."

"When it's off the record and I'm the host at our country house, it's off the record. If there were no such thing as that kind of privacy and silence, then our whole government would collapse in a few hours. And since I think your father will agree, I'm trying to get what I want—a break for the Sanctuary people."

"Then Leonard can be there?"

"If he keeps his mouth shut and understands the rules."

Dolly sighed with relief. "Thank heavens. Shall I talk to him?"

The senator hesitated, then he said, "No." Pause. "No. No, I'll talk to him myself."

"Yes," Dolly agreed. "That's best. I must run."

Dolly entered the kitchen. They were waiting, like a tableau. She dropped onto a chair and put on her shoes. "You know, I could forget to put them on," she said to Ellen. "I've done it before, it feels so good to get out of those damn shoes. All right," she said, turning to the others, "this is the way it goes. I take the ladies into the library, and you, Nellie, bring coffee and mints, two pots, decaf and regular. Ellen will have it for you. Meanwhile, Mac, coffee at the table and brandy and port. Oh, yes," turning to Nellie, "offer the ladies brandy or Baileys cream, just those two unless they ask for something else. I'll be there, so we'll have that under control."

"And nothing else at the table?" Mac asked. "I mean if they ask?"

"Whatever they ask for, of course. And when you pass the humidor, make sure you have at least three shapes."

"I always do. I'll mix the Don Diego and the Flaminco."

"Of course. Then leave the humidor and the coffee at the table and close the doors behind you. Privacy after that, unless the senator calls you."

"Right. Don't worry, Miss Dolly. Smooth as silk." MacKenzie agreed, thinking that he had done this dozens of times, which she would have remembered had she been less taut. Why now, he wondered? Why was this evening so different?

"Your mother buzzed," Ellen said. "She wants you."

TWENTY-EIGHT

Just as he had a hundred times rehearsed his offering to the Senate, so did Richard Cromwell go over what he would say to his son. But it didn't work the way he planned it. He tapped at the door to his son's room.

"Come on in," Leonard said.

The senator entered, closing the door behind him. He stood awkwardly, clearing his throat. Leonard, dressed except for his white jacket, which was draped over the back of a chair, was sprawled on his bed. He rolled over now and got to his feet.

"You know, Lenny," the senator said, "the way I feel. . . ." No, that wouldn't wash. Why in God's name couldn't he speak to his son, straightforward and direct, and say what he meant and nothing else?

"Lenny, I've been a rotten father," he said straight out.

Leonard stared at him, as if the senator had come naked into his room.

"You know," the senator went on, "I'm no great shakes at anything. If I weren't a senator, I don't know whether I could earn a decent living."

"No, Pop!"

"Let me tell the truth for once in my foolish life. I love you. I haven't said it since you were a kid. I was never able to. I go around with my head on the Hill in Washington, and I don't see you. I don't see anything. I don't see your mother. I don't see you, and I never had the guts before to ask you to forgive me." Then he stood forlorn.

Leonard, his eyes filling with tears, asked himself, Why now? Why does he give me something that has to be taken away? He moved to his father and put his arms around him, tentatively at first and then clutching him in desperation; and in turn the senator held his son to him, the first time since Leonard had been a small child, feeling his ribs, the bony vehicle of his trunk, clutching at his bones, his life, his flesh, his spirit, for now Leonard was laughing through his tears.

"Are you all right?" the senator asked him.

"Oh, Jesus Christ, Pop, I'm all right, I'm as high as a kite and I'm laughing and crying because I have to die and I don't want to die— I want to stay with you and work with you."

The senator took his son by the shoulders,

tenderly yet firmly, moving him away to arm's length. "What did you say?"

"I'm going to die," the boy whispered. "I didn't want to tell you. I have to tell you. Please forgive me."

"For what? What do you mean? What are you talking about?"

"Pop, I have AIDS."

"No. What are you trying to tell me?"

"That I have AIDS. The disease—A-I-D-S," spelling it.

"Oh, God, no—no, you're crazy, Lenny. You can't have AIDS."

"Why?"

"Come on. Don't toy with me."

"Dad—"

"You look fine. You're not sick. . . ."

Leonard pulled loose from his father's grasp, dropped into a chair, raised one trouser leg and pushed down his sock. There was a small purple spot, the size of a blueberry. "That's it," he said. "Kaposi's sarcoma. You can't turn it off, Pop. I have about six months, maybe a little more."

Like a somnambulator, the senator moved to his son, knelt, and touched the small purple spot. "Does it hurt?" he asked inanely.

"Not much."

It became harder for him to speak. "Lenny, you're telling me the truth? This isn't a punishment? If it is, all right, I deserve it."

"It's the truth."

Still kneeling, the senator put his face on his son's lap. He was crying uncontrollably now. Leonard stroked his hair and begged him to stop. "Please, please, Daddy."

The senator climbed to his feet, nodding, his head shaggy with hair in every direction. Leonard rose and gave his father the handkerchief from his jacket pocket. The senator accepted it and rubbed his eyes.

"We don't leave it at that!" he said suddenly. "No, sir, we fight it right down the line. There has to be a way. We have enough money to really go at it, and we're going to lick it, Lenny, we're going to lick it."

"Sure, Pop," he agreed. "Both of us. You'll help me?"

"That's my life—from here on."

"Thank God. That's the best thing I heard today. Oh, I was afraid that you'd be so angry with me."

"Angry? How could I be angry? I'd give my life to help you."

"Pop," Lenny cried, almost in abandon, "Don't you understand—I'm a homosexual. I'm gay."

For a long, long moment, the son and the father stared at each other, Leonard sick that he had said what he said, Richard Cromwell groping through eternity until he managed to say, "I don't give a damn about that. You're my son. I love you, and we're going to find a way to beat it." The senator moved close to Leonard. "Do you believe me?"

"I'm trying. You won't turn on me because I'm gay?"

"Stop that!" The senator enclosed him in a bear hug. Then he remembered his wife. "I'm going to send them away. The dinner's off."

"Oh, no—don't do that. You'd have to tell Mother."

"Yes, I have to."

"But not today, please. Not while her folks are here. I can't go through it with them."

"Lenny, she'll know. Does Elizabeth know?"

"Yes."

"Poor kid—that's why she's so quiet."

"You can handle it," Lenny pleaded. "I don't want to face Gramps and Grandma. That's too much."

"I don't know whether I can handle it."

"You can. Look at me—just telling me that you're with me—it's like giving life back to me. I thought you'd hate me, and that would have been worse than having AIDS. Can't you do it—please?"

"Are you all right?" the senator insisted. "Are you in pain of any kind?"

"No. I'm all right now. Look at me."

"And you really feel that you can go through with this?"

"The way I feel now. . . ." He shook his head, groping for words, "I feel good," he said quietly. "I'm all right."

"Then, since you want to, we'll go through with it."

"Sure. Don't tell Mother today. This is going to hurt her so much."

The senator was thinking that his son was dying and yet his son was protective. He was trying to understand that, and at the same time still reacting to the sentence of death, numbed inside, sick inside, screaming inside against the fate that was taking his son away from him. His son came to him and embraced him. "I'm all right, Dad." The arms were protective and the voice was cool. In one day he had been Father and Pop and Dad and Daddy. "I'm a homosexual," but Richard Cromwell had known that all along. There was the wall that had grown up between them, and why could he see it only now when he had known for so long? Why did it take this cold horror to bring them together? Words and memories stabbed at his mind, like fire from a gun that shot cold slivers of pain, and somewhere in that far away part of the brain called remembrance a voice screamed, Would God that I had died for thee, O Absalom, my son, my son. Now, not minutes ago, it came through to him. His son was dying.

"Oh, Jesus, Dad, don't take it that way."

The senator nodded, his face full of loose flesh that had lost the will to stay together and be a face. Leonard drew back, but the senator clutched for him.

"God damn it," Leonard said sharply. "Don't do that. You're leaving me alone. I don't want any fucking grief. I want love."

The senator nodded, still unable to speak.

"Don't go away from me. Your grief takes you away. Don't you understand?"

Death was new to the senator; it was old to Leonard.

"Father," Leonard said gently, "do you know what I tell myself? I tell myself that this thing must come to all men, sooner for me, later for others. But it comes, and we must face it. Sit down, please." He led the senator to a chair, which the senator dropped into, still a man in a waking coma.

Leonard went to his desk and took a piece of paper out of a drawer. "I wrote you a letter."

The senator came awake. "Oh, God, no! You don't take your own life. I said we'll fight this. I meant it!"

"Not suicide—I love this thing called life so much I'll fight and scrabble for every minute of it. But I didn't know how to say this—I didn't have the courage to say it." He read from the letter. "I'm facing an awful thing, and I won't make it unless you can tell me that you love me. If you can't, crumple this up and throw it away. . . ." He crumpled it and tossed it into the wastebasket. "Stupid letter. I wouldn't have finished it. Please, come on, be my friend."

"Always," the senator whispered.

"You look like hell," Leonard said, smiling at his father. "Some cold water on your face and comb your hair," pointing to his bathroom, "and then we'll go to meet the foe."

The senator went into the bathroom. Someone rapped at the door. Leonard opened it, and there was Elizabeth who said, "Is Daddy with you?"

"In the bathroom."

"They're here. Big stretch caddy, and two fat S.S. men in front."

"Just now?"

"Five minutes ago. Funny thing to see them face to face, like seeing a cartoon character walk out of the strip." In heels, with her pale brown hair piled high on the top of her head, Elizabeth was almost as tall as her brother. She wore a white voile dress with a full, many-layered gathered skirt, white kidskin shoes, and a single long strand of pearls her father had given her for her sixteenth birthday.

"What a beautiful woman you are," Leonard said.

"You noticed."

"I always noticed."

"What happened?"

"I told him," Leonard said.

"Did you? Lenny, was it terrible?" she said, whispering now.

"Quite terrible."

"Is it all right now? I mean, is anything all right?"

"It's as all right as it could ever be."

She kissed his cheek, lightly. "I'm downstairs."

"No word to Mother—remember."

She nodded and fled. Leonard closed the door and turned to his father, who had just stepped out of the bathroom. "How do I look?" he asked.

"Good. That was Liz. They're here."

"Let the bastards wait. One thing, Lenny—your friend, Jones, does . . ." He let the word hang. He couldn't go on. He thought about it, and the whole order of things collapsed.

Nodding, Leonard clutched for words. "Yes. He says no, because he doesn't want me to carry the guilt. He can't weep, he can't let his terror out of him. . . ." His eyes filled. "I don't like to talk about that. It's just too fucken terrible."

He wiped his eyes. The senator took his arm, and they walked out of the room together.

TWENTY-NINE

MacKenzie told his wife that her trouble stemmed from the fact that she was not political. He had told her this before, informing her that she was not properly conscious of being a black woman, to which she replied that if being black and being a woman did not make her properly conscious of being a black woman, she would turn to MacKenzie whenever she required information on the subject. He brought it up again this evening before he left the kitchen to take his place at the front hallway.

"That is all right," Ellen said. "I am tired to death of being a black woman, so when you look at me tonight, just you see a white woman, and that solves the problem and I am busy." Then she added, "Too busy to quarrel."

"No quarrel," MacKenzie assured her. "No way." He spread his arms, and Ellen had to admit that he made a handsome figure, six feet and one inch tall, quite impressive in his white jacket and creased black trousers. "But just suppose you have to explain this to your kids, which I will. We had a lot of dinner guests in our time, but this is different, very, very unique. These two gentlemen run the United States foreign policy which just makes them two of the most important folk in the world."

"Senator's more important," Ellen said flatly.

"No way. I wish, but no way. These two make the decision and run things. Oh, I'm sure they wake up the president now and then. Mr. President, here's what happens past two days. They read it off and then he goes back to sleep."

"Will you stop bothering me. I got work to do. Furthermore, you get up there in front or they will come and just be left standing at the door."

"Also," MacKenzie said slowly and judgmentally, "they do not like blacks."

"For heaven's sake, this country is full of people don't like blacks. Now will you get out of here."

As he marched through to the hallway with its wide curving staircase and its rich old Persian rug, MacKenzie saw Augustus and his wife descending the staircase. He ushered them into the sitting room, where Nellie,

bright and perky in her starched, freshly
pressed white uniform dress, awaited them.
Augustus eyed her with appreciation, while
Jenny said, "You do look handsome tonight,
Mac."

"Trying my best," he said. He went back to
the front door, where he had a full view of the
driveway, and at exactly half past seven, a
long, black stretch Cadillac came down the
driveway and pulled up in front of the house.
A Secret Service guard leaped out of it almost
before it had stopped moving, snapped his
glance here and there, on the house, the door
way, the ornamental taxus and rhododen-
dron, as if behind each bush in the lovely evening sunlight an assassin crouched, doubled
around the car, and then opened the rear
door. The driver of the car, also a large man,
the size of his partner, and displaying the
same wide, expressionless face as his partner,
the same black suit and white shirt and black
four-in-hand tie as his partner, leaped out of
his side of the car and took a position between
the house and the guests, so that he might
have a clear line of fire should the terrorists
attack.

No terrorists attacked, and in the early twi-
light a rose hue fell on the old, rambling Colonial house, turning the white clapboards pink
and violet. The four passengers were caught
by a trick of light that enveloped them in a

golden glow, and being human, they reacted with pleasure.

"So that's the old homestead," William Justin said. "It's a pretty place," dropping a small compliment toward a man he did not actually like. Justin was a small man, not terribly small, five feet and seven inches in height, but giving an impression of being shorter because of his bald head. It was his pride that he would not wear a toupee, and it worked for him since he was the only one of his contemporaries who did not hide his weakness under a rug. He had tiny, gimlet eyes, very dark, and he gave no impression of being either young or old—although he was, in fact, forty-nine years of age. The media never referred to him as either Young Bill Justin or Old Bill Justin, bowing to his agelessness. Like the ferret, he was compulsively driven to triumph and to kill, wearing his marine background like a medal of honor. His wife, Winifred Lackover Justin, came of a Louisiana family that had once owned one of the huge, ostentatious Mississippi river houses with the Greek-revival columns and numerous slaves. A blue-eyed, blonde southern girl, she had turned sour over the years as she came to realize that the presidency would never be within her husband's reach. Not only was he woefully nonphotogenic, but in his past there was the shadow, true or not, of an unwed grand-mother.

Webster Heller, the secretary of state, was out of a different world, a world of new and very oily money. A Texan, he was tall, gaunt, with eyes so cold that the blue was almost white. The senator felt that there was nothing behind those eyes, no soul, no heart, only a brain that was not unlike the very best of computers. In height, he matched Augustus, but without Augustus's bulk and wide muscu-lar chest; he was a long, lean man in the Gary Cooper tradition. His wife was an odd con-trast. Heller was sixty-three, his wife eleven years younger, white haired, full breasted, with a timid, apologetic smile and a thin, diffi-dent voice. She could have posed for the pic-tures they put on frozen apple pies, boxes of cake mix, and tins of cookies. It was bruited about that she existed in permanent panic, but no one really knew much about her ex-cept that she chattered. Her prissy, printed silk frock appeared perfectly proper for her, although on anyone else it might have looked ridiculous. But it retreated in utter defeat be-fore the ruby red silk gown that enveloped Winifred Justin.

MacKenzie took the ladies' wraps and then ushered the four guests into the living room. It was a beautiful room, with its eighteen-foot silk Chinese rug, gray-green walls and white woodwork. A courtly and restful room, the evening light slanting through the windows vying with the lamps. MacKenzie disposed of their wraps, saw that Dolly had the situation in hand, and then sped outside. The two Secret Service men were sitting obediently in the front seat of the stretch Cadillac.

"Follow the driveway around to the back of the house," MacKenzie told them. "You can park just outside the garage, and you'll see the kitchen door, and then over a ways on the right, there's a screened-in porch. You can make yourself comfortable on the porch, and Mrs. MacKenzie will have your dinner brought to you there."

"What about security?"

"Oh? What about it?"

"There's the front door."

"We got a German shepherd. I can tie him up out here, you want me to."

"Mister, are you putting me on?"

"My goodness, no," MacKenzie protested. "You mean terrorists and such?"

"I mean security."

"Well, I can lock the front door."

"You know, Mister, you are beginning to be a pain in the ass."

The other Secret Service man said to his partner, "Take it easy." And to MacKenzie, "I think we better keep our station right here. If we can have bathroom facilities?"

"I'll leave the front door open."

"No! You don't do that. We'll go around to the back if we need a bathroom."

MacKenzie said to himself, What you mean is that you'll piss on the grass once it's dark. He stalked back into the house, full of anger, calming himself as he entered the living room. Dolly's eye signals said, For heaven's sake, get them drinking. He poured the Pavillon Blanc for Winifred and accepted Frances Heller's request for a Perrier, while Dolly hissed to Elizabeth, "Will you run upstairs and get them down here!" Frances was explaining to MacKenzie, "I don't drink anymore—oh, I'll have a glass of wine at dinner, but not real drink. Mr. Heller is very secretive, and when I drink, I can't be secretive." The pink apple-pie face smiled up at him, and though it was quite insane, MacKenzie had the feeling that the plump little lady with the white hair was coming on to him. Heller and Augustus both had Scotch and soda, and Justin had a wine cooler. The thought of diluting the Château Margaux with soda water horrified MacKenzie. When he turned to Dolly, she whispered, "I'll wait. Mac, where are they?"

"Shall I go?"

"Oh, no. No. I sent Liz."

"It looks to me," Augustus boomed from across the room, "like a couple of barely ambulatory Republicans have driven my son-in-law to cover."

Heller protested that he still got onto a golf course at least once a week.

"Riding the cart or walking?"

Justin insisted that he himself walked. Heller confessed to getting on and off the cart. Mrs. Heller was admiring the wallpaper. "It looks real," she said to Dolly, who wondered what she could possibly mean by that.

"It is real," Dolly said lamely.

"She means blocked," said Winifred. "But your house isn't that old, is it?"

"Oh, no. Mother built the house. It's simply a passable reproduction." The kitchen and the pantry are the remains of a very old house, but modernized as they are, they can hardly claim antique vintage."

"If you can think of a reproduction as being passable?"

"Well, perhaps not with houses," Dolly agreed with Winifred. "Certainly not in terms of face-lifts and such. But furniture can be almost perfect."

It was a stiletto into a very tender spot, and Dolly would have swallowed her tongue to have the words back. It was not the kind of thing she would ordinarily have done—smack in the face of the two bouts of surgery that Winifred was said to have had, and whose small, hardly hidden scars about the ears bore witness to.

"Yes, yes indeed," Winifred agreed, smiling thinly. "Just as some women are almost perfect. I have heard it said about Joan Herman, but I don't think she's quite that perfect—I mean, being a tall blonde doesn't forgive all sins."

"Touché," Dolly murmured. "It's a long evening. Shall we be friends?"

"One tries."

"I always try," Frances Heller said. "You know, it's basic to the practice of politics."

"Really? I hadn't noticed."

"I'll never need it—unless I go on some dismal diet—which I have no intention of doing."

"What won't you need?" Dolly asked, and once again wished she could gulp the words back.

"A face-lift."

"Of course, darling," Winifred said acidly, "you're too lovely."

But Frances Heller, too high for acid to touch her, simply smiled and nodded. "Thank you," she said. When she was six, her mother had told her never to contest it when anyone said she was beautiful, but accept it and say thank you. "Frank Bixbee says that a little pudge keeps the lines and creases away. Does Frank do your hair, Winnie?" There was no contrived bitchiness in Frances. She was still the six-year-old who everyone said was so very pretty.

"Pudge?" Dolly wondered.

"Fat," Winifred said flatly. "No. I don't use Frank. Seventy-five dollars for a haircut is beyond my fantasies."

"I would perish without Frank. Do you, Mrs. Cromwell?"

"I'm afraid not," Dolly confessed. "When it gets too long, Ellen takes a pair of shears and lops it away."

Elizabeth entered the room now, and Dolly realized she was too young and too beautiful for the moment, putting the older women on the defensive, making them unhappily aware of themselves. It was not going to be a good evening. Elizabeth whispered to her mother, "They'll be right down."

"Nothing wrong?"

"Oh, no. All systems go." Lies. How could she lie to her mother in this fashion? The sorrow would pile up. The sorrow was something that belonged to all three of them; it was wrong to separate it, cut it apart, save it so to speak. How could she or her father live through the remaining hours of the day? But she couldn't deal with this question; she was still trying to comprehend that her brother was dying, and the decisions belonged to her father. She was amazed by the manner of her pretense. Was she born to deceit? Who was it who had said that "only a woman could properly engage in deceit"?

Elizabeth was introduced to the secretary of state and to his assistant for Central America. Justin responded stiffly. His problems with women came out of a fantasy world where all women desired him, and such was the sexual enticement of power that it was bruited about that he had made a new record of swift, short-lived conquests—even for Washington, where the competition was stiff indeed. But the presence of Winifred stilted his efforts; she made him aware of his physical self. Webster Heller, on the other hand, was a handsome Texan with a valid southern accent. In the media, he was frequently described as a courtly gentleman. He bowed and gushed properly, informing Elizabeth that the little girl had become a beautiful woman.

Elizabeth inferred by this that he meant they had met before. She had no memory of it, but Heller was quick to inform her that she had been no more than six or seven.

"Little girls become big girls," Augustus rumbled. "Fact of life. It's also a fact that horny old men appreciate. Why not? She's as beautiful as the first good day in April."

Jenny was used to it, and she apologized by offering a long sigh to the other women.

"You remind me of my mother," Heller told Elizabeth. "She was the first beauty queen ever to be crowned in Texas—a true flower of the old frontier."

Winifred whispered to her husband, "His mother's family kept a feed store in Dallas, and his mother was horsefaced."

"Will you shut up," Justin hissed.

"Will you drop dead," his wife whispered gently.

"Webster is charming," Frances said to Dolly, regarding her husband with affectionate awe. "Don't you think he's charming?"

"Yes," Dolly agreed. "Both he and my daddy—both of them very charming."

Jenny was whispering to her, "Where are they? This is dreadful."

But then the senator and his son entered the room.

THIRTY

Dolly's first reaction was pleasure and pride at seeing them walk into the room together, two tall, good-looking men, so alike even though the senator was broader and at least fifty pounds heavier than Leonard. Her mood pleased and annoyed her at once. Richard Cromwell was the same man who had ripped her to shreds emotionally at least a dozen times, who had taken other women to bed, who at times had totally ignored her and her children, and who had given her periods of utter misery. What had changed? Or had anything changed? Had she ever let go of it, stopped loving him, considered divorce? His position was not a reason for staying married to him, it was an excuse.

Once in the room, the senator became another person. Dolly recognized the change; she had seen it a hundred times before, likening it to the man by day who turned into a werewolf at night.

In the case of the senator, it was the political animal. His body relaxed. Everyone in the living room became a part of his extended family. He was gracious, he was charming. He told Heller that he had never looked younger, Justin that he had read with great interest a piece he had written for the *Washington Post*, Winifred that she was ageless—"You evoke a dream of youth"—and Frances that if she could market the secret of her skin, she could make millions. He introduced Leonard with pride, left him under the protection of his grandmother and his grandfather, and kissed Dolly very tenderly.

She recalled a talk the senator had given some years back at Yale. The subject was politics, and the senator had begun by saying, "Politics, from the Latin *politicus* and the Greek *politikos*, the art of the people, the art of belonging to the people."

Did he believe it? Had he ever believed it? But there were so many things that were neither black nor white, but rather defined by a fluid field of changing grays; and he always specified, in his dislike and frequent disgust with the people who ran the government from the White House, taking it out of the president's hand and into their own, that they lacked the only virtue any government could claim, the process of election. They were not elected. They had never gone before the people. They had never touched the people or felt them. They were of the old, wretched world of kings and courts.

"I think your son is perfectly beautiful," Frances said to Dolly.

"Yes. Thank you."

"I never had a son," Frances said, "and Webster still feels that life dealt unfairly with him. But they do say that a son's a son until he gets him a wife, but a daughter's a daughter all of her life."

Richard had warned her about Frances Heller. "She comes off as a total idiot. She may not be smart, but she's damn cunning and anything you let slip comes right back to Heller. That's why he brings her along. She's useful, a sort of ambulatory wire tap."

Dolly could not think of anything said here that could be useful to Heller. All her life she had been exposed to the conversation—better called chatter—of the rich and the powerful, and unless it dealt directly with the business of being rich and exercising power, it was filled with inanities; and since their women were excluded for the most part from the business of getting richer or increasing power, they spoke of little else other than inanities. Never had she heard, in the chatter over cocktails and across dinner tables, philosophy, personal or otherwise; curiosity concerning the universe and its ultimate mysteries; thoughts, however puerile, about the fate or hopes of man; points of ethics or hints of brotherhood. Yes, books, when they were marked as best sellers by the *Washington Post*, films and plays occasionally, but without depth and without wit. Long ago, she had ceased to be a participant and had become an observer.

"One treasures the young," Heller was saying to Elizabeth and Leonard.

"Of course," Elizabeth agreed. "Which is why we have wars and atom bombs."

"Defense is our gift to the future," Heller said. He was not tuned to sarcasm.

Dolly signaled to Richard, and the senator took Elizabeth's arm and announced that dinner would be served.

As they marched into the dining room, Richard Cromwell fought for every step and every word, and he fought against his inclination to put his face in his hands and weep. MacKenzie was already in the dining room, playing the role of a proper, sensitive British butler, just as he had seen it done in British films. As the senator was seated, MacKenzie whispered, "Senator, sir, them two mothers in the big caddy won't move. They just sitting there outside, waiting for terrorists."

"Fuck them," the senator whispered back into MacKenzie's ear.

As was most frequently the case, both these men were in perfect accord with each other.

THIRTY-ONE

He should have called it off, the senator decided. He should have called it off the moment Leonard told him. He should have met the car outside and turned them away—but exactly what was his position in this damn party? He was still puzzled about Augustus's need for the dinner party. Why had Augustus agreed to it so readily? Prior to this, it was Augustus himself who made the decisions to visit the Cromwells. When he wished to appear and see his grandchildren, he informed Dolly of his intentions. If it conflicted with the senator's plans, Dolly would spread her arms hopelessly and ask Richard what could she do? Richard might make a point of their never taking a cent from Augustus, but he was well aware that large contributions to his campaigns had come from Augustus via Dolly, who was the last person in the world to be pledged to keep a secret. In later years, money had come directly from Augustus, who said flatly, "You can't be a politician without being a beggar."

So whether this dinner party was of great or small importance to Augustus was a question that puzzled the senator—just as he was puzzled by his own compulsive anxiety about the Sanctuary trial going on at this very moment in Tucson, Arizona. The Sanctuary arrests and indictments were not the first injustice and indecency to sicken at least a part of the American public. The creation of martyrs out of people who fought for the best elements of American democracy was apparently endemic to the nation; and as they had hanged John Brown, executed Joe Hill by a firing squad, murdered Sacco and Vanzetti in the electric chair, so were they determined that a simple pastor and his wife and their friends, who had given sanctuary to the pursued and threatened, should pay for this by being sent to prison. His own only son was dying—and still this matter of Sanctuary obsessed him.

In the end, this was it—this and the fact that his son had taken the issue in hand. Leonard had asked him to go on with the dinner. He realized through his agony that this was possibly the first time Leonard had asked for anything from him. Now he asked for love, for help, and for his father to finish the day. The extraordinary thing that sometimes happens had happened to the senator; he had become the child of his son.

THIRTY-TWO

Justin was knowledgable about the quenelle. He was a man who had applied himself assiduously to the mastery of sophistication. He knew he was disliked. He had once pointed out to his wife his physical resemblance to John Adams, who was also, as Justin assured her, disliked. Justin read *Gourmet* magazine. He read Emily Post. He was married to a snob, and he envied her easy snobbery. He wanted desperately to be admired for knowing about the very small details of living. "Absolutely splendid," he declared, voicing his judgment of the quenelle. His wife allowed herself to be charitable enough to join in his praise; although, as she pointed out, in Virginia the quenelle was usually of veal.

"Really?" Dolly said. "How interesting!" It was the kind of quiet cut that evoked envy in Justin and challenge in Winifred.

The senator sighed and accepted the fact that swords would not be sheathed. He knew his wife that well, and he found himself irritated and pleased at the same time. He could control his dislike for Winifred Justin and her husband; Dolly on the other hand controlled only her face and voice. The round doll's face with its dark, patient eyes and tiny nose and gray bangs appeared to be made of innocence, and the voice, rather thin and high, bespoke simple, dull honesty. It was a mask many had accepted to their subsequent regret.

Augustus tasted the wine. "By God," he thundered, "Château Margaux. Nineteen seventy-eight, Richard?"

Of course, the senator said to himself, he read the label. The same wine had been served in the living room. Richard also realized that Dolly had changed the seating, switching Jenny and Winifred, so that his mother-in-law sat between the senator and his father-in-law, while Winifred Justin was encased between Augustus and Leonard. Had Dolly done this, the senator wondered, to keep Winifred within earshot, or to flatter her by putting her next to a very handsome young man?

Augustus offered a toast to Dolly, the hostess, and the senator squirmed a bit. The toast should have gone to the secretary of state, but then Richard Cromwell had been in the family long enough to know that everything and anything Augustus Levi did was calculated and a part of the image he would never surrender.

"It's a lovely table," Jenny said, admiring the gleaming mahogany, the old silver with its flat, unadorned surface, the glassware and the dishes. It almost hurt her physically to see the place plates sitting so casually; but sighing and accepting this, her pride overcame her trepidation. Jenny loved things and she loved to talk about her things. *Architectural Digest* had once devoted seven pages to her things, her china and silver and rugs and paintings and seventeenth- and eighteenth-century furniture—things that were her defense against her husband, whom she had never understood, the world, and, of course, people who did not measure up to her yardstick. Jenny felt uncomfortable in the world that was the habitat of Augustus as well as in the world that surrounded her daughter. Her *things* were a shield and a sword, and a plea for what she felt was the only proper way of existence.

Frances Heller understood this. "Such a beautiful table," she agreed. "But the plates!"

"Aren't they wonderful? I shudder to think that one of them might break."

"I'm dying to turn one over."

"After dinner," Jenny promised.

"What are you two plotting after dinner?" Justin wanted to know.

"Very innocent—to look at place plates."

"You worry too much about plots, Justin," Augustus said. "We're all becoming a little plot crazy in this country."

"With reason."

"Tell you something. There aren't any secrets. The big plots are out in the open. Nobody gives a damn."

Frances Heller looked puzzled, and Jenny shook her head. She felt that Augustus let things drop simply to befuddle a situation.

"Interesting man, your grandfather," Webster Heller remarked to Elizabeth, who was seated beside him.

"He's a great man," Elizabeth said seriously.

"Oh? Then you reject your father's persuasion?"

"I don't understand," Elizabeth said, wondering whether he could be gauche enough to refer to the fact that the senator was not Jewish.

"I was thinking of the Democrats. Gus is a rock-ribbed Republican."

"Oh—no." Elizabeth smiled. "I have no persuasion in politics, neither Democrat nor Republican. I'm a Buddhist." She failed to add that only this morning she had meditated— for the first time.

Nellie was removing the place plates and the first course, and behind her MacKenzie followed with the dinner plates. Dolly whispered to him, "Is Ellen carving?"

"Right now."

"That's hardly political," Heller said to Elizabeth. "Buddhism's a religion."

"Not really. Not in the Western sense. Wouldn't you say so, Leonard?" she asked her brother, who was sitting across the table from Heller.

"I suppose that since you can be a Buddhist and a Christian or a Jew, you could be a Buddhist and a Democrat or a Republican. I don't think that's what Liz means."

"I would like to know what Elizabeth means."

"Really, Webster," Frances said, "is the dinner table a place to discuss religion?"

The exchange at Dolly's end of the table had drawn the attention of the entire company. Other chatter died away, and the secretary repeated his request.

"Buddhism," Winifred said. "What an odd thing!"

"I'm not dodging the question," Elizabeth said. "I just have trouble putting it properly. Could you, Lenny?" she asked her brother.

"I could try," Leonard agreed. "I heard about a discussion between Allen Ginsberg and Helms—it was some time ago, and I think that Mr. Helms was then the chief of the C.I.A. They were talking about meditation and Buddhism, and Ginsberg told Mr. Helms that if he were to meditate seriously for six months, he would resign as head of the intelligence agency."

"And did he?" Frances asked.

"Oh, no, no. If he did resign, it was not for that reason. Oh, no—he never took up meditation. As I heard the story, he was very indignant about the suggestion and declared that he loved his work and wouldn't he be a damn fool to go in for something that would make him unfit for his job."

"Is that what you're talking about—something that makes you unfit to serve your country?" Justin demanded of Elizabeth.

"Don't jump to conclusions, Bill," Heller said. "They both look fit enough to serve their country. But just what did you mean?" he asked Leonard. "I've been to Thailand. That's pretty much a Buddhist country, isn't it? I never got the impression that would lead me to accept what you say about Ginsberg and Helms."

Leonard didn't answer. He had closed himself off, turned inward, and Dolly, observing this, watching her children intently, felt a chill of fear, an instantaneous vision of both her children torn from her, gone forever, an ugly vision that passed as it came, in a matter of seconds.

"Let me see whether I can answer that, Mr. Heller," Elizabeth said, very cool and controlled. "I don't think Leonard meant to imply that any magic or subversive forces were at work. I know that subversive forces always suggest themselves in such a situation, but I'm not even sure what subversive forces are. What could happen, I suppose, is that if Mr. Helms or someone like him were to meditate seriously in the Buddhist fashion for six months, he just might find that an act of violence was impossible. I don't suppose you could run the Central Intelligence Agency without violence."

"She's got you there," Augustus said, "although I don't know what the devil she's talking about."

"What are you talking about?" Justin wanted to know. "Pacifism?"

"Not exactly," Elizabeth said.

"Are you and your brother incapable of an act of violence?" Heller asked Elizabeth.

"That's such a personal question," Jenny said. "I think we ought to drop the subject."

"Oh, Granny, it's all right," Elizabeth smiled and patted Heller's hand. "I don't mind questions. Questions have become very 'in' since you were a child. As for Lenny and me and violence—who knows? But I do like to *think* that neither of us are capable of it."

"Too deep," Winifred said. "Much too deep and provoking. When I was a kid, we talked of other things."

"I'm sure you did," Dolly said pleasantly. "On the other hand, it was a long time ago."

"Do you agree?" Heller asked Leonard.

"Oh? Yes, I think I do." He had come awake.

Dolly, watching her son, began to sense that something was wrong, terribly wrong. The threads that linked the two of them had suddenly become tangled; nothing was right, nothing that she could pin down was wrong, but the threads had become tangled. She glanced across the table to where the senator sat and felt that she saw her own fears in his eyes without knowing exactly what she saw.

The meat was being served. Delicious pink slices. She had forgotten that Leonard would not eat meat. It would have made no difference in the menu, but she should have remembered. Why was she so nervous? Why this talk of Buddhism and meditation?

"Delicious beef. Tender," Heller said appreciatively.

"It's not beef. It's lamb."

"I can't believe that," Frances said.

"It's marinated and broiled, as you would do a steak."

Frances would have gone on to the recipe and that might have kept her through the main dish, but the senator, realizing that she would have to monopolize Dolly across the length of the table, diverted her with questions about the Hellers' recent trip to the Soviet Union. Frances responded with a story of a rash that Heller had contracted on his visit. "It itched so, I'm afraid it gave our relations with Russia a turn for the worst. Webster says it came of their having no comprehension of what we mean by clean. It spoiled everything."

"For want of a nail, the shoe was lost," the senator mused.

"Oh?"

"Nothing. I'm sorry?"

Jenny saved him with a compliment for Frances's clothes. At sixty-nine, Jenny with her height, her great mop of white hair piled on her head, and her dress of ivory-colored silk faille, was doing her thing as a doyenne of snobs. She had the equipment for a role she assumed only when she felt that Augustus was threatened, and her method of operation was to destroy with faint praise. Indeed, it was the only weapon she had—since beneath her shield of class lived a soft and sentimental person—and she used it sparingly. Her praise, dropped upon the tasteless dress Frances wore, was devastating. Frances lowered her eyes, mumbled a word of thanks and then brought her lips together tightly. Jenny was enveloped in guilt.

At the other end of the table, Heller pressed Elizabeth. "About this meditation thing, if it does all you say it does, it sounds like a dangerous thing."

"In what way?"

Heller studied her keenly. Was she playing a game with him, this slender pretty girl? He smiled and said that it might wreak havoc in the armed forces.

"But soldiers don't meditate," Elizabeth assured him. "So you have nothing to worry about."

Both the senator and Dolly were listening, Richard straining to hear Elizabeth's soft voice from where he sat at the other end of the table. Even MacKenzie, who was pouring the Lafite-Rothschild, paused to listen.

"How do you know that?" Justin demanded. Elizabeth was seated between Heller and Justin.

"It's very simple. If they meditated seriously, they wouldn't be soldiers, would they?"

"Vietnam is full of Buddhist pagodas, but they fought like devils."

Elizabeth shrugged. "I don't imagine the fighters came from the pagodas."

"And I've heard that story about Helms and

Ginsberg," Justin said. "I don't put any stock in it."

Heller, who had tasted the wine, held up his glass. "Suppose we talk about something civilized—namely wine. It's splendid, Richard. What is this red wine, if I may ask?"

MacKenzie exhibited the bottle, and Heller nodded. "Splendid."

"You're a connoisseur, Mr. Secretary," Dolly said.

"Hardly. But it is part of the job."

"I think it's brilliant. I have only the vaguest sense of the difference between a good wine and a bad wine."

"No need to apologize. It's a matter of little importance. But tell me, Mrs. Cromwell, how do you feel about your children's profession of Buddhist belief?"

"I never regarded it as belief. It's the way they are. I have no complaints." She glanced at Leonard, who had put on his plate a spoonful of flageolet and another spoonful of spinach.

"I'm not very hungry, Mom."

"Please try to eat," she whispered.

"Sure."

Augustus lifted his glass and proposed a toast. "To our two eminent guests and the land they rule!"

"Come off it," Justin growled.

"I drink to the land," Heller said, and after

he had tasted the wine, "not to an old friend's sour sense of humor."

Not funny by any means, the senator reflected, and what is the old devil up to tonight? He's rehearsing for something.

For moments he had forgotten or put aside or shunted into the area of disbelief the fate of his son. His mind had done one of those curious tricks and directed his concentration toward the wit and poise of his children; thrust back into reality, he felt the tears beginning in his eyes. He hid for a moment behind his napkin, but when he looked up he realized that Dolly was staring at him and that she had missed nothing. He was transparent. He always had been. It was a rotten habit for a politician.

"What land would that be?" Augustus asked, grinning. "El Salvador, Honduras, Nicaragua, Guatemala? Trouble with my sour sense of humor is that it's not shared by the fifty states. My sense of humor, I mean. If it were, Webster, you and your pals would be laughed out of existence."

"That's uncalled for," Justin remarked, his tone treading the thin edge of anger.

Heller, older and wiser than William Justin, grinned back at Augustus and reminded Justin of the old movie called *The Virginian.* "Not when he says it with a smile, Bill. You remember the film? Was it Gary Cooper? I think so. The bad guy insults Cooper." He glanced around the table inquiringly. Augustus's speech had stopped all other conversation.

" 'When you say that, smile,' " Elizabeth said sweetly.

"Oh?"

"The late show. That horrible little box lets our generation live two lives."

"And at the same time, young feller," Augustus said to Justin, "it propounds the virtues of the Republican party. We can say our piece and never ripple the water. A Democrat wouldn't dare come out and say we run and own Central America, body and soul. No, sir! He'd be denounced as a Communist, tuck his tail between his legs, and run like hell."

The long moment of silence that followed was broken by Winifred Justin who said to Augustus, "But if that's the case, Mr. Levi, and you are not teasing all of us, which I am sure you are, I mean teasing the lot of us, but if that is the case, where does virtue lie?"

"With a well-bred woman. Where else could you find it?"

Jenny, doyenne to the table, the enduring wife of Augustus Levi, shook her head to still the waters. "My dear Mrs. Justin," she said, being one who saved first names for either servants or those she considered her equals, "you must not take my husband seriously. He enjoys shocking people."

"But I must take him very seriously," Heller said lightly. "I've known him a long time." He turned to Leonard suddenly, "And don't you take him seriously? How about that, Son?"

Leonard hesitated, and for a moment the senator thought he would make no response whatsoever. Then he said, smiling slightly, "Gramps and I had a different relationship. He used to carry me, or get down on his knees to play with me, and steal candy for me behind Mom's back—but do you know, sir," pausing, "we never talked about murder."

"Murder?"

"Of course, it's only my point of view," Leonard said apologetically. He wanted to leave it there.

"Why would he talk to you about murder?" Frances Heller wondered. "Unless it's another joke?"

"No, I didn't mean it that way. I was thinking. . . ." He faltered, as if he were confused.

"Go ahead, Lenny," the senator said softly.

He bent his head for a moment, then looked at Heller and said, "I meant politics and war—I mean to me, the taking of a human life is an act of murder."

THIRTY-THREE

In the kitchen, MacKenzie, sotto voce, was berating Nellie. "Serve left, remove right, serve left, remove right—can't you understand, you silly girl? This is your right hand, this is your left hand."

"I know. I know which is my right hand. But the corners—"

"I know about corners. I don't give a spotted catfish about corners. You serve left, you remove right."

"Oh, leave the poor child alone." Ellen handed Nellie a silver boat of hot bread. "Check the bread." And when Nellie had departed, she said to her husband, "If you didn't have such hot pants for that child, you wouldn't be putting her down all the time."

"She's no child and my pants are cold as ice right now."

"That'll be the day. How is it going in there?"

"Interesting. Smooth so far."

"Go check the wine again. Don't just stand here with your teeth in your mouth."

"The old man, Gus, he just put down the secretary of state like Mohammed Ali did it to all challengers in his good time."

"Mac, get back in there. I'm not going to tell you again."

The fourth bottle of Lafite-Rothschild had emptied itself through MacKenzie's careful pouring, and Frances, unexpectedly, was allowing her knee to tip toward the senator. Knee to knee, she asked him what he had seen of the theater in New York. Richard was schooled in that diplomatic book of procedure that says that one never knows what one can do for whoever, or what whoever could do for one, and therefore one does not reject a knee. Ignore it, but don't reject it; and meanwhile explain that you rarely get to New York.

"In London," Jenny put in, "we do the theater with ferocity. But of course Gus does everything with ferocity. In New York, somehow, we don't operate that way. New York is different."

"And it does come to Washington sooner or later," Frances said.

Richard Cromwell accepted the general condition at his end of the table with equanimity. There had been times when the senseless chatter would have irritated him; now it was meaningless. There were no more small irritations, only the dark horror that had overcast the day; and Jenny, who sat to his left, was never an irritation. Early in his marriage to Dolly, when Jenny had been in her forties, a great, strapping, high-breasted woman, he had engaged in sexual fantasies about her, and even though his delicious lusts were unrealized, they added to the charm he displayed toward her. Jenny loved him for this and would hear no word against him, possibly sensing his mood and finding a response in herself for the unthinkable. Jenny was pleased by his tolerance for Frances Heller; not that she liked Frances, but it did give Richard points in Jenny's image of him.

Justin, on his fourth glass of wine, and finding Elizabeth unresponsive, stirred the little snakes that had taken residence in his mind so long ago, and asked Elizabeth whether, in the light of what had been said, Leonard had registered for the draft? He was not drunk. Justin did not become drunk in the usual manner, slow, funny, foolish. In fact, he did not become drunk at all, only more unpleasant.

"I haven't the vaguest idea," Elizabeth said. "Why don't you ask him?"

Justin glanced at Heller, who pursed his lips and shook his head slightly.

"Question?" Leonard asked across the table.

Stepping in with the first thing that leaped

to mind, Dolly said, "I was amazed the other day to hear the president quote poetry."

"Did he?" Heller said.

"Well, hardly the greatest poet. Robert W. Service as a matter of fact. An odd little poem called *The Cremation of Sam Magee*. He had memorized it, for some reason."

"Nothing wrong with his memory," Augustus snorted. "He'd memorize the dictionary. and read it as his State of the Union address if someone put it in front of him."

Justin was set to react in anger, but the secretary laughed and reminded Augustus of the eleventh commandment.

"And what's that?"

"Love thy fellow Republican. No low shots at the party. He's ours and we love him."

"You got me, Web. I love him too."

"Augustus always loved cowboy films," Jenny said sweetly.

Softly, half-singing, Elizabeth said, " 'But we are endowed with a mushroom-like cloud, and one happy day we'll all blow away—' "

"That's uncalled for," Dolly said quietly.

"Yes, I apologize," Elizabeth agreed.

"Yet," Leonard said, pausing to search his memory, "there is this." He recited slowly:

"When our children's children shall talk of war
As a madness that may not be;

When we thank our God for our grief
today,
and blazon from sea to sea
in the name of the dead the banner of
peace
that will be victory."

"Same poet who wrote the tidbit your president quoted. But after having served in
World War One, he was no longer cute."

"I don't know what that has to do with anything," Dolly said, troubled by the turn the
conversation had taken.

"Something the president didn't memorize. I think some things that he didn't memorize are important," Elizabeth said, smiling.

"I think this has gone far enough," Dolly
said. Heller smiled tolerantly. Anticipating
Justin, Richard pointed out that this was another generation. "The thing is, Bill," he said
to Justin, "that when twenty years goes by,
which it does in ten minutes or so, you find
yourself with a new generation, new notions,
new ideas—and certainly a way of speaking
up."

"Don't think we're immune to that," Frances said. "You know Sylvia Palmer, don't
you?" she asked of Jenny.

"I haven't seen her for ages. We don't get to
Washington that much."

"Well, her daughter, Claire—well, she just

took off and married a black man. Well, a black man—in my day, we would have called him colored, but today you call them black. Not that he's black, kind of light brown color and good looking. He has an important position in the general accounting office. Do you know that Sylvia came to me to see whether I could get Webster to do something for her new son-in-law. And when I asked her wasn't she devastated, she said, no. Suppose she had married a Jew."

Unfortunately, Frances had a voice that carried, one of those high, piping little-girl voices, and while the other end of the table had not been listening, the tail end of her remarks caught them.

The senator had a reputation for being imperturbable, because in moments like this he took refuge behind a blank, expressionless mask. Rather than exploding to the cause, this gave him time to consider what should be said, as opposed to what could be said.

Jenny was controlled. That suited her. Having been raised in a milieu where reactions were properly controlled, she said nothing and simply stiffened her face. So when Frances cried out, "For heaven's sake, forgive me," Jenny's expression did not change, nor did she respond in words. Afterwards, Richard would recall her expression as *withering,* a word he had previously considered to be merely a literary device. It was sufficiently withering, and he decided to leave the ball with his mother-in-law and say nothing that would smooth these troubled waters.

At the other end of the table, Dolly went into a frantic tale of her difficulties in trying to recreate a Colonial herb garden. But she prefaced her remarks with, "It's quite all right, Frances. It's an understandable slip of the tongue."

Winifred, leaning against Augustus, said, "Never thought the little old pigeon was that silly." She was controllably drunk. The senator had wondered earlier why Justin had brought her. "Usually," he had said to Dolly, "he doesn't bring her." But nothing was usual tonight, and the senator had the feeling that it was becoming more and more like Alice's tea party. Augustus chuckled with pleasure, and Dolly, armed with years of political diplomacy, was in animated conversation with Heller and Justin. Leonard and Elizabeth had become spectators. And Frances was driven to compound her distress, mentioning that Jenny was not really Jewish, and therefore should not feel hurt.

"Of course, my dear," Jenny said graciously. "That's why my name is Levi."

The lemon mousse was served. The senator realized that the dinner had come to its final moment. For this he was grateful.

THIRTY-FOUR

When the ladies rose to go into the library, leaving the men at the dinner table, Leonard whispered to his father, "I can't stay here, Dad."

"Yes, I can understand that."

"I think I'll step outside. I need a breath of fresh air."

"Sure. I'll see you later?"

Leonard nodded.

Dolly was preoccupied with three women in various degrees of annoyance, petulance, and alcohol. Leonard waited until the women had left the room, and then he slipped out through the living room and into the front hallway. As he came out of the house, he saw that the big limousine was still parked where it had been when it first pulled up. One of the Secret Service men got out of the car and faced him.

"Who are you?"

"Leonard Cromwell."

"Do you have identification?"

"I live here."

"I asked you, do you have identification?"

"I live here. We had a dinner party; I'm wearing black tie; and I'm at home, so I have no identification. If you're so crazed on the subject, I'll go inside and get some." He turned toward the door.

"Hold on! You don't go in the house!"

The other Secret Service man got out of the car and said, "For Christ's sake, Hinton, that's the senator's kid."

"How do you know?"

"How do I know, how do I know—I know." He said to Leonard. "Forget it, kid."

Leonard started off toward the pool.

"He swallowed the book, kid. Forget it."

Leonard walked on through the night without looking back. The moon was almost full, and a wonderful silver glow lit the grounds. He felt that he was walking in a dream. The guard was mad—obviously mad. The guard had taken him for a terrorist. They were all mad, caught up in a giant neurosis, a nation gone paranoid, and the disease Aids was a part of it. Out of a kettle of insanity an insane disease had been brewed, and where once simple, bony witches had danced, now there was a dance of driven clerics screaming that abortion was a sin, that Aids was a punishment from a God who burned souls in hell forever and who would cheerfully burn mankind to make a biblical prophecy come true. It was a nightmare. Only in a nightmare could madmen rule the world with thousands of atomic bombs—which in a spell of petulance or frustration could destroy mankind.

He dropped down cross-legged on the warm stone terrace of the pool. The house was beneath him, down the slope, and in the moonlight it was lovely. Yet this was no nightmare. There was the black stretch Cadillac, and leaning against it one of the Secret Service men smoking a cigarette whose tiny glow was a firefly—up with a puff and then down.

The thought that he, Leonard, was to leave this place, nightmare or not, step out of it forever into cold eternity, still clutched at his heart and awoke the inner pleading that it should not be so. There was enough beauty to soften the nightmare, the silver world below and all around him, the lights from the house, a doll house with a candle flickering inside, the faint smell of wood smoke on the wind, and the icy moon, dominating the wild array of stars, billions of stars and billions of planets, and billions of cultures and here, a dust mote called the earth, where madmen proclaimed themselves the vicars of God. Beauty and the beast, or was it that only what the beast touched lacked beauty? It had all been beautiful once; whatever else the Maker was, the Maker was an artist.

He took a pallet from one of the lounge chairs, folded one end of it, kicked off his shoes and positioned himself to meditate. No guru had taught him meditation, but a small Japanese gentleman who taught philosophy at Harvard. A student had come to a rashi, who was a teacher of meditation, and asked him why one should sit and meditate, and the rashi had answered, so that you will not be afraid to die. A story very old, as old as the fear of death.

A chill had come into the summer night. Leonard let the cool air caress him. The air was inside of him and outside of him, without separation. He watched his breath rise and fall, and gradually his mind cleared and his fear went away.

THIRTY-FIVE

The women had left the room, and the four men, the senator, Augustus Levi, Webster Heller, and William Justin, sat at one end of the dining room table. MacKenzie had poured the drinks, brandy for Heller and Augustus, Baileys for Justin, and port for the senator; and now he was offering the large humidor of cigars.

"I see no Cuban," Justin complained.

"No, I don't use them."

"By golly," Heller said, "you must be the only member of Congress who is a cigar smoker and doesn't come up with Cubans."

The senator was troubled; it took all the effort he could muster to focus on the matter at hand, working out his own fantasy that Leonard was mistaken, that the boy had invented the story, that he simply used it for its dramatic effect. He had not been shaken by the news that his son was a homosexual; it was something he had sensed for many years. But the news about AIDS—that couldn't be true, it must not be true—

"Senator?"

"I am not a smuggler," he said harshly.

"Oh—oh, come on, sir. Those are harsh words."

Augustus had come to realize, during the dinner, that something was deeply wrong. He knew the senator, but this man tonight was not the man he knew. MacKenzie was at his side now, and Augustus chose a Flaminco panatela. "These damn things," he said, "are pretty near as good as the Cubans. I don't have the virtues that the senator has, but I think it's just too fucken stupid to pass a law and then have every rich cigar smoker and half of the Washington crowd breaking it. You have Flamincos and Don Diegos here, and I'd like to see the Cubans that are any better."

"I hardly think you have to lecture us, Gus," Justin said.

"No? Well I'm not the host and you're not in my house, so I can break some rules. I know old Web here for twenty-five years, but I never met you before tonight, and I'll be damned if I'll sit here and listen to you call me 'Gus.' It's Mr. Levi. Levi. You call me that, and you can get your jollies by saying to yourself that this old Jew has to be humored, and what more can you expect from a lousy Jew?"

"Oh, hold on," the senator said. "Please,

Gus, that's not called for, and if you don't apologize, I certainly will."

Justin, on his feet, exclaimed, "I don't have to hear this."

"Sit down," Heller said. "We're family. Gus was in our party before you were born. He's the nastiest sour old longhorn bull in the crowd, but that's the way he is."

"My apologies, Mr. Justin," Augustus said lazily, lighting his cigar and grinning. "Webster is right. I call them as they fall. You should sit in the House of Commons in London for a few hours and hear those Brits go at each other. They pull no punches. When a man's their enemy, they specify."

"Gus, we're none of us enemies here."

"On the other hand," Augustus said, "when I listen to our Congress, it turns my stomach. 'My esteemed colleague.' 'My learned opponent.' 'My old friend.' Bowing and scraping to some of the worst, brainless, ignorant bastards that ever polluted Washington—and nobody willing to open his mouth and call a son of a bitch a son of a bitch."

"I think," Richard said coldly, "that no one here is an enemy."

"He's right," Heller agreed. "Don't divest us of the few trappings of civilization we still retain."

Justin was pulling himself together over his Baileys and cigar. Now he looked up at Augustus, his eyes narrowed and angry, his voice controlled. "I understand your position, Mr. Levi. You are an old man and entitled to your perquisites. I have erred."

"Good boy." Gus nodded.

"And I think," Justin added, "that we should get down to the business of this evening, the matter of the road." He was good, the senator realized, very controlled, very calculating.

"I'm sure," Justin said, "that you have guessed the purpose of this dinner, which your daughter was gracious enough to provide."

"I'd be a horse's ass not to. How often do you think I am summoned to take counsel with two of the gentlemen who rule my country."

"We don't rule your country," Justin said.

Heller sighed. "Relax, Bill," he said to Justin. "These are good cigars and this is damn good brandy and even that Irish swill you're drinking is potable. We've had an excellent dinner, as good as any I've ever tasted—and that meat, Richard, succulent, succulent. Hell, we're as comfortable as a chigger in a lady's tit, so just ease up and let a couple of old-time Republicans shoot the breeze."

The senator had never heard this kind of country boy talk from the secretary, nor did it have the feel of validity. It sounded like a little from here and a little from there, not to mention a few words from the television screen.

"Before we get down to the road," Augustus said, "I'd like to argue a little piece for my son-in-law here. Do you mind, Richard?" he asked the senator.

"You have the floor," the senator said.

Augustus took a deep drag on the cigar, and then let smoke drift slowly around the chandelier. "A woman is only a woman, but a good cigar is a smoke. Nothing a politician dares say these days, with the women's organization at your throat, and it never made much sense anyway. A good cigar is a consolation; it makes you believe, if only for a moment, that love and compassion abound—but we know better. My son-in-law, Senator Cromwell, is what we call a damn liberal. But he's a little more than that; he's an honest liberal who doesn't give an inch, and he's been a pain in our backsides for years. He's a man of principle, and nothing makes fellers like us as nervous as a man of principle."

"Is this going somewhere?" Justin asked.

"I think so, if you're patient and give me a chance to pull a few loose ends together. You see, Richard figured out that the only thing that could bring you fellows here for an off-the-record meeting with me was the road, and that you were going to ask me to dump it, and since you'd be asking for a big chunk of something, he'd ask a little bit of an off-the-record favor for himself. Now I don't want it to hang on what I do or don't do, so I'd like to have Richard present his case before we get down to the business of mine."

"I have no objections," Heller said. "It's Richard's house. He's our host."

The senator had to fight to put his fractured thoughts together again. He wished he had thought to see whether Leonard had returned, either to his room or to the library, but it was too late for that now. Augustus had given him the best shot he could have had. "I want to begin," he said, "by admitting that I could have brought this up in the Senate. But we're not in session now, and even in session, it could be months or never. Since you were coming, I thought perhaps we could do this quietly and quickly. I'm talking about the Sanctuary Movement, about the hundreds of churches and synagogues that have formed an underground railroad to help and shelter and give sanctuary to the poor devils, men, women, and children, who are fleeing from the murder squads of El Salvador."

"We don't know that they're fleeing what you call the murder squads," Justin said.

"I won't argue that," Richard replied. "You both know the facts of the case better than I do, and we're four of us, alone in this room, no bugs, no press, no media."

"He's right," Heller said. "We're not convincing a crowd. We'll say our pieces, straight on."

"All right," Justin said. "I grant it."

"Almost fifty thousand murdered already."

"Your figure is high," Justin said. "Forty thousand at most. They're Marxists."

"They don't know Marx from Santa Claus. Six-year-old peasant kids are not Marxists."

"That can be argued."

"And if they're sent back, it's to the death squads, armed and kept in business by us."

"That too can be argued," Justin said. "What is your point, Senator?"

"Simply this. In arresting the eleven people who are on trial, we did something that never happened before in the history of this nation."

"Richard," Heller said, "we do lots of things that never happened before in the history of this nation."

"Do you know how the evidence was gathered for their arrest?"

"Of course I know. We did what we had to do. We wired up a couple of these refugees and sent them into the churches. They recorded what went on. What went on was a conspiracy to evade and break the immigration laws of the United States."

"Spies for the federal government to record prayers in churches for evidence to send people to prison. Doesn't that chill your blood, Mr. Secretary? Can you think of another incident as disgraceful, as obscene, in all the history of this country?"

"Can you think of another country as obscene as the Soviet Union?"

"Which doesn't justify anything. We have faced enemies before and fought wars—with the British, with the Confederacy, and twice with the Germans, but never did it require that we sneak into the churches and bring their prayers into court as evidence against them. My God, what have we done to ourselves? What have we become?"

"All right, Richard," Heller said. "We've heard you out. What do you propose? What are you asking for?"

"I'm asking you to stop it, to end it. All you have to do is say a word to the attorney general, and the judge throws the case out of court and it's over."

"Suborn a judge—a federal judge?" Justin was smiling. "Really, Senator, suppose I were to publish that to the four winds. Senator Richard Cromwell asks conspiracy in the suborning of a federal judge."

"I'm serious," the senator said. "I am deadly serious about a tragic and important situation. I don't enjoy seeing it turned into a joke."

"I am serious too."

"I told him," Augustus boomed, "that there wasn't a chance of a snowball in hell for you two buzzards to bite on that compassion line. Hell, Richard, compassion has no business in politics, and nobody ever got rich pushing compassion. They want El Salvador and they want Nicaragua, and you can line up every church in America and they'll bulldoze the lot of them, and that includes your precious moral majority too, the moment they stop dancing to the right tune."

"Is that it?" Richard asked.

"Senator," Heller said, his voice quiet with reason now, "the case is in court. I can see your argument, and I don't for a minute agree with that cynical old coot you have for a father-in-law. I admire your pain when you contemplate this, but we are a country of law. That's all we can cling to when you come down to the final line. Law. It's the cement that holds us together and makes us different from any other country on earth. I can't abrogate the law. You know that, and neither can Bill here. They will be tried by a jury of their peers. Let it rest there."

"I thought we had agreed to cut the bullshit," Richard said slowly and deliberately. "Don't give me that shit about the law, sir.

Say 'no' with some dignity. Tell me to fuck off
—but do it with honesty and dignity. They're
your filthy death squads, and that's why
you're running that farce in a courtroom in
Tucson, Arizona. Now I asked you here, and
you're my guests and you have business to
discuss. You don't need me." And with that,
the senator stood up and left the room.

Like his son, the senator avoided the library
and left the house by the front door, where,
like his son, he encountered the two watch-
dogs that had arrived with his guests. When
one of them asked him to identify himself, he
burst out, furiously, "You dumb bastard, I'm
Senator Cromwell and this is my home and
who the hell are you to ask me to identify
myself?"

As before, the other apologized with, "Senator, I'm sorry. We're given orders—"

"I don't give a damn what your orders are.
You're parked in front of my house and you
knew whose house you were coming to, and if
common sense doesn't tell you that if someone comes out of this house in dinner clothes,
he likely enough belongs there, then turn in
your badges and get yourselves jobs sheep
herding—"

"Senator—"

"No! You've both said enough. Now which
way did my son go?"

One of them pointed, and Cromwell strode

off in that direction. His anger was like a coiled snake, not directed toward two stupid men with government jobs, but mainly toward himself and his naiveté and also toward the men sitting in his dining room, drinking his brandy, and smoking his cigars, men who ruled America for a cardboard-cutout leader and sniggered at a silly ass who whined about compassion. The senator was not enjoying a pretty picture of himself; in fact, since he had awakened some sixteen or seventeen hours ago, his self-image had steadily deteriorated, enlarged only during those moments when he held his wife in his arms. He was entirely within himself, unaware of the beauties of the night, unaware even that he was walking so freely at night because the extraordinary moonlight lit the earth and his way, and even unaware of the path he had taken. His mind was filled with fear and pity, pity for his son and pity for himself, and almost as an afterthought, pity for his wife, Dolly. But the reality of his pity eluded him; he was too imaginative; as he was unable to face his son's death, so did he see Dolly as being even less able to face the death of her son. Out of this, he extrapolated a situation in which Leonard, unable to deal with any more of it, had decided to kill himself and spare his mother the knowledge of either his AIDS or his homosexuality.

As his imagined situation superseded reality in his mind, so did the senator respond in grief, grief for the son whose life he had truly shared only this night, grief for Leonard's suffering during the months ahead, and grief for the lost love that could have been. Now the senator returned part of himself to reality, running toward the swimming pool where he half expected to see his son's dead body floating on the surface.

So intent was he on the awful fulfillment of his fears that for a long moment, as he stared at the still surface of the swimming pool, he failed to notice Leonard, sitting cross-legged in meditation. When he saw him and realized he was alive, a shiver of relief went through the senator. He didn't move, standing absolutely still and watching Leonard for perhaps a whole minute—until Leonard turned his head and murmured, "Dad?"

"I don't want to disturb you."

"It's all right." He got to his feet.

Suddenly, the senator felt the cold and he shivered and asked his son whether he was cold.

"No, not really. Are they gone?"

"No. They're still here. I walked out on them. I blew it."

"The Sanctuary thing?"

"You know about it?"

"Yes—sort of. Is it very important to you?"

"I don't know anymore. Things have

changed, orders of importance, the whole process of wanting. . . ." The senator dropped into a chair. "Sit down, Leonard, or do you want to go back?"

"No, I'm in no hurry to go back." He sat down next to his father. "How long will they stay?"

The senator looked at his watch. He was cold, but he was determined to sit here and talk to his son. "It's almost half past ten. They can't be staying much longer. We should get down there before they go. It leaves Dolly in a rough spot."

"Mom can handle it. If she can't," Leonard said, smiling, "there's Grandma Jenny. She'll look down her nose at them until they gratefully crawl away."

"She could do that," the senator admitted. "Still, I've made two bad enemies tonight."

"What can they do to you, Dad? They were the enemy to begin with."

"Well, yes and no. They had a certain attitude toward me, but they had the same attitude toward lots of other people. Now it's special for me."

"Do you mind terribly?"

"No, Lenny. Not so much—not so much at all." He hesitated, groping for words. "That thing you do. Meditation. What is it, actually, I mean other than what I see? I see a person

sitting cross-legged." He peered at his son.
"You don't mind my asking?"

"No. No, I don't mind at all; I'm glad you
asked me. I suppose part of it is what you see,
someone sitting cross-legged in a certain way.
It's a natural position, the way kids sit. We
forget how to sit that way, we become wed-
ded to chairs. Then things go on inside you.
You try to be aware of your whole body, you
watch the rise and fall of your breath, and
then, after a time, you stop being afraid to
die."

"And can you stop?" his father asked him.
"I mean the fear."

"Not all the time. But when I meditate—
yes."

After that, they sat in silence for a time. The
cold breeze had stopped, and everything was
very still. The senator was trying to comprehend something that was beyond his comprehension, but instead of tossing it aside as nonsense, he tried desperately to think as his son
thought. But try as he might, he could not
relate the simple process of sitting cross-
legged to his world and the demands and ter-
rors of his world. Now and then in the past,
conscious of the almost effeminate gentleness
of his son, he yearned for the kind of a boy
who'd rather play baseball or football than do
anything else and who was macho enough to
fight with other kids; and when Leonard grew

to his slender six feet and two inches at the age of seventeen, Richard put up a backboard and net behind the barn and tried desperately to make a basketball player out of a boy who was totally indifferent to the game. It was all so meaningless now, as even the homosexual designation was meaningless; death had split his mind wide open, emptying it of all his prejudices.

Groping for a connection, he asked, "Is it what the Japanese call *satori?*"

"That means enlightenment."

"Oh. I didn't know that. How do you define enlightenment?"

"I don't know," Leonard said. "I've never been there."

"I don't understand," Richard said hopelessly.

"I mean it's a state of being. I suppose you could call it a state of consciousness. But what it is, I don't know. I've never experienced it."

As if driven by his own desperate need, the senator pressed the point. "But if you've never experienced it—"

"Dad, I've talked to people who have."

"And what do they say?"

"They don't say very much. It's not anything you can describe."

Then, again for a while, silence, until Richard asked, "Some day, next week or so, will you show me?"

"Sure."

"I won't give up the Senate? I mean—if I go on with it?" he said half humorously, offering a joke that was not a joke.

Leonard shook his head, grinning for the first time in hours—or so it seemed to the senator.

THIRTY-SIX

You've driven my son-in-law out of here,"
Augustus said. "Not very diplomatic, Web.
You remember what old Dave Dubinsky used
to say—punish your enemies, reward your
friends. Richard isn't your enemy—or
wasn't."

"Just hold on, Gus. He was asking me to
interfere with immigration and to interfere
with the courts."

"And with a trial in progress," Justin put in.
"You don't do that."

"You're talking to old Augustus Levi. I been
around a long time."

"You know I couldn't say 'yes,' " Heller said.

"Couldn't—no. Wouldn't—yes. I told him
that, Webster. It's not just that you're a cold-
hearted bastard, which you are, but you want
that trial to go on. You want Sanctuary broken."

"Of course I do."

"I told him that. Trouble is, Webster, that

Richard doesn't understand people like you
and me, and he's never going to. I leave you
out, Bill, because you're something else. You
will blow with the wind. Webster and I are
brick shithouses, top to bottom. The wind
doesn't even touch the smell of us."

"I heard you use my first name," Justin said,
smiling thinly.

"You damn well did, Sonny. My preroga-
tive, not yours. You need a few laps more on
your track record. And don't get your ass up.
I'm old enough to be your daddy."

"It's not easy," Justin said. "I'll try—for the
common good."

"You're learning."

Webster Heller lit his cigar again, and admitted that Flaminco was just about as sweet
as some Cubans. "What do you pay for a cigar
like this, Gus?"

"You'd have to ask Richard. I'd guess three
dollars."

"Lot of money. Things cost too much."

"Always did."

Justin looked at his watch and said, "Let's
talk."

Heller nodded at Augustus.

"Let's talk," Augustus agreed. "We're on
our way to Switzerland. My daughter, Dolly,
said to stop by for the night and break bread
with two elegant gentlemen. Well, here I am

at your command, one poor old Jew facing the powers that be."

"I was waiting for that poor old Jew routine. Let's come right to the point. We don't like that road, we don't want that road, and we don't need that road."

"We?"

"That's right, Gus, we."

"You're short-sighted," Augustus said, watching the smoke curl up out of his cigar. "You might need that road more than you imagine. Suppose a bomb took out the canal —you wouldn't even need an atomic weapon to blow one of the locks. Then a road linking the two oceans through Central America might be worth its weight in gold. And we intersect the Pan-Am highway. Think about it."

"We thought about it, Gus. It wouldn't be our road. It would be their road, and if we wanted it we'd have to put together a little war to get it. And believe me, putting together a small war in Central America is not as easy as it used to be."

"My heart bleeds for you."

"I'm sure. If we want a road, we'll build a road. We still have more money than you do, although sometimes I question it."

"So you want me to drop it? That's the long and short of it."

"Right."

"I like you, Web. You don't crap around. You know, I have a lot in that project."

"How much?"

"Over two hundred million."

"Come on. You haven't really started."

"I know your lads are watching me like buzzards, but consider. Four years of surveys and selling the project. Clearing. Ordering special earth movers. Six different machines designed just for the job. Building a terminal where we can unload ships. Cement and sheds to house it. Sand—it's just the beginning, Webster, and right now I imagine it's closer to a quarter of a billion. That kind of money is real, even to me."

"You have guarantees."

"From those countries? Come on. Yes, once we start construction, we'll put out the bond issues, and that will bring in the money. It's a business proposition, a high-toll road, and eventually it will pay off, but right now I'm bankrolling it. It's my dream and I'm not asking anyone to dream with me until a little reality sets in, and don't sit there and tell me you want me to swallow a quarter of a billion dollars because you live with some kind of a nightmare of Russians grabbing it."

"We're not stupid, Mr. Levi," Justin said. "We would be stupid if we asked you to swallow it."

"So you come bearing gifts. Tell me about them."

MacKenzie came into the dining room. "Can I bring you anything?" he asked Augustus. "Coffee?"

Augustus glanced at Heller and Justin, both of whom shook their heads.

"Nothing, Mac. Tell the ladies that we'll not be too long."

He placed the humidor of cigars on the table and then left the room.

"You know," Heller said, "you could swallow that quarter of a billion very nicely if you had to. Your earnings this year will be four times that. You have the tax loss, and we could sweeten it through Internal Revenue."

"Thank you," Augustus said sourly.

"Not finished, Gus. The Russians are feeling us out about putting together two off-shore platforms for their Siberian coast. We'll give you the contract. It's bad water and at least half a billion for each platform. It's a damn good tradeoff, and you'd come out with a neat profit—over and above what you write off on the road."

"Beautiful."

"God damn it," Heller said, "don't look at me like that. You know what's going on. We rub their back, they rub ours. We sell them wheat and we sell them a lot of other things.

Time comes when we might need that Siberian oil."

"Oh, I do admire you gentlemen."

"Now don't go holy on me, Gus."

"Heaven forbid."

"You know damn well that if we don't keep this country hopping with the threat of war breaking out in the next twenty-four hours, we won't get twenty cents out of the Congress. Don't play innocent, Gus. We have a war economy without a war, and it works and everybody eats. If we ever went to war with the Soviet Union, it would last about twenty minutes, and after it's over, even the cockroaches wouldn't find anything to eat."

"That's as neatly put as ever I heard it, Web. So you want me to dump a road that might bring some prosperity down in that sink hole we call Central America, and go to work for the Commies. You want me to build them two off-shore platforms." Now Gus's cigar had gone out. He studied it to discover whether it was worth retrieving, decided in the affirmative, and lit it thoughtfully. "Can I say my piece?"

"That's what we're here for, Gus."

"I ramble a bit. That's the price that time exacts. Well, I got to go back a bit. I once hired a scholar, at the behest of my dear wife, Jenny, to look into my family past. The first Levi, the fellow who started our line, came to

New York in 1669, and his son settled in Philadelphia in 1710. Went into the retail business, something I never cared for. He opened a little shop and sold ribbons, cottons, linens, thread. Did fairly well, and a hundred years later, the family owned three houses in the city and were the biggest linen and cotton merchants in Philadelphia. I paid that young man from Swarthmore eleven thousand dollars, a lot of money before inflation, to find out everything there was to find out about the Levis. Aside from money and a secretary of state after the Civil War, a vice president in the 1830s, there was not a hell of a lot to boast about. Two brothers who were captains in Washington's army, a college president, nothing very big."

"I hope," Justin interrupted, "that all this gets to the point eventually."

"It does, yes indeed. Be patient, young fellow. Tell you something else this researcher dug up. He found over a thousand Jewish families in the colonies at the time of the Revolution, and only three of them could be traced to today. The rest had gradually turned Christian or whatever to a point where most of them had no memory of ever being Jewish— or so they claimed. Our family had done the same thing, except that they preserved the memory because the Revolution had put them into the history books. However, in the eighteen-seventies, they changed the family name to Livia. Can you imagine—Livia? And then, twenty years later, they were inspired to change Livia to Livingston, and that's the name I was born with. This young scholar I hired had a long, busy nose, and he worked out the fact that I was one sixteenth Jewish, which is pretty good after two hundred years of indifferent rutting. During World War Two, I was an infantry captain and there was a Rabbi Hirschman attached to our regiment, and one day I mentioned to him that I was one sixteenth Jewish. He blew his top at me and said that no one was one quarter or one eighth Jewish, or anything else Jewish. You were either a Jew or you weren't. 'All right, Rabbi,' I told him. 'What do I have to do to be Jewish?' He says to me, 'Are you circumcised, Gus?' 'I am indeed.' 'Then you're Jewish, and anyone who doubts you, send them to me.' Well, it's no tea party being Jewish. First thing that happened, I got busted to lieutenant."

"For being Jewish?" Justin demanded.

"You are damn right, for being Jewish. There was a captain in the regiment who was as mean a foul-mouthed son of a bitch anti-Semite as you'll find, and he let go at one of the enlisted men, and since I was now Jewish, it became a personal affront, and I beat the hell out of this captain, and he went to the

hospital and I was court-martialed and busted
down to second lieutenant."

Heller burst into laughter, choking over his
cigar, taking a minute or so to clear his throat.
"Why didn't they bust you down to private
and chuck you into the stockade. That would
have been proper."

"Yes, I suppose so. But things were delicate.
The concentration camps were being liber-
ated."

"I still don't see where this gets us. We listened to your family history. It's not what we
came here for, but we listened."

Nodding at Justin, Augustus said, "Webster,
this is someone you have to work with?"

"I do, and for God's sake, Gus, he's right.
You're diddling us."

"No, sir. I am finishing my story. When I got
out of the service, I got together with the
family lawyers and had the name changed
back to Levi—and by golly, I like being Jewish. Civilized. You know what's the blood of
civilization—trade. Commerce. Roads. That
road down south is my dream. It's what a
piece of sculpture is to an artist. I'm making a
passageway for the goods of the world."

"I'd think a bit before I said anything
more," Heller told him. "I'd just think this
over."

"You know why I like being Jewish—because I'm apart from you. I can see what

you're blind to. I'm not talking about religion, ethics, ideals, loyalty—neither of us have any of that. I'm talking about the sheer, nasty pleasure I get out of sitting here and telling you and that little man to go fuck yourselves. I'm building a road, and I intend to go on building it. I know what you'll do. You'll get your C.I.A. down there and you'll kill my workers and blow up my supplies and maybe in the end you'll stop me. But I'm going to use everything I have against you. I'm going to fight you in Congress, I'm going to fight you in the press, and I'll fight you in the media. Not because I give a damn either way about your stupid dance with your fellow lunatics in the Kremlin, but my road is cement and steel and not politics. It will be built because it has been waiting to be built these three hundred years, and I'm going to build it."

There was a long, uncompromising silence after Augustus finished speaking. The three men sat and held onto the silence until it felt like a material thing that would break with a thunderous crash. In the end, it was broken quietly, even mildly, by Heller, who asked, "Is that your last word, Gus?"

"It is."

"I wish you could have said it without all the name calling. We're both in the same party. You gave a cool million dollars to the president's campaign. We're not enemies."

"We're not friends," Augustus replied. "I enjoy life, and I don't delude myself into thinking there's anything else. You and your mirror image in the Kremlin could have stopped this lunacy years ago, but neither of you had the brains or the guts. There's no way to rectify it now. You've doomed this lovely little planet of ours. Sure we're enemies. You damn fool, it's not communism that's going to destroy us—it's plain, old-fashioned ignorance and stupidity."

THIRTY-SEVEN

Winifred Justin was drunk. She confided to Dolly that in Washington she was never drunk in public. "Once," she said, "once, and that little bastard beat the shit out of me." Frances was horrified and Jenny was disgusted.

"He really beat you? Oh, no. Our set doesn't."

"Under the rock, where his set lives, they do."

Jenny could not face drunken women. To her, a drunken woman was in violation of every tradition she believed in, and she reacted with unbearable tension. "I have a dreadful headache," she said to Dolly. "You will excuse me, won't you—and you too, Frances?"

"I'll excuse you," Winifred said. "You want to pee, go outside and turn left. You're excused."

Dolly went to her mother and kissed her cheek. Even though she wore heels, she still had to push up to reach Jenny's cheek.

"Beat you—you mean with his fists?" Frances asked eagerly.

"Go upstairs, Mother, and lie down," Dolly said.

Jenny bent to kiss Frances, who was an inch or so shorter than Dolly. Each time Dolly saw Webster Heller, six feet, three inches tall, along with his small fat wife, she felt that they were both unreal, a cartoon come to life.

"I do hope your headache goes away. Headaches are dreadful. Webster gets headaches, I don't."

"You need a head for headaches," Winifred muttered.

"Good night, Winifred," Jenny said.

Sprawled on the couch, Winifred clucked at her, "Nighty, night, Mrs. Levi."

Dolly suggested some freshly brewed strong coffee, to which Winifred replied, "Shit, no. Get me a drink." Elizabeth, curled in a chair and watching and listening now got to her feet and embraced her grandmother. They were of a height. "Lovely people," Elizabeth whispered into her grandmother's ear. "Don't let them get to you, Granny."

"Never." Jenny tossed her head, and then swept out of the room. Her passage in or out of a room always filled Dolly with envy, yet Dolly knew no one else of whom it could be said that she swept in or out of anywhere.

Dolly adored her, a sort of icon out of a long-ago, forever-lost era.

"That drink," Winifred reminded her.

"What would you like, Mrs. Justin?" Elizabeth asked her.

"Mrs. Justin. Sweet. I think a brandy. One little stirrup-cup for the road." Elizabeth buzzed for MacKenzie. "Do you remember," Winifred went on, "that congressman's wife who took off her clothes and went skinny-dipping in the fountain. That's for me."

MacKenzie came in, and Dolly said, "Mac, please bring Mrs. Justin a brandy."

"Anyone else?"

"No." She glanced at Frances, who shook her head. "Just a brandy."

When MacKenzie returned with the brandy, Winifred had fallen into a deep, drunken slumber. "And you know, you can't wake her," Frances complained. When she complained, her high-pitched voice turned into a whine. "I've seen this before. Webster and Bill will have to carry her out to the car. Do you think he really beats her?"

"It's been done."

"But not by civilized people," Frances protested. "I do suppose it happens among working classes, coal miners and such, but not civilized people. I think Webster would perish before he raised a hand to me. Of course, you don't have to worry because you're Jewish.

Jews don't beat their wives—or is that just something I heard?"

"Daddy's not Jewish," Elizabeth said. "His name is Cromwell, unless he's changed it from something. In our family, they only allow the women to be Jewish. That's why Daddy can't beat Mother."

"Elizabeth!" Dolly exclaimed. "How can you say such things! Forgive me, Frances. She's making a silly joke."

"I'm sorry, Mother," Elizabeth said dutifully.

"How strange," Frances persisted. "I mean, why would they only allow the women to be Jewish?—Oh, you're teasing," she said to Elizabeth.

"Yes. I am sorry."

"Shouldn't we let Mr. Justin know about his wife?" Dolly asked, desperate to change the subject.

"It's happened before," Frances said, pleased to find a moment of superiority.

"Do you suppose they'll be much longer?" Elizabeth asked.

Dolly had no idea. "It's twenty to eleven."

"Then it won't last much longer," Frances decided. "Webster always tries to be in bed before midnight."

THIRTY-EIGHT

At the terrace beside the swimming pool, the senator sat with his son, sometimes silent, sometimes talking. Richard Cromwell realized that this was the first time he had talked to his son, not to ask or instruct or order, but simply to talk and allow each flow of words to set another into motion. And then to allow the silence to stay instead of rejecting it or fleeing from it. They talked about the senator's plea for the Sanctuary workers, and Leonard asked him whether he had expected any more than what actually happened.

"No, not really. Gus told me it was hopeless. It's hard to believe that everything is so damn hopeless."

"Is that the way you feel—about everything?"

"Sometimes. I was just a kid when we fought against the Nazis, but I can remember. We saved the world from the worst horror it had ever known, and then I grew up and all I

ever wanted to be was a member of the
United States Congress. That's all I ever
wanted." The senator covered his son's hand
with his, thinking. And to have a son. But he
left that unsaid.

A gentle wind began to stir the leaves of the
trees around them. After a while, the senator
said, "We were poor when I was a kid. I was
born into the Depression."

"You always feel like a stranger here."

"How do you know that."

"I feel that way."

It surprised him. How could Leonard feel
that way? The night was becoming colder.

Leonard pointed to the house. The front
door had opened and sounds reached them. A
flood of light splashed over the driveway.
"Shouldn't we go down there, Dad? Say good
night to them?"

"No!"

"Then Mom takes the brunt of it."

"All right, we'll say good night to them."

Elizabeth was calling them. "Dad! Lenny!"

As Richard and his son approached the
house, they saw Webster Heller and William
Justin come through the open doorway. Winifred was a limp sack, dangling from their
arms. The two Secret Service men rescued
her, lifting her and placing her in the car.
Augustus stood outside the door and said,
"Will you shake hands, Web? I don't want to

see you go off like a frustrated fox in a chicken house."

Webster Heller held out his hand and said softly, as Augustus took it, "We're going to make it very hot for you, Gus."

"I got that impression."

Justin walked past and into the car without saying a word.

Frances was almost ready to grant Dolly and Elizabeth good night kisses, but Dolly's set, uninviting expression broke her resolve. She squeaked her thanks and good night, and darted into the car.

"Good night," Richard Cromwell said, shortly and with no apologies.

The car door slammed, and the big stretch Cadillac drove off down the driveway. The group at the open door stood in silence for a moment or two, and then Dolly said, "How could you do that, Richard?"

"He had good reason," Augustus said.

And Elizabeth said, "Well, Grandpa, did you give them the road?"

"Like hell I did! Where's Jenny?"

"She lied about a headache and went to bed, leaving Liz and me with those two creatures."

"Then I guess I'll join her. Good night, children." He stalked through the door into the house without another word.

Dolly turned to Richard. "I will say it again.

How could you do it and leave me to wind up this dreadful evening?"

"There are other things to talk about."

"What other things?"

"Dad," Leonard pleaded.

"No, Leonard," the senator said. "This can't wait. We're a family, we're together. Your mother's angry at me now and she's been angry at me before, but I love her very much, more than she'll ever understand."

"What on God's earth are you talking about?" Dolly demanded.

"Come into the library. We can't stand here outside and talk about this."

"About what?"

Ignoring her insistence, Cromwell led the way into the library. They passed through the dining room, where MacKenzie was removing the brandy glasses and the dirty ashtrays. "Will you want anything else?" he asked the senator.

"Thank you, Mac, but I don't think so. Finish up and go to sleep. You and Ellen have had a day." In the library, Richard closed the doors. Leonard went to Dolly and stood beside her. Elizabeth crossed the room, turned to Dolly and watched, her face tight.

"You are terrifying me, all of you," Dolly said. "Please tell me what has happened. Is it Webster Heller?"

"No," the senator said. "When our guests

came, I was late. When they left, I was late. I was with Lenny both times. A few minutes before the guests came, his effort to keep a secret collapsed, and he told me that he had AIDS."

Dolly shook her head. "I don't know what you're talking about. Are you crazy?"

Leonard put his arms around her and said, "Mommy, listen. Don't be frightened. I'm not frightened. I have AIDS."

"No!" she screamed. "No! No! No!"

"I'm sorry, Mommy. I'm sorry." Dolly clung to him, and now he was crying, like a small boy who had done something terribly wrong and wept as a defense against his punishment. "Oh, I'm so sorry," he sobbed, his own fear gone and replaced by a new anguish for the hurt he had inflicted on his mother.

"It's not his fault," Elizabeth cried. "Mother, tell him it's not his fault."

In Dolly's mind and body there was only pain. She heard nothing, and made sense of nothing. Richard went to her. "Baby," he said, "poor baby." She was clinging to Leonard. "Let me take her," Richard said. Leonard let go of her, and Richard moved her around so that her tearful face was turned up toward him, her mascara and make-up smudged, her lips trembling.

"Where's Leonard?" she cried.

"Here, here, Mommy."

"You won't leave me?"

"No, never."

Her body began to slacken, and before she could collapse, the senator cradled her in his arms and lifted her, whispering, "All right, Darling. We'll work it out."

"How? How?"

"We'll work it out." And to Leonard and Elizabeth, "I'll take her upstairs to her room. We'll talk. She's stronger than you imagine. Better if the two of us are alone."

She felt light in the senator's arms. Leonard opened the door, and Richard left the room, Dolly cradled in his arms like a child.

THIRTY-NINE

Leonard and Elizabeth sat in silence for a time. Then Leonard said, "It was worse than I thought it would be."

"Poor dear Leonard, poor dear Dolly."

"Still," he said, his voice thick with emotion, "there are some advantages, small gifts."

"Tell me."

"Love. Giving. Wanting."

"Yes, I can understand that."

"Do you have anyone, Liz? I don't mean those kids you date—I mean someone for real?"

She thought about the question before she shook her head.

"Find someone."

"Ah, yes, find someone—someone who is not gross, boring, stupid, angry, arrogant, sniveling, or macho."

"Don't try to do it alone."

"Let's play tennis tomorrow," she said suddenly.

"What?"

"Exactly. I don't give you up, and we don't give up life. Anyway, it will do Mother good to see that we're playing. We can offer her a set."

"She's awful," Leonard said, smiling.

"Hooray. Anyway, she's not too bad. I could let her win."

"Oh, no, you couldn't. Lizzie, do you think there's a chance, even one in a million, that they'll beat this before I die. I have six months to a year. That's not long."

"I will tell you something. When Gramps hears about this tomorrow, he'll endow a lab of a hospital or a research center."

"They have all that and they come up with nothing."

The talk ended. The big grandfather clock in the hallway began to strike the twelve tones of midnight. When the tones stopped, Liz asked, "Tonight—did you go out right after dinner?"

"Yes. I couldn't face them any longer."

"Where did you go?"

"I went up to the pool terrace, and I meditated. It helps me a little when I do."

"I saw you and Dad come back together."

"Yes, he joined me there after those two bastards turned him down. We talked about meditation."

"I think he lost out tonight. He wanted so

much to stop the drive against Sanctuary, but it wasn't that alone. He has nowhere to go."

"Have we?"

"I don't know, Lenny, I just don't know."

FORTY

Jenny was still awake when Augustus crawled into bed next to her. She pulled back away from him. "You stink of those vile cigars."

"A woman is just a woman—"

"No! Stop! Don't ever dare say that to me again. That's the most wretched, stupid line that was ever invented, and I am going to insist that Dolly put twin beds in this room."

"I like a king-size bed."

"You like anything king-size."

"Why," Augustus wondered, "are you so angry?"

"Why? You dare to ask me why after bringing those contemptible people here, and then holing up with those two men and leaving Dolly and me to deal with those creatures they married."

"Oh—that's pretty damn snobbish."

"You have your kind of protection. Let me have snobbery as mine."

"Granted."

"Do you know," Jenny said tiredly, "you are absolutely impossible. You're arrogant, insensitive, strident, and without a shred of manners."

Augustus chuckled. "That's because I'm Jewish. I stay married to you because you have those gorgeous big tits. Why do you stay married to me?"

"For your money, and I'm tired, and go to sleep."

"You old biddy—you love it when I talk about your big tits."

"You're not simply a dirty old man. You're a filthy old man."

"My love, we've been married over fifty years, and I still get horny as a kid when I crawl into bed with you."

She muffled her laughter while he pressed his face to her bosom.

It was well past midnight before MacKenzie and Ellen had emptied the dishwasher for the third time, cleaned the dining room, opened the windows wide to allow the fresh air to wash out the cigar scent, cleaned the kitchen, packed away the leftovers, sent Nellie Clough off to bed, and then climbed tiredly to their own rooms. MacKenzie paused in his undressing, lost in his thoughts, his face grim and inwardly fixed.

"What is it, old man?" Ellen asked him. "Come to bed and stop brooding."

"That beautiful young black boy—you know what he reminded me of, of the painting of the young Zulus in the old times."

"Everything reminds you of something. I'm too tired to jabber with you. I'm too tired to keep my eyes open."

"I think of the illustrations in the novels of H. Rider Haggard. Got him out of the library. I used to read a lot when I was a kid. I don't read much anymore—my poor suffering god, Ellen, don't you know what was here tonight. Both them boys got AIDS."

"What?"

"Yes, yes."

"Oh, you stupid ox, you and your crazy ideas."

"No, no crazy ideas. I wish it was just crazy ideas. Oh, my, I wish on the birth of little Jesus that it was so. But it ain't that. The two boys, our Leonard and that fine Jones boy, they got AIDS, both of them and both of them will die, God help us."

"How do you know?" she whispered: terrible trouble is whispered.

"I heard them talking."

"Maybe you wrong."

He shook his head. She began to sob, and he sat down and stroked her hair. "It's a bad world, baby, a lousy stupid place."

FORTY-ONE

She had thrown up three times. Her body was ravaged, and looking at her, as he half-carried her out of the bathroom and back into bed, the senator realized how small and frail she was. He had given her a Valium. It eased her, and now she begged him to take her to Leonard. "It's late, darling. Tomorrow, you'll handle it better," Richard said to her.

"He could be dead tomorrow," she sobbed.

"Oh, no—no. He has months and months and maybe years ahead of him," he lied, trying desperately to believe his own lie. "By then, there could be a cure."

"Do you think so, Richard?"

"I do. Sure. They have hundreds and hundreds of people working on it. And we're putting money into it."

"But, Richard, they have no money. Everything goes to the Pentagon. You know that." Her voice was heavy and slow.

"There's enough. And good heavens, when

we tell Gus, he'll build his own research center."

"He will, you know." She yawned and closed her eyes. "Don't leave me tonight, Richard, please."

The door opened slowly, and Leonard poked his head in the room. The senator motioned him in. He entered with Elizabeth close behind him and both of them went to Dolly. Elizabeth sank down next to the bed, taking her mother's hand and pressing it to her lips. Leonard bent over and kissed Dolly. "I know it's you," she said before she opened her eyes. "You won't go away, Leonard?"

"No, I like it here. Lizzie says I should play tennis with you tomorrow, but you're not much good, and I know that when Liz beats you, you get upset."

"No. I don't get upset. That's not so." It was difficult for her to keep her eyes open. "Give me your hand." He held out his hand, and she pressed it to her lips. She was utterly exhausted, and feeling the effects of the Valium, she dozed off. Elizabeth rose and kissed her father, and he embraced her and then Leonard.

"Go to sleep, kids," he said softly. "I'll stay with her."

When they had gone, he took off his clothes down to his undershirt and crawled into bed next to Dolly. Her instinctive response was to roll toward him, her face against his shoulder, her arm over his chest. He lay on his back, breathing quietly, considering the fact that this long, awful day was finally over. He had only underlined his impotence and achieved nothing. His son would die, and there was nothing he could do about that. He sat on the most powerful and important legislative body on the face of the earth, and there was nothing he could do—nothing to stop or slow a world gone mad and hurtling to its doom. He was not a brilliant man, but he was a decent man, a good man, full of love and hope and compassion—the final link in a line of such men going back through all the ages of man, to Socrates, who sat with a cup of hemlock in front of him, yes, and to a time before then; yet he could say, as had been said once, that the fault was not in the stars; the fault was in him. It was a flashing moment of illumination that allowed him to realize the truth, and then he closed his eyes and wept, for his son and for himself.

In the quiet solace of his own room, Leonard was wide awake; in a manner of speaking, more awake, more conscious than he had ever been. He sat cross-legged on a small round pillow, watching the rise and fall of his breath, listening to the question, Where were you before you were born? For this moment, his fear was gone. His mind was filled with the knowledge that he was here. Here was holy ground. Here was eternity. The meditator was once asked, "What is the difference between your way of being and mine?" He was answered, "In your way of being, you look upon your skin as the outside of you which separates you from the world. In my way of being, I look upon my skin as that which connects me with the rest of the world."

Leonard watched his breath rise and fall.